ALL THE BRIDGES BURNING

Neliza Drew

Blinking Neon Press

BlinkingNeon.com

Drew, Neliza

All the Bridges Burning / Neliza Drew

ISBN: 978-0-9975502-1-4

Library of Congress Control Number: 2016941956

1. Fiction —Crme. 2. Fiction — General. 3. Fiction— Mystery & Detective

First Edition

Cover art: girl photo by Oleg Gekman; boats by topdeq; fire photo by Rafael Valeev; font 4990910 by Phillip Cavette

Interior text font: Adobe Garamond Pro. Chapter font: Eordeoghlakat by Bumbayo Font Fabrik. Date and page number font: Fresco Stamp.

Edited by Elizabeth A. White (elizabethawhite.com)

For Lumpy, my favorite unicorn.

CHAPTER ONE
Tuesday, February 7

The first time I saw someone die, I was almost thirteen years old and still naïve enough to hope our mother, Charley, would keep us safe. The first few moments after walking into a gun range still made my hand itch and my self-preservation instinct kick in until my systems realized we'd come this close to gunfire on purpose. Despite spending lunches shooting with my friend, Tom, at least once a week, my involuntary responses meant I always insisted he go first while I loaded my old revolver with care bordering on meditation.

I'd been foolish to think Tom hadn't noticed. "You gonna shoot that thing or what?" Tom noticed everything. The hazards of having a former cop for a best friend.

I eyed him.

"You're getting an autoloader for Christmas."

"Fine." I pulled up my ear protection, sighted the target, and squeezed off the six rounds I'd just loaded.

Tom hit the button to bring the target up and wiggled his fuzzy white eyebrows at the centered grouping. "You still shoot like a champion. You know, you could probably win some competitions again, you ever wanted to get back into that."

I handed him one of the silhouette targets he'd bought without comment. Competitions were something I'd done with my uncle, who wasn't really my uncle. And after all the destruction I'd seen guns do, after all guns had taken from me, I had trouble seeing them as just so much sports equipment anymore. Yet, I still showed up with Tom because he needed to keep up his skills, and I guessed some part of me worried I might need to as well.

Tom pulled out a new pistol and held it up. A grin spread across his face. "Can Marilyn pick them or what? How's this for an anniversary gift?"

I smiled. "You know your old partner helped her, right?" Tom's wife knew Cuban food, golf clubs, and databases. Her love of firearms stopped at her wedding band and her proficiency hovered around the knows-enough-to-be-terrifying mark.

"Maybe."

I gave him a look that said he owed his old buddy a beer.

My phone vibrated in my pocket as I watched Tom shoot. I pulled it out and checked the display just in case my boss had misplaced something again in the fifteen minutes I'd left him alone in the office. Unfortunately, it wasn't my boss.

Tom's voice broke my thoughts. "What?"

I looked up at the neat grouping of holes in the silhouette's center mass. Not as tight as mine, but certainly not bad. "Charley."

"Your mother?"

Biologically speaking.

I tried to steer the conversation back, pointed at his target. "Pretty good for someone your age."

He raised a fluffy eyebrow. "You're the one with the old man gun. You want to try mine?"

"Ah, semi-automatics. Hot little projectiles in my cleavage and burning through a week's salary in five minutes."

He gave me a brief look that said I'd feel differently if I ever had to rely on one in a pinch. It shifted into the puppy dog eyes that usually convinced his wife to let him have dessert and ridiculous man-toys.

I accepted his gun and forced half a dozen of his rounds into the magazine. Another thing I disliked. The way the force required made my hand ache and reminded me far too harshly that I had limitations. I ignored the look he gave me that encouraged loading the thing to capacity.

Tom loaded up another of his silhouette targets and I shook my head. He eyed me like he was divining something in my preference, but stuck on another bull's-eye just the same.

"I've never a shot a person," I said. "I don't really intend to. Isn't that what you're always telling me? 'Don't point at anything living unless you aim to kill it'?"

He sighed. "Sometimes we don't have a choice. Even when we want one."

I stepped up to the center of the stall and sighted the target so I wouldn't have to see the pain on his face and he wouldn't be able to find any on mine. The first two rounds strayed to the edge of center. I adjusted my aim, quieted my head and breath. The next four hammered through the middle of the paper and left a ragged, oversized hole.

Tom hit the button and whistled when the target got closer. "Damn, girl. You are just no fun."

I set his anniversary gift between us. "It's my only legal talent." My phone vibrated between the boxes of ammo. The screen said it had a new voice mail.

His expression grew serious again. "Call her back, Davis."

I stared at the phone, the ammunition surrounding it. Tom knew a lot about me, as much as anyone not related to me could. He knew I'd been a stripper, that I'd been an escort before becoming a paralegal. He knew I'd used the money I made to buy real estate I didn't live in. He knew I was leery of touch, that I had little contact with my family and spent holidays running or swimming alone despite Marilyn's invitations and efforts. He knew there were marks on my body I didn't try to hide, but didn't bother to explain. He also probably knew whatever he'd dug up on his own.

"At least listen to the message." His voice was too gentle, like he was talking to a suspect. Or a victim.

"Don't. You know better." I picked up the phone and left my ear protection on the counter. Outside the stall, I dialed voice mail and listened.

Charley sounded drunk. "Nik? Nik, why don't you pick up, Nik? They took Lanie. Police. They said awful things. Why won't you talk to me? I deserve better than this, Nik." She pushed buttons and swore until the voice mail cut her off.

I wanted to ignore her. I knew I wouldn't. She'd invoked the magic word: Lanie.

I pinched the bridge of my nose and called her back. When she answered, I said, "Charley."

"Speaking." She sounded cheerful. I wondered if she even recognized my voice.

"You left a message for Nik?" The few times she'd called me in the past few years, she'd called me by older sister's name.

Hearing Nik's name seemed to trigger her outrage. "The cops, those pigs, they came for Lanie. They took her away. They said she hurt someone, that she killed her boyfriend. That's not true. That's just some lie. I saw it on the shows."

"Can I talk to Lane?"

"Are you as stupid as Davis was? She ain't here. Gone."

I swallowed the insult. "Lane's with the police?"

"They took her. Said she murdered her boyfriend. Shot him. Right in the head. Made her sound crazy as Davis. Why don't you ever call me? Write? Something? Didn't even see you for Christmas."

"Nik was there for a week at Christmas, Charley. Do you remember which police department you talked to?"

"Why would I want to talk to the police?" She sighed heavily into the phone and gulped something. "If you can't talk to me like I'm a person, I might as well not talk to you at all." She punched some buttons until she figured out how to turn the phone off again.

I walked back to the stall in a haze of bad memories, confusion, and anger. Tom took one look at my face and slid both guns closer to him. I rolled my eyes at the gesture.

"Look, can you give your buddy, Rubelli, a call after we're done here? See if he can find out if a girl was arrested for murder in Carteret County up in North Carolina?"

"Lane?"

I nodded. "Lane Groves. She's seventeen now. Guardian of record would be Charlemagne Allister Groves."

He studied my face. "If you're that worried…" He took a deep breath. I knew what he wanted to know. Why'd I leave? Why'd I leave Lane behind with Charley? I'd made some terrible decisions in my life, but leaving ranked up there. Then, I hadn't felt I'd had a choice.

He patted my hand. "Tell me later." He held up his phone and disappeared.

I watched him leave and wondered how to explain my childhood without engendering pity or disgust. Rather than dwell on it, I called Nik, the real one. Nik, the perfect Groves kid, who was probably the sole reason I was alive and in possession of a GED and associates degree. Even that she was a bit disappointed with.

She answered on the third ring. "Hancock and Associates. Nik Groves speaking. How may I help you?"

I'd been chewing my lip while it rang. Her voice caught me off guard she sounded so normal. "Have you heard from Charley?"

"Davis?"

"Who else?"

"I don't know, Davis. Any of the five people I've left messages for? My advisor calling about my dissertation? My boyfriend? The friend I'm supposed to meet for lunch?"

"Nik, it's what? Nine a.m. there? Look, have you heard from Charley?"

"She left a wad of crazy on my phone last night. Something about a show she saw that upset her."

"She told me Lane'd been arrested."

"That's ridiculous, Davis. Lane?"

I had to admit it sounded weird. Lane had always been soft-spoken and sweet, trusting and, well, normal. I mean, sure she'd had a rebellious phase, but it hadn't been serious. We hadn't involved her in any of our schemes or disasters. We'd always protected her from danger and strife.

"You still there?"

"Yeah."

"You can't do the no-talking stoic thing on the phone, Davis. For one thing, I don't really have time, but mostly I can't read your face if I can't see it."

I nodded even though she couldn't see that either. Nik always had suffered some ability to nearly read my mind no matter how much I tried to hide things from her. "I have a friend looking into it. I just, I wanted to see if she'd talked to you."

She sighed into the line. "She hasn't."

"She never calls me by name." I couldn't figure out why I cared, but something inside hurt when I thought about my mother not knowing my name.

"Well, all things considered…"

I tamped down the things to be considered. There were a lot of them.

Tom walked back in, his expression grim. He nodded, whispered, "Beaufort has her. Homicide."

"Nik, Charley wasn't fooling around. Lane's been arrested for murder." My voice sounded calm, cold, even to me.

She must have heard the change. Of course she did. "Do you need me to fly out?"

"Not yet. Take care of your calls and your advisor." She had a life in Arizona. It didn't make sense for her to drop everything. Especially since I wouldn't let her go alone. "You were there Christmas. Did everything seem okay?"

"Lane was distant, quiet, but she's always been quiet and she's a teenager. They're surly by nature, right?"

I shrugged into the phone. Had we been surly? Hell, I was still surly.

"Charley had a boyfriend. She was taking some new meds."

"Prescribed?" I asked.

"I saw the bottle. I saw the dosage. I think they're both smoking pot, though."

"I'll call you when I get there, sis."

Her voice shifted, grew melancholy and weary. "Be safe, Davis."

I hung up and looked at Tom.

"Are you going to be okay?"

I nodded. He only had an inkling of the things I'd been through. It had been a while since I'd had to rely on the survival skills I'd spent my life honing, but I knew they were still there.

"You're heading north, aren't you?"

"Please tell Marilyn I'm sorry I'll miss her cookout this weekend."

He smiled wryly. "Yes, because I know how much you enjoy a raucous party."

"Hey, I attended the last one. Even kept that urn in the hallway in one piece. Rubelli's cousin can drink." I faked a smile I didn't feel.

He patted my arm. "Be well. Call me if you need anything."

I nodded, forced down the mixture of panic and resignation. "I'll be fine."

After he left, I sat in the car and looked and my hands. There was blood there no one else could see. A lot of it was mine.

I'd made sure Lane never suffered any of the things I had as a child. Or at least I had until I'd left. She'd been innocent. Maybe too much so.

"Lane, what have you done?" I started the car and put my hands on the wheel. I had a bad feeling in order to save Lane I was going to have to face the past I'd tried to forget.

CHAPTER TWO
Wednesday, February 8

I pulled into Charley's driveway seventeen and a half hours later. It had taken me a few hours to get my boss set up for my absence and to toss a few things into a duffel bag, but I'd driven through the night, only stopping for gas and coffee. At some point, I'd called my boyfriend Matt, told him where I was going.

His response had been confused. "I kind of thought you were an orphan."

"Close enough."

"So, you'll be gone how long?"

"I honestly don't know."

"Oh, well, call me if you need anything. I'll miss you." He sounded sincere. I pictured his boyish face and shaggy version of a business cut.

"I will. I'll miss you." I didn't mean it, but he didn't seem well-versed enough in my lies to know.

I stretched, straining the seat that was already shoved back as far as it would go, and looked up at the house. From the outside, a 1940s copy of an old farmhouse with mix-matched additions. We'd bought the place with blood money, paid for it outright, and Nik and I had been slipping utilities and tax collectors money ever since. The inside would smell like dust and pot smoke, soured milk, cheap beer and sex. Because it always did.

Spanish moss hung from the two scrub oaks sticking out of the overgrown, brown grass like cypress hammocks in the Everglades. Across the street, Old Lady Hathaway's house sat uninhabited and creepy on its sagging frame. The area in general felt abandoned, neglected, and depressed.

A cold drizzle settled in the hairs on my bare arms and I reached back in the car for my bag. In it, I'd stuffed my few long-sleeve shirts, a pantsuit in case I needed it, and underwear. I'd moved to South Florida—fled, really—five years earlier with nothing more than stolen clothes and someone else's credit card. First in Miami and then in Fort Lauderdale, I'd learned that the coldest days of the year could still be survived in a light jacket, but had bought a single leather coat to blend during the handful of days the locals bundled up.

I left the coat on the back seat. Let the cold settle into my bones and find old breaks and bumps. It seemed only right to face my mother cold. I'd spent so much of my life ill-prepared and poorly dressed, making sure Lane and then Nik had what they needed before I did.

The key was where I'd expected, and inside the air was still and musty except for a lone ceiling fan covered in enough dust to make it look like a spinning cat.

"Charley?" I tossed my duffel into her cluttered old studio. It knocked over a stack of dusty paintings, blank and stained canvases, and an empty glass jar smeared with paint and the cloudiness of long-evaporated turpentine. I couldn't remember the last time she'd produced new work. Could barely remember her sober, remotely whole.

Down the main hallway, in the obnoxiously purple kitchen, I heard water running upstairs. I glanced at the empty jug of wine and half-eaten Pop-Tart.

"Charley?" Still no answer.

I headed up the back stairs, sucked in a breath at the memories embedded in the cheap paneling. "Charley, it's not such a good idea to leave the key on top of the mat. Kind of defeats the purpose of locking the door."

From the bathroom came crashing and a feral screeching that could only be Charley. "No!"

"Is there someone in there with you?" I raised my hand to pound on the door, then stopped myself.

"No!"

I tried the doorknob. Locked. I looked down. Reddish water puddled from under the once-white door.

My heart sank and sped up in a way only Charley could cause. I ran down the hall to my old bedroom, where I knew Uncle Phil's former belongings sat piled up. Obviously ransacked boxes told a story I didn't have time to process.

In a box of old tools, I found a camping ax to use on the door. Had I been at home, I could have used the lock pick set my downstairs neighbor had given me. Hell, at home I could've just kicked in the cheap door. Course, at home I wouldn't have had this freaking problem.

Then again, maybe home for all of us would always end up being wherever Charley had last fallen off a proverbial wagon no matter how far we ran.

I whacked the wood near the lock. "Charley, I'm not going to hurt you. You have to talk to me. Tell me what's going on in there."

"Nik? It's not my fault."

I sighed. "It's okay."

"You wouldn't understand." She ripped the shower curtain off its rings. "Stop it!"

"Are you with someone?" I could see through a crack I'd created so I had an answer to the question before I'd finished asking it, but it always helped to see if she and I were on the same mental page.

"Hands. So many hands. Like spiders. Everywhere."

We were not only on different pages, but in different books. I got a hole big enough to stick my hand through to unlock the door.

She moved away and curled up in the corner beside the toilet.

She'd slashed her wrists. Again. As usual, she'd cut across just deep enough to make a big mess, but not deep enough to really kill herself absent copious amounts of blood thinners and some extended, unsupervised time. For a second, I wished she'd figure out how to do it right already.

I grabbed her wrists and wrapped them in a towel. "Old scars get too faint?"

"You!" She stared at me, terrified, and tried to back away. She slipped, hit her head on the toilet tank, and started screaming again.

I reached behind me and turned the water off, keeping her cornered. "You feeling okay?" I checked her eyes, but they didn't seem abnormally large or small. "Did you take something?"

She shook her head without taking her eyes off my face. "You're not real."

"Do you remember why you cut yourself?"

She rocked. "I can't even do this." Tears fell out of her eyes and I noticed bits of broken glass in the greasy spikes of her inky-indigo hair. She suddenly yanked her right wrist away and grabbed a stray piece of glass. "You're not here. I'm in hell."

I grabbed her wrist. Blood squished through my fingers. I felt disgust and a simmering rage.

"You fucked it up!" She squeezed her fist around the glass.

I pried her fingers open and threw the glass across the blood-streaked tile before yanking off some toilet paper. "Hold this."

She threw it in my face and spat.

I tried again, holding her fist closed around the paper as I jerked her up.

I frog-marched her across the wet floor to the hallway. "You haven't tried to off yourself in almost seven years, Charley. What the hell?" I knew I was trying to reason with the unreasonable. Old habit.

She dragged her feet and wriggled like a giant toddler.

I dumped her writhing, bony frame on the bed and dialed 911. She had the bed shoved in the corner, covered with mounds of garbage and dirty clothes. The whole place smelled like a seedy motel room. I told the person on the other end of the phone I had a suicide attempt near Newport and rattled off Charley's address.

Charley, her features distorted and puffy, her lips cracked, skin splotchy, screamed, "I hate you!"

The dispatcher asked if this was a domestic dispute.

Charley kicked me in the leg and ran for the door.

"No," I told the woman. "It's an addict."

I dropped the phone, launched myself at Charley. Tackled her around the waist, sent us sliding on a cheap rag rug. She reached for a dresser she shouldn't have been strong enough to move and pulled on a leg until it toppled toward us. Drawers fell, clothes spilled. I pushed her out of the way and rolled up against the wall as it crashed to the floor. "Dammit, Charley."

She ran for the hall and I followed her. My feet sloshed in the water and my leg hurt. The place looked like a stupid horror show: blood smeared on the floor, the doorframe, me.

At the end of the hall, she beat the glass out of the door leading to the balcony with a footstool and threw it through. She grabbed a chunk of glass and held it to her neck. She stood, in her dingy white cotton panties, looking more deranged than she had in years. "Fuck you."

I searched my brain for the tricks we'd used on her when we were younger.

Tears streaked her face and her hands wavered. "I'll be good. I swear." She wasn't talking to me, if she ever had been.

"Charley, please don't do this." *Shit.*

"I tried so hard." Her eyes were glassy, unfocused. "He's dead."

I nodded and shook my head, not sure what to do.

"You're not real."

"Then you can tell me, right? If I'm all in your head, you can tell me anything."

Her eyes swam into focus. "Shut up." She backed up through the metal doorframe, not even noticing the glass under her bare feet. "Get out of my fucking house!" She stamped her feet in the glass and scrunched her face. Held the glass out like a knife.

"Please put the glass down." I inched forward.

Her eyes went through me. "Why?"

Behind me, the wall still bore a bullet hole from a moment like this years ago. The look on her face was the one she should have been wearing then.

I stepped closer.

She put the glass back to her throat.

"It's okay." My voice betrayed none of the anger I felt, none of the pain.

She tightened her grip. Blood flowed down her already bloody arm. Her eyes grew crazier and her hand wavered.

I ran.

She stared at me. "I hate you," she whispered as I charged.

I dove and a feeling of déjà vu washed over me.

Charley held the glass in front of her. It caught me in the left shoulder when we collided. Pain shot through, then radiated. She let go of the glass and grabbed my ears, clawing at old scars.

We hit the deck of the balcony so hard it knocked the wind out of me. Slid on broken glass. She howled and left a bloody smear. My forehead slammed into the railing, which stopped us from falling two stories into a rose bush.

She grabbed another piece of glass and jabbed it in my back. I gasped, despite years of steeling myself against things that could hurt me.

I rolled her and tried to pin her, but the drugs were making her strong, the blood was making her slippery, and the crazy was making her wily.

She grinned, triumphant, picked up another piece of glass, tried to jab it in my arm.

I shoved her arm over her head and yanked the shard out of my shoulder.

She reached for it and I jerked her to a standing position, wincing as the glass in my back moved with the muscle.

She twisted herself free. "One of us has to die."

I pulled her down into a modified wrestler's hold. *How many times had we been in similar spots or worse? How many times had she tried and failed? How many times had we stopped her? How many more before we failed?*

She wailed and struggled and peed.

CHAPTER THREE

Somewhere behind us, sirens stopped. I watched the lights bounce off the trees, splashing the house and lawn in red. Parts of me hurt that hadn't hurt in years.

A voice, rich and baritone, accompanied pounding downstairs. "Hello?"

Charley kicked me in the shin and lunged for the edge of the balcony.

"Out back!"

Charley screamed and shook the metal railing until screws rattled.

I couldn't hear what the baritone said in response, but a few seconds later he ran around the jutting front corner of the house. He wore jeans and a plaid shirt under the bright orange volunteer rescue squad vest, and looked oddly familiar.

The railing broke; Charley plunged. I grabbed her wrist and a piece of the next section of railing as we tumbled off the deck. When gravity kicked in, the jolt felt like it ripped my already-bleeding arm out of its socket, but I held fast. I couldn't feel my hand, but it worked on its own.

Charley continued screaming, kicking and making matters worse.

"I don't even want to know how you two ended up like this." He easily grabbed the flailing Charley around the knees. "You okay?"

I nodded and let her go.

"Super," I muttered. I looked below me over my shoulder. "What the hell's under me?"

"A piece of railing and a bunch of weeds. Why? You're not going to—"

In answer, I dropped and cushioned my landing with a loose-limbed squat. "I hate this place."

I got to my feet and pulled my shirt up to look for damage. I had a few nice bruises forming in addition to the bloody shoulder. I reached behind me and tried to pull the glass out of my back. It was wedged pretty tight about six inches below the base of my neck, a little left of my spine, and it moved every time I did, making my stomach churn.

I looked at the new guy in front of me, a short blond "Got any tweezers?"

He nodded and disappeared. I examined the various cuts on my arms and hands. None seemed life-threatening. I rubbed my face but found no major damage there either. My clothes, on the other hand, were filthy, ripped, and probably needed to be burned.

Another day with the world's greatest mother.

They'd driven the ambulance as close as they could and it looked like another weird addition to the house. A squishy woman and the runty blond fought to push a stretcher across the dead, overgrown lawn. I didn't see the baritone.

I held my shoulder and felt dazed.

"Ma'am, are you sure you're all right?" A hand touched my good shoulder. I tensed and nearly attacked him.

"Yeah, fine." I wiped my face with the back of my hand and slowed my breathing.

"Can I see that?"

I turned. "Craig Silvano?"

"You probably need stitches." He gestured at the bloody hole in my shirt.

I covered my shoulder again with my hand. "Stitches are overrated."

The blond trotted over, handed Craig a plastic package. He looked up at me and held out his hand. "By the way, my name's Scooter."

"Davis." He wore gloves and didn't even flinch at the bloody paw print I left on them.

Scooter winked at Craig and took off.

I suddenly felt self-conscious, ridiculously so. I tried to smooth my hair with tragi-comedy results.

Craig didn't look shy or self-conscious. Or bloody and rumpled. He wrinkled a dark, bushy eyebrow. "She gonna be okay?"

I grabbed the package and pulled out the tweezers. "Probably not."

"You want some help?"

I reached over my shoulder. "Ow. Fuck."

"Something set her off."

I stared at the bloody shard.

"I haven't seen her like this since prom." He gave me a nervous, fake laugh and his eyes wandered first to my hand and then to the ambulance as the woman slammed the doors shut.

"She wasn't this bad then. Well, different anyway."

He made a noise like he disagreed, but didn't push it.

"She'll be fine. Always is."

"And you?"

"Never better." I dropped the bloody glass on the grass.

"Still full of family secrets?" He looked hurt, angry.

"I don't need this, Craig." I stepped past him. "I don't need any of this."

"What do you need, Davis?"

"It's not your problem. Never was." I felt kind of lightheaded.

"That's low."

Craig started to look kind of fuzzy. Drunk fuzzy. "How's the wife?"

"We divorced. She lives in Claremont with the kids, but you're changing the subject."

"Things change. Even subjects." I started across the lawn, feeling weak in the knees.

He closed the gap between us. "You should sit."

Wooziness hit me and I stopped. "I'm just tired. It was a long drive."

"Uh huh. Let me help you inside. Please?"

I realized the ambulance had left and we were alone. "You sent them away?"

"I know you. I knew I'd have to knock you out to get you to a hospital."

I pushed off and headed across the yard to the back porch. A broken piece of railing caught my eye. "She tried to kill me. Again."

"She was on something. She didn't mean it, Davis."

I turned and looked into his dark brown eyes before heading into the house. "She doesn't even know who I am."

"You're shivering."

"It's cold." I stumbled inside and collapsed on the eggplant-colored linoleum

"You need a doctor."

"It's just blood, Craig." I pulled off my shirt and used it to wipe off as much as I could before reaching for a filthy dishrag.

He snatched the dishrag away from me and put the bloody shirt back over what seemed like a relatively small hole. "Stay here. I'll clean it up."

I sat. I still felt dizzy. I needed breakfast and probably a nap since I'd driven all night. I crawled to the fridge, opened the door and let my teeth chatter.

Nothing. Half a bottle of ketchup, a box of baking soda, and an empty vodka bottle. I yanked out the Popov with my good arm and hurled it as hard as I could at the opposite wall where it left a dent and bounced onto a cheap rug. To ensure that together we'd made a complete mess of the house, I threw the ketchup bottle after the vodka. The cap broke off and reddish brown splotches filled in the dent.

Craig rounded the corner with a small tackle box and a box of gauze pads.

"I should have let her. I sound like a horrible person, but I should have let her." I pushed Craig away and crawled over to the nearest cabinet so I could lean against it.

"It's the blood loss, Davis."

"It's not my flesh wounds. I'm a selfish, rotten human. And I'm tired." And I'd seen the way she looked at me. And I remembered how she'd looked at me prom night. And I recognized the hate.

"She gave birth to you."

I shook my head. "I left her here. With Lane. I thought I had to. I thought it was best. Now she's in jail."

"Lane's in jail?" He moved closer, dabbed the shoulder wound with a gauze pad.

"Will you just fix that already? I have to do things."

"You need stitches."

"It's a tiny cut."

"It's…" He gave up and dug around in his tackle box for something labeled sutures. He didn't look so sure about that idea.

"That should work. Hell, butterflies, needle and thread, Elmer's glue, bubble gum, whatever."

"I don't have a topical anesthetic."

I took the package and jerked it open with my teeth.

"It's gonna hurt."

"It already hurts. Just do it so I don't have to." Rage and disgust and a pain deeper than skin all swirled in my head. I slowed my breathing, controlled my emotions with it, and watched Craig lay out the contents of the packet on a layer of gauze.

He moved my hair and examined the jagged hole. "You could have severed something."

"I can move everything, no nerve damage." I eyed the web of scars on my hand. "I'm not dead, so I assume she missed anything major."

"Do you not understand how serious this is?" He cleaned the blood from around the wound and pinched it closed. "Or do you just not care?"

"It's not serious, Craig." I felt drained, empty, but it wasn't the blood loss, spent adrenaline, or lack of sleep.

"I'm sorry, Davis." I watched the back of his neck ripple slightly. I smelled his shampoo. He touched a faint scar just below my ear, one I'd forgotten was still visible when my regrown hair was brushed aside. "Davis? Are you sure you're okay?" He sounded petrified, like I'd gone off the deep end Charley-style. He fingered the scar again and I could feel his eyes following the stick-straight path my strawberry hair usually took down my back to find older, worn-out scars he'd seen before. And new ones.

I bit my lower lip. "Just because you mean well enough to try to keep me from bleeding to death this time doesn't mean I have to tell you."

"If wherever you were, if it was helping… Maybe you should leave this for someone else to take care of. Maybe—"

"Who, Craig? Lane? You?" I turned my head so I could see him in my peripheral vision. "This is my job, Craig. It's just like the one you volunteer for: fixing people who fucked up."

Craig looked at me with his serious-discussion face. The same one he'd always worn when he was getting ready to deliver an after-school special speech. "Just what *is* wrong with Charley?"

"Does it matter?"

He nodded.

"You really want a label? There isn't one. We moved around too often for her to get regular treatment. One guy diagnosed her as schizophrenic, wanted to have her committed if she wouldn't take her meds. Another thought she had multiple personalities and wanted to study her like a lab rat. Nik thought he was a quack. Some other woman claimed Charley suffered from drug-induced psychosis. And another thought she had a psychotic break stemming from childhood sexual trauma. She worked for one of the jails Charley was in for prostitution, so there's that."

"What do *you* think?"

"She's certainly fried her synapses with the drugs. Basically, she's just some wannabe artist, who mostly didn't have a stitch of talent for anything other than holding their liquor and painting with their toes, giving each other sponge baths in the park—that kind of crap. She's never made anything anyone wanted to look at or listen to, but she's affected a helluva persona trying. Doesn't matter what you call it. Doesn't change it." I left out the day she'd gone from casual drug use to hard-core, suicidal abuse. That wound still hadn't healed for either of us.

I tried to stand, but immediately grabbed the countertop.

"You can't keep abusing yourself." He dragged a stool over and stuck it under my ass. "Sit. I promise not to let the secret slip." He set his supplies on a relatively clean section of countertop.

"Craig, I know you can't understand, and that's good." I watched him open my palm and tape a fresh piece of gauze over a gash he seemed to know I would reopen half a dozen times. He didn't bother commenting on the melted whorls in the shape of a stove burner that refused to disappear.

"I can't tell you how to live." He squeezed the cut on my arm that I hadn't really noticed and put in two neat little stitches. I watched and ignored the urge to wince.

"I've done worse."

"I can see that." He cleaned up the shoulder wound, not commenting on the long white line running under it from my armpit to my collarbone, and started on another row of stitches. I took a long, slow breath and thought about the first aid kit Nik used to keep in a Hello Kitty pencil pouch, how she'd insist on sewing up cuts just to make me "think twice about doing that again." It never worked.

"You've seen me naked before. You've seen me bloody. What the hell?" I closed my eyes tried to remember a time when I wasn't in some kind of pain, tried to imagine a life where it didn't seem necessary.

"And Charley was the cause then too, wasn't she?" He waited to see if I'd admit it.

"You don't know that."

He shook his head like he was clearing mental cobwebs. "Forget it. Keep this clean, will ya?"

I shrugged and regretted it. I hadn't realized how often I shrugged to avoid answering questions, or as an answer when further explanation seemed pointless.

He put down his scissors and peeled off his rubber gloves. "We were friends for years. Why didn't you talk to me about this stuff?"

"*Because* we were friends."

"We were more than friends, too. Or don't you remember that?" He slammed his box closed, wouldn't look at me.

"We went to the prom together. Or, we were supposed to. Prom's about parties and getting drunk and having some awkward sex. It's not about watching your mother get drunk, having some awkward sex, and never even making it to the damn dance. And it doesn't mean you have to tell your date your life story."

"I sat with you at the hospital. You never mentioned any of this. You never talked at all." He paused for a second. "Wait, who'd you have sex with?"

"It was inconsequential. It still is."

"You cheated on me. On prom night." He gathered his stuff in silence. "I'll see you later."

I let him think whatever he thought because it was a much easier explanation, and I had things to do besides open old wounds for no good reason. I'd been in town an hour and I already had fresh ones.

"Thanks," I called as he shuffled down the hall. "Really. For everything."

He ignored me.

CHAPTER FOUR

I hadn't driven nine hundred miles to confront guys I'd had sex with in high school. I showered, slapped some bandages on the worst cuts, and threw on the pantsuit I'd brought. I found a fuzzy aspirin in my purse, along with a half-melted mint, and washed both down with water cupped from the bathroom sink.

Then I called my boss and had him draw up a simple power of attorney and guardianship papers. Since he considered my friends to be his friends and thought a few of Tom's might be useful should he run for mayor, he was oddly pliable most of the time. Either that or it was his aggressive mood disorder that had scared off a record twenty-three legal secretaries and paralegals the year before he'd hired me. I'd been there almost two years because I basically treated him like Charley and reappeared at work every time he fired me in a crazy rage.

I had him fax the papers to a copy shop halfway between Charley's and the police station, found a notary willing to bend the rules for a sob story, and disappeared long enough for her to think I'd gone to the hospital for Charley's signature instead of forging it like we'd been doing it since we'd learned to write.

Tom was right when he said I'd have ended up locked away for life had we lived in any one town long enough for the law to catch up with me. Of course, who knew how we'd have turned out had we stayed in one place long enough for people to get to know us, for social services to catch up, or for Charley to get help.

Downtown Beaufort was more charming than sprawling. I found the police station, a small brick building with two cruisers out front, on Broad Street next to what looked like a boarded up train depot from a theme park. I parked next to a cruiser and stared at the department logo. Ignored the uneasy feelings it generated.

At the reception desk inside, a pretty, uniformed black woman offered me a massive grin. "Hi, may I help you, ma'am?" Her nametag read Winters and she had talons, all painted for the season with hearts and fake diamonds.

"I'm here about Lane Groves. I'm her sister." I pulled out my wallet and showed Winters my driver's license. Next to it was my conceal carry permit.

Winters tapped the counter with a pink nail. "You usually carry?"

"Not really, no."

She didn't look like she believed me.

The permit had been Tom's idea, "a just in case you ever need it" thing. So far I hadn't.

"You aren't the legal guardian." She picked up a nearby clipboard and flipped through logs or notes, rows and rows of the same cramped-capital cop handwriting. "Charlemagne Groves – the guardian – has been informed of the charges and all pending court appearances. It's up to her to divulge information as she sees fit."

"Our mother is in the hospital." I reached into my bag and my usual assortment of toiletries, gym necessities and half-finished tasks jostled as I pulled out the folder.

She looked at me warily. "You just got these drawn up?"

"My boss is an attorney; he agreed to help me out."

"He has a Florida address like you?"

"He's admitted to the bar in North Carolina, too." I gave her a look that said I didn't really get it. Experience had taught me to only give them the information I had to.

She walked away, back into the semi-concealed office part of the building and returned a few minutes later with a file folder and a stack of reports. "She's been arraigned. Judge wants her held for observation."

An older white guy appeared on her heels from the bowels of the tiny building and gave me the full eye-fuck. "Looks like you got a little boo-boo there."

"Fishing accident."

"Girls shouldn't be guttin' their own fish."

"I was helping my boss release a hundred-pound tarpon down in the Keys, but thanks for your concern." I turned back to Winters. She hid the smile on her lips well, but not well enough. "Can you walk me through this real quick? My boss handles real estate, probate stuff, so he was a bit fuzzy on the system here. Down there, you do something too bad as a juvenile – multiple felonies, murder, run out of juvenile program levels – the judge holds you for twenty-one days in detention while the prosecutor decides whether to direct file you to county."

"You know this from personal experience?" she asked.

"I have law enforcement friends."

"Honey, I'd look for a lawyer," she said. "Sheriff's department found her at the scene covered in the victim's blood. Vomit."

"Is she still in the juvenile system?"

"Technically, yes, but she still gets to talk to an attorney if she wants to. We can't question her without a parent or guardian present." She gestured at the papers I'd brought. "Guy heading up the case may be giving you a call in the next day or two."

"Did you try to get Charley in here?"

She flipped through the file. "Took us a while to track her down—she wasn't home the first time we stopped by. When we did, she told us her name was Ramona Wilkerson. She seemed lucid, but her ID said Charlemagne Groves."

I noticed a copy of a search warrant, but couldn't make out what they'd been looking for. "I suppose you want me to let you talk to her."

"Whether you do or not, it gets transferred to adult court and you get no say anymore, guardian or not." She made it sound inevitable and I worried she might be right. "Since you're here, though, want to consent to letting us ask her a few questions?" She smiled warmly.

Good luck. Lane had once gone almost a year without talking.

On the other hand, it would give me a chance to study Lane, maybe figure out what she'd been up to. And let her know I was there and to keep quiet.

I nodded.

"I'll go arrange it. We'll have to meet over at the jail. No reason to have her transferred for a little chat."

The guy who'd been in earlier returned, his nose and ears pink. The smell of cigarette smoke clung to him. "Any idea why this guy was shot with your gun?"

"*My* gun?"

He leaned on the counter where Winters had been. "Dan Wesson 1911 Series Commander Classic Bobtail .45 caliber. Previously owned by Philip Lockhart, deceased. Transferred to you."

I wondered just how bored they all were that they seem to have memorized the case. Not to mention the fact that the gun had never been transferred officially. It'd been left to me in Phil's will and his relatives had shipped it without legal documentation. "Why do you even know that?"

"I make it a point to know things. Like how Mr. Lockhart died."

"Am I under arrest?"

"Should you be?" He cocked his head.

"I was in Florida when this guy got shot."

"You sure about that?"

"I was in Florida when you all talked to Charley. I was in Florida when Charley called me."

He hitched his belt and leaned on an elbow. "You know it's a misdemeanor to improperly store weapons around minors, right?"

"Well you locked up the minor. Problem solved."

He gave me a look that said he didn't like that answer.

"Charley was supposed to keep them stored properly while I was in college." I had no compunction about blaming Charley, even if she and I had never had such a conversation. She owed me a few.

"Don't worry your pretty little head about that." He grinned and I noticed he had bread stuck in his yellowed teeth.

I dug my fingernails into my fist in an effort to keep from telling him which part of hell he could take himself to and how. When I drew blood, I stopped and fought the urge to wipe it on my pants.

Winters walked back up. "I'll have Detective Huber meet you over at the jail in forty minutes."

"And visitation?" There was only so much I could gain from Lane with a cop in the room.

"Visitation's for family, Sundays only." Winters picked up a cheap pen and scribbled information on a Post-it note. I marveled at her ability to maneuver the decorated daggers. "The jail's close." She handed me the note with hours, directions and a crude map. "Oh, and here's a card for the public defender."

"Thanks for your help."

She gave me the sort of sly smile I associated with being sized up. "Something tells me your friends aren't the only reason you know about the juvenile justice system."

I gave her my best innocent expression and wondered if that warrant in Texas had expired.

CHAPTER FIVE

About a block away from the police station sat a giant red brick courthouse reminiscent of an antebellum South, with flaky, painted columns and bell housing, minus the actual bell. Inside, it held a bureaucratic labyrinth of industrial tile floors and dirty beige walls accented with dark paneling and a million little plastic signs leading visitors to courtrooms, offices and restrooms.

I followed the signs to the public defender's corner of the building and waited on a gray plastic chair for the lone attorney, a small man with a neck like a turtle who looked like he'd take any opportunity to duck down into his brown suit jacket and refuse to return.

He led me to his office, stacked so full of files it was surely a fire hazard, and flipped through the guardianship papers. "I'm not sure I have time for this today." He gestured at a folding chair opposite his desk. "Groves, right?"

"How many child murderers could you possibly represent a year?"

"Murder, not so many. Vehicular homicide, drug possession, domestic disputes…" He waved his hand at the stacks. "I'm not saying her case isn't important, but," he handed back my file folder, "she already had her secure custody hearing. Next step, they decide if she's tried as an adult. When's she turn eighteen again?"

"May."

He made a face. "That's not good."

"Likely not, no." I waited for him to offer some useful piece of information beyond the utterly obvious. When he didn't, I tried a new tactic. "Look, all I know are the basics I got from the police. Any chance you could give me a little more insight on what happened?"

He shook his head and rummaged through a stack of folders. "They decided to hold her. I'd expect filings for a probable cause hearing any day now since it's a felony case and she's over thirteen. From there, they'll probably transfer it to Superior Court and that's when you're going to want to hire her an attorney or come back and see me for an

Affidavit of Indigency."

If Charley were still Lane's guardian, that wouldn't be a problem. I nodded like that sounded great and planned to look for private counsel.

"If, and it's likely, they transfer it, she'll be eligible for bail, but I wouldn't count on that."

"Because they think she murdered this guy." I gave him a look that said I expected him to elaborate.

"Because they found her at the scene, gun in her hand, bullet in the guy's head."

"In? I thought it was a .45 caliber."

He thumbed through the file. "Right. 'In' is kind of a colloquialism here. William Guthrie's head was mostly on the wall. The neighbor heard the shot around one-thirty and it looks like they made the first attempt to notify Charlemagne Groves after they finished the initial processing. Looks like they had to come back around eleven."

"Yeah, Charley's … not always herself. They recovered and tested the weapon?"

"One bullet fired. Seven left. Ballistics aren't in yet, but early assumptions are the gun at the scene did the shooting."

"Fingerprints?" I asked.

"Lab reports aren't back yet. State lab should have early results by tomorrow or the day after. If you're leaning toward a private attorney, they'll get copies of all the reports as they come in."

"But if she took the gun from our mother's house and it turns out that's what shot this guy, they'll claim it was premeditated and she's—"

"Looking at life in prison, if she's lucky."

I sighed and thanked him for both his time and the Affidavit I knew wouldn't do me any good.

On the other end of the building, after some frisking and metal detecting and identity proving, I was shuffled into a small room with three mix-matched chairs, a seventies-era wooden table, and scarred acoustical tiles on both wall and ceiling. I picked one of the molded plastic chairs, leaving the one with the exposed cushioning.

A detective entered first and held the door while a corrections officer led Lane in, handcuffed and shackled. Lane looked at the leftover chair and sneered. "Of course you took the good one."

None of them looked comfortable, so I assumed it had something to do with hers being the only one without arms. I shrugged and held back a wince.

The detective, a classic Old White Man from his nearly-bald head to his slight paunch, wore wrinkled khakis, blue collared shirt and tie. He motioned for Lane to sit.

She glared at him, but sat.

I stared at her. We no longer looked very much alike. She'd cut her hair short and dyed it black with a streak of orangey-red. The way it had grown shaggy told me Charley's darker locks had been an imitation of Lane's. The bags under her eyes seemed more an imitation of Charley's.

The detective looked back and forth between the two of us. "I'm Wilson Huber. You can call me Detective Huber. I'm going to ask a few questions, and if your older sister here doesn't object you can answer whichever ones you want. Got that?"

Lane snarled and I noticed the hole where a nose ring had been. "Fuck you. And her. She don't care. I don't even know why she's here. And you can ask whatever the fuck you want, but I ain't gotta say shit."

Detective Huber didn't bat an eyelid at her. "Did you bring a gun to the victim's house?"

Lane stared at him, bored.

"Did you intend to shoot the victim or was it an accident?"

Lane moved her tongue around like she had something in her teeth.

"Were you in a relationship with William Guthrie?"

Lane twisted her mouth sideways.

"Did you shoot William Guthrie because of what happened to Amber Martin?"

My head tilted. "What happened to Amber Martin?"

Detective Huber glanced at me, then back at Lane, waiting.

She said nothing, just rubbed her arm and stared.

"So, if it wasn't a relationship gone wrong and it wasn't about Amber, why would you shoot William Guthrie? Had to be some reason, right?"

Lane picked at her thumbnails, making the chains rattle.

"Maybe a burglary. Someone searched the bedroom upstairs. Was that you? Or are you covering for someone? What did you go to steal?"

Lane rolled her eyes.

"Did you go there alone or did someone help you?"

Lane smirked and stared off at the wall.

Huber leaned back in his chair. "So, you have nothing to say. You went, alone and armed, to the house of a guy who for all the world looked like he was a friend of yours and you shot him in the head for no reason. That's what you want me to believe."

"Ask Murphy," Lane said without taking her gaze off wall. From the side, I could see remnants of hurt I knew I wasn't projecting and wondered how long she'd been drugging herself to numbness.

CHAPTER SIX

I stopped for coffee on the way back to Charley's. My phone had three messages from my boyfriend, Matt, but I ignored them. I had less idea what to say to him than to Charley. While waiting in line, I picked up a local paper from one of the yellow boxes and then settled in an overstuffed chair. The newspaper wasn't thick, but one story caught my interest.

Local Man Shot

William Guthrie, a beloved employee of menhaden magnate and former commissioner, Eric Wright, was found dead in the early hours of Monday morning. Police responded to a call shortly after midnight but have not released further details.

Wright was not available for comment. Business partner Vince Zellner said, "Our hearts go out to the family during this time."
Guthrie, a manager at the Downeast plant, leaves behind his mother, who works at Carteret General Hospital.

Eric Wright and Vince Zellner. The names grabbed some dangling thread of memory and tugged until a whole tapestry of carefully constructed lies lay in tatters.

Vince had sat on a sunken, stained couch in the corner of a warehouse loft in a questionable section of town. His face said he was confident and deeply concerned about whatever minor problem my roommate, Jackie, had been telling him about. His eyes told me something else. They always struck me as guarded, as hiding something dreadful. I was never sure how I felt about his eyes because I was never sure if what I was seeing was really him, or just a reflection of myself. And either way, it scared me.

Vince filled her head with doubts. Told her he'd caught Eric looking at me. Showed her pictures he'd taken of me working out, convinced her there was no way she could keep Eric away as long as I was around. Eventually, he'd done much worse.

I smelled blood that wasn't there and pulled myself back to the coffee shop feeling sweaty and cold. I looked down and realized I'd set the coffee cup on the edge of the table so the slightest breeze or sneeze would send it crashing to the floor. I pushed it farther onto the table and took a long, slow breath.

It's okay. You survived. The memories can't hurt you.

It was another one of my lies. My memories hurt me all the time. I'd wake up in the night shaking and crying. I lived on the fringes of other people's lives, even Tom's and Matt's, making sure they didn't get too close. Tom thought he understood. Matt didn't know he was supposed to.

I picked up my phone and called information, got a number for Wright's Seafood and let them patch me through.

"I'd like to speak with Eric Wright, please."

"He's unavailable at the moment; would you like to leave a message?"

"Do you expect him back soon?" I asked.

There was a pause. "I'm not sure, ma'am. Would you like to leave that message?"

"No, thanks."

I reread the newspaper article, forced myself to stay in the moment.

A shadow fell across my corner of the coffee table. "Davis? Davis Groves? Oh, I do declare. It's been a dog's age since I've seen you."

I looked up to find woman with straight blonde hair holding a toddler and smiling like she'd found a diamond ring in her soup. I had no idea who she was, but she sort of resembled a chunky cheerleader.

"Do I know you?"

"It's Jessica. Jessica Darber. Well, used to be Hutchinson. Married a Darber from up near New Bern. Met him at ECU." She beamed and plopped down next to me. "You went to Wilmington, I heard. It's so pretty down there, but I always wanted to go to Chapel Hill. Still root for the Tar Heels, you know. I can't help it. Didn't have the grades to get into UNC. Isn't that where your sister went? The little one? What was her name?"

"Nik."

"That's it! Y'all always had such weird names, you'd think I wouldn't forget them."

I nodded like I'd never been accused of having a weird name before.

"I heard you left Wilmington. Headed to the mountains? It's pretty there, but I guess I'm just a beach girl at heart. Never could picture myself going away from the coast for too long."

"Yeah, well…" There was no way to explain to her that after Jackie's suicide attempt had triggered memories of every time I'd found Charley strung out on the floor or the bed, I'd decided I couldn't do it anymore. That after Vince had held a knife to my throat, I'd had not just enough, but too much.

She didn't let the silence play out long. She leaned forward, letting the toddler hang off her hip behind her. He reached out and wiped something on the upholstery. "I heard your little sister shot somebody. Did that really happen?"

"If it did, why would I tell you?"

She looked hurt. "You don't have to be rude." She sat up straight. "Now that I think about it, you were always rude in high school, too. Thought you were better than everyone else. But you know what else I heard? I heard you were a slut, masquerading as some Goody Two-shoes like we were all so stupid. I heard you'd been arrested, even." She sniffed her nose at me, gathered her kid, and got up.

"I wasn't a slut."

She turned, her nose already in the air. "Not what I heard."

"I was a whore. The difference is cash."

She stared at me in horror and stomped away.

CHAPTER SEVEN

Since I couldn't figure out why Lane had shot Guthrie, I decided to find out more about Guthrie. In my experience, sometimes people had personalities that just lent themselves to eventual execution or accidental death. Many would argue I was one of them.

A shelf under the glass top of the coffee table held several stacks of old magazines. Under one was a small phone book. I pulled it out and looked up Guthrie. The listings took up half a page, which meant his mother would have been hard to track down if I hadn't seen the address on the police report. Finding her in the phone book led me to believe she wasn't too paranoid. I figured I could use that to my advantage.

I dialed her number and waited. The coffee house was cozy and smelled of desserts and sweaters. I inhaled deeply and tried to fill my soul with some of the sweetness and comfort.

She answered on the third ring, breathless and expectant.

I slathered on a Southern accent from no particular sub-region. "Hello, my name is Amy Sylvester. I'm a reporter with *The News and Observer* in Raleigh. Am I speaking to Sally Guthrie?"

She paused, and when she answered I knew it was because she'd been holding back a sob. "I don't know anything."

"I'm not trying to intrude on your grief or anything ma'am. I usually handle op-ed pieces. You know, fluffy, feel-good stuff." I inserted just enough pause to seem understanding, but not enough to give her time to think. "We picked up the story from the *News Times* there in Carteret County and, well, the story just seemed so sad and short. I'm sure you can understand how readers would want to know more about William."

"He was a good boy." She blew her nose and I could tell she was fighting tears. "He didn't deserve this."

"It does seem a shame more people didn't get a chance to know him." My voice was so syrupy I could've used it to sweeten lattes.

"You want me to tell you it's okay to use my boy to sell papers."

"Not exactly. There's never even a guarantee any particular story won't get bumped by another. But readers—and juries—tend to empathize more with the victim if they feel they know him, like he's one of them."

"I don't want his named mixed up with any of the rumors I've heard about that guy running the plant right now."

"Eric Wright?"

"Nah, he's not so bad. He tries to help. Only reason Billy would go work for him. Ain't too many fishing jobs left and Billy wanted to be in the industry because of his dad. Tried to tell him that's no way to live. Wanted him to go to the college, even if just for a couple years. I thought… I just thought he'd end up struggling too hard, like his dad." She paused and I could tell she was reliving some past argument. "Never figured on this."

"Manager, right? Sounds like a good job."

She snorted a little, a polite Southern, feminine snort.

"So, not a good job? Wright's. Seafood company, right? People eat lots of seafood." I was taking notes in the margins of a stray newsmagazine geared toward tourists. I doodled a top hat on the cartoon fish in a coupon.

"People *eat* seafood, but they like to get it cheap. Billy always complained about it. Even the hospital cafeteria orders from some company in California." This brought new tears and sniffles.

I waited, letting her move back from hysterical to wistful on her own.

"When I was a little girl, the air around this place was so polluted with the smell of the fish factories you'd almost choke on the oily stench. Smell of money, folks called it. They'd rush down to the docks whenever a menhaden boat would come in, hoping to get some roe."

"Fish eggs?"

"Shad roe. My daddy'd fry it up and savor every bite." She paused. "Doesn't matter no way. Only factory left is Wright's. Billy said things were pretty good when he worked there in high school. After Eric took over fulltime, started running for office… well, the old manager, the one Eric's daddy left in charge, just wanted to keep the place afloat. People done changed, too. Nobody wants to eat a spot no more when there's 'mahi-mahi.'"

I thought about restaurants at home in Florida. Dolphinfish, mahi-

mahi to keep tourists from confusing it with Flipper, ran off the coast with sailfish and marlin and tarpon and a lot of other things that seemed to end up on plates and trophy walls faster than it seemed nature could spawn them. "So he had image problems?" I was trying to figure out what that had to do with Billy's death, but figured letting her ramble might get us back there.

She snorted, and this time it was cynical and rough. "Billy used to get upset about how people couldn't eat what was in their own backyards. How people had to get all fancy but still wanted everything to cost a dollar-ninety-nine." She blew her nose violently. "But he was a good boy, made a lot a sense. Tenderhearted, he was. World didn't deserve him maybe, so God called him home."

Silence hung between us, so I asked if Billy'd had any friends I could talk to.

"He was a bit of a momma's boy, I guess. We took care of each other. Talked about Ricky Gillikin and Rex Wittman. They worked together. Got on pretty well. Had some friends from school, Amber Martin and her brother." She sniffed again. "Used to be close to Lane Groves, too."

After she'd hung up, I stared at my notes. Something didn't fit, but I wasn't sure what.

I flipped to the yellow pages and called several attorneys without getting anyone to take my call, much less the case. One paused before asking, "The William Guthrie case? Absolutely not." He followed it up with a click.

I felt the beginning of a headache stretching across the middle of my head. Seemed like time to call my boss for something harder than forms. He answered, annoyed. "Erickson. Talk to me."

"Your clients pay you by the hour, Dick. You can afford complete sentences."

"Davis, what the hell do you want now? I have some temp in here who can't seem to find anything and Belinda Huffington just died."

"The Huffington files are in the second cabinet from the wall with the Miró print. Third drawer down. Midway the drawer. The file's huge. You can't miss it." I rubbed the scar behind my ear. "Be-Huffy covered her ass and her assets years ago. Not to mention, everything you need is on your laptop."

"The family's arguing over the corpse."

"Sounds about right. Look, I could really use a bit of a referral."

"Why do I even keep you?" He sounded exasperated. The Huffington family could do that to a man. Or a lawyer.

"Because you threw a vase at the girl I replaced and the only reason the temp agency agreed to send anyone this time is because I told them you'd pay double."

"You what? Dammit, Davis." The sounds of flapping folders told me he'd put me on speakerphone.

"I need a good criminal attorney up here and I can't get anyone to return my calls. You know somebody?"

The folder flapping stopped. "What the hell'd you do? You've only been gone a day."

"Not for me." I hated needing help. Felt like begging. "It's for my sister. The police up here say she murdered someone."

"Did she?"

"I don't know. She's not talking to anyone. Can't see her alone until Sunday." Not that I thought she'd talk to me any more than she'd talked to Detective Huber. Something had changed in her that wasn't just teenage angst.

"You know, generally even gang members' mamas and nephews come out of the woodwork saying there's no way little Shaquan could've hurt anyone. Don't you watch the news?"

"That's racist bullshit and I'm not looking for a lawyer who cares one way or the other."

He paused and I figured he was calculating my assets since he'd prepared my will shortly after I started working for him. "How much you looking to spend on this?"

"I could sell a condo or two if necessary."

He whistled. "I ever tell you you're the smartest stripper I ever met?"

"Considering how many strippers you've met, I'll take that as a compliment."

"Get MacQuayde to help you with the evidence. He's respected. Got friends in lots of places."

"Uh huh." Tom's friends were like a shiny gold ring Dick wanted in his pocket.

"You gonna be back in town soon? I got a couple new people coming in next week. Could be big money. I don't want them to have to meet this temp. She's hot, but..."

"You're a pig, Dick."

He laughed the laugh of someone who gave even fewer fucks than I did.

CHAPTER EIGHT

There were as many Gillikins as Guthries in the phone book, so I shoved it in my purse for later and called the glass repair place advertised on the back page of the newspaper.

Matt texted again as I hung up. *Are you okay?*

I sighed and considered what I should tell him. Matt was a good guy, but my relationship with him had been superficial at best. I decided to go with the easy lie and told him things were great.

Tom, I called while eating a protein bar on the way to Charley's to meet the glazier. I summarized my chat with Dick.

"You're going to stick your nose in places it doesn't belong, aren't you?"

"Kind of my specialty, Tom. Seeing as that's how we met."

He sighed the way the parents of a precocious child did before they finally gave in. "I'll start with financials on Guthrie."

After he hung up, I tried Wright's Seafood again. The same woman told me she still hadn't seen him. Something in her voice made it sound out of the ordinary, but I couldn't be sure. I told her to tell him Davis called.

"Would you like to leave your first name, ma'am? We got a lotta Davises Downeast."

"It's my first name. That should clear it up for him. Thanks."

The glazier turned out to be an older guy, nonplussed by the mess. I left him working and went off to finish cleaning up. When I ran out of towels and sheets in Charley's room, I loaded the mess into the washer downstairs and went in search of more fabric to ruin.

Nik's bed was still made just the way she'd left it. I sat and held a discarded stuffed animal. The house was the first place we'd lived for longer than a few months since we'd left San Francisco when I was five. We bought it with the blood money of my uncle, who wasn't really my uncle, and my father, who'd been declared dead without a body.

Nik had picked the location because I'd been tired of mountains, afraid of cellars, and because we'd both found ourselves worn down by cities and interstates. Nik and I found the realtor, talked to the banks, used the insurance money from dad's death to pay for it, and worked part-time jobs to keep the utilities on. Charley lived there with us like a teenager. She drank too much, used up all her tips on drugs and junk food. She stayed out too late, brought home strange men, and sold herself because that's what she was used to. What we were used to.

When we'd moved, I'd tried to transform myself, reinvented myself as best I knew how. I may have been a bad girl who skipped too many classes, smoked pot a little too often, but I'd gotten my As and Bs. Nik made sure of that. She wasn't having a dummy as a sister. She saw me as her eldest kid and she wouldn't let me be a failure. Not on the surface, anyway.

She hadn't been thrilled when I took the GED, but she still took pride in my perfect score. She'd graduated a year later, but with honors recommendations for everything.

When I'd left for college, I'd gone to Wilmington because my new best friend, Jackie, was going there and I'd thought she needed my protection. She'd been so innocent and sheltered, so happy when we started at the same college—a college that let me on a limited scholarship and probation as a non-traditional hardship case. I always wondered if they'd believed my admission essay.

She met Eric Wright almost immediately and fell hard.

At first, I'd been happy for them. Later, I'd felt foolish, but held on to hope that she'd be okay, that she'd find her own strength. But she found it too late, and I failed to protect her.

I'd failed a lot of people.

My old bedroom, bare mattress and scattered boxes, hadn't been preserved like Nik's, but still carried the weight of my existence. Old sweatshirts still covered the closet floor. The dresser top still held dried-up lip gloss and hair ties.

Craig thought he wanted to know the truth of prom night, why Charley hated me, and why things had gotten messy and wrong. Like most people, he thought the truth was just an inconvenient tidbit, some minor tragedy that could be washed clean with time and the healing powers of antibacterial ointment and sutures. People could relate to things they saw in sitcoms or heard about from friends, but the real confessional privilege, with the deep-dark-dirty secrets, only extended to strangers on television.

Or maybe I just didn't feel like seeing the look of pity on his face.

I stared at the pile of boxes and refuse in my old bedroom. Most of the boxes had been Uncle Phil's, but the contents had been slashed, tossed and scattered.

Phil Lockhart. Daddy's boyfriend after the divorce from Charley— something I tried to resent them both for, but I found I couldn't. Surrogate uncle. Former Marine. A conflicted man hidden in layers. A man who couldn't live with the things he'd done, seen, survived. I'd failed him like I'd failed Jackie. He was dust somewhere like she was.

I wondered if things would've been different if I hadn't been the kind of girl Uncle Phil thought needed survival skills, needed to learn the discipline of sport. Would Lane have been better off if I hadn't inherited a box of guns? Would she have been better off if I'd let Charley handle her own problems?

I walked to an open box and squatted, examining the contents. I'd shot everything in it, a couple in small tournaments, most just on Phil's wilderness property since competitions for tweens and teens largely focused on small-bore rifles or Wild West exhibition things with little revolvers that made other parents coo and clap. I pulled out the cases one by one, opening them and pulling out the guns. None had been used recently. All had been meticulously cleaned before being put away. Uncle Phil had always taught me that. He'd taught me a lot of things.

And then, he was gone.

I noticed all three .45-caliber guns were missing. I wondered why the cops hadn't confiscated all the others, too, but figured maybe they'd decided removing the minor solved the problem, too. Personally, I'd have thought Charley was more of a danger to the citizenry, but maybe they weren't into preventative measures.

I avoided the black case at the bottom, empty except for a sheet of paper. The paper explained what became of the weapon, but not why. The longer letter, the one written in Uncle Phil's hand and splattered with Uncle Phil's tears had burned away in a fire the year Jackie died. Gone. The hollow feeling remained. I didn't have to fight back tears. Anger and resentment had long since settled into the place where sadness had once reigned.

I heard footsteps in the hallway behind me and jumped up to meet the glass guy, pulling the door shut behind me.

I had decided I'd rather get shot again than finish cleaning up the mess, even if it would improve the resale value when Charley finally managed to off herself, when Nik called.

"All right, what's happening? Charley called me from the hospital."

I rolled my eyes. "Now who needs phone etiquette?"

"What's wrong?"

I registered the change in her voice, but didn't answer.

She waited. Always the patient one.

"You know I…" I gave up. "Charley tried to commit suicide this morning. Again."

"Damn." She paused. "Drugs or razors?"

"She was high as that proverbial kite when I got here. Talking to voices. She slit her wrists. Flooded half the house. Broke the glass door to the balcony."

"And Lane?"

"I've been busy cleaning up, getting stitched up – you know, all the fun stuff. But, yeah, Lane's fucked. And…different." I described the Lane I'd met at the jail.

"You sure it's not just a teenage thing? You think that's what set Charley off?"

"I don't know. She didn't seem quite dialed into this reality."

"Fuck."

"Yeah." I glanced at my watch.

"I can fly out if you need me to."

"Some things should be left to me."

"I hate it when you act like that. I'm stronger than you think I am."

"I know that, Nik. But she was worse than I've seen her in a long time. Maybe ever." I pictured Nik trying to calm Charley in the past, saw her trying to stop her today. "If she'd called you instead of me… She could've killed you, Nik. Or at least managed to kill herself."

"I'm sorry, Davis."

"Don't. No one's bleeding anymore. It's fine."

"She was that bad?"

"Yeah."

"Worse than Daytona?"

I thought about that one. In Daytona she'd been curled up in the fetal position—half dressed in an old vinyl child's-sized Halloween costume and covered in boozy vomit—on the landing of a cheap motel. She'd had an empty bottle of pills in one hand and some bloody, cocaine-dusted cash in the other, her face pulpy. "Let's call it a draw."

"What are you gonna do? What if it's her mess that got Lane in trouble? You're going to check it out, right?"

"My name is not Nancy Drew, you know. In real life, people don't go around snooping in murder cases with a magnifying glass, spunk, and a never-ending supply of daddy-purchased cars."

"Smartass."

"I'll keep you posted."

"Davis?"

"Yeah?"

"I'm glad it was you again and not me."

CHAPTER NINE

For lack of better ideas, I called Tom, who expressed more concern over Charley than Nik had because…well, because he hadn't grown up Groves.

I pulled out my notes. "Got a few names of Guthrie's friends." I rattled off the people Sally had mentioned. He told me he'd call me back in half an hour with something.

Half an hour seemed like a long time. Nik was good at doing nothing. Nik could sit for hours thinking about what we should do and where we should go and how to solve a problem. I sucked at doing nothing. I was good at beating things up, running away from things, and making snap decisions that tended to run the gamut from not-bad to stupid-crazy, with a much higher percentage on the crazy end. Problem was, I'd run out of things to do.

I hadn't come close to running out of crazy, yet. Evidence suggested I probably wouldn't run out of that until about fifteen-to-twenty minutes after I died for good. The fact that I'd already died once, for almost two minutes, was just more evidence of my bad decision making. Maybe it was the genes.

Luckily, Tom called fifteen minutes later with an address. I had been expecting it would be at least an hour away since Wright's main plant was on the other end of the county. Instead, it turned out to be on the other side of Newport, down a road that was more of a suggested hunting path, the driveway a muddy rut in the woods with piles of pine straw over the biggest holes.

The truck at the end was a rusted-out pickup with a flat rear tire. Beside it sat a small boat on a trailer, a tiny sailboat that didn't really look like it had done much sailing, and the chassis of an ATV with a splotchy camo paint job. Overall, the toys didn't seem beyond the range of possibilities for whoever lived in the single-wide since it was a fair guess he didn't have Nik's student loans, but I was a little curious about what might be in the semi-attached wooden garage.

I stepped around a pile of firewood and followed a worn path up to the front door. It opened before I'd reached the cinderblock steps and the brownish-gray hair of a man who looked to be in his mid-to-upper thirties appeared. The rest of him hid behind the door, but his head hovered roughly six-feet from the ground.

"You Ricky Gillikin?"

"What're you sellin'?" He moved to fill the doorframe, wearing an old navy blue tee shirt with jeans, bare feet, and his weathered face. He cocked his head at me slightly. "You kind of look like someone."

"Lane and Charley Groves?" I extended a hand. "I'm Davis."

The cocked head grew a frown. "Ain't you dead?"

I looked down at my upright frame. "Not yet."

"Hmm." He stroked his graying brown beard. "You sure you ain't some cousin trying to fuck with me?"

"Pretty sure." I reached for my purse. "I could pull out my license and check."

He waved a calloused, meaty paw. "Nah. What's up? Ain't seen the girls around for a few days."

"You spend a lot of time with them?" I asked, trying to figure out why a man maybe a decade younger than Charley would be hanging out with the two of them.

He nodded and rubbed the back of his bedhead. "Well, um…this is kind of embarrassing, I guess. I was kind of…" His face turned pink behind the leathery tan.

My face settled into my this-figures look. "You were paying Charley for sex."

The pink deepened. "Kinda."

"You paid her in drugs."

He nodded like he'd been caught diddling my mom or something. Guess he thought he was the first. "I mean, I threw a few bucks her way." It came out like he was trying to justify himself. "She didn't really ask for more."

My expression turned to wry. "That sounds about right. She think you two were dating?"

"Hey, I cared about her."

"As a hooker."

"As a friend. We have similar interests." Defensive. He'd fallen for her. Great.

"Look, she can get a little clingy. She think this was something more?"

He shrugged and looked vaguely sad. "I think the new wore off things. Saw her stalking younger prey, you know what I mean."

"You know who?"

"Some widowed do-gooder out to Mill Creek. Still came around to me to get wild, if you know what I mean." He gave me his best lewd smile.

"So, did you notice her getting a little extra crazy lately?"

He rubbed his beard and stared at the doorframe. Smoke may have risen off his brain. "I don't know. We were always kinda…busy. Besides, she'd shoot up and mellow, you know."

"Yeah, I know." I sighed because it seemed like the right thing to do. "So, you shoot up, too?"

"No way, man. That ain't my thing. I stick with the grass." He nodded like this made him freaking spiritual.

"So, why aren't you high now?"

"Gotta get to work."

"Yeah, about that. Were you buddies with William Guthrie at work?"

"Kinda." He shrugged. "Hey, it always helps to make nice with the boss."

"You guys used to go get beers or whatever?"

"Look, lady, I don't know what your deal is, but I ain't no nark. I talked to the guy a little, to get better schedules."

"His mom thought you two were friends."

He started to shut the door. "His mother's nuts."

I put my foot in the door. "Lane friends with him?"

He stopped. "What'd you hear?"

"I heard they were friends up until she shot him."

He chewed his lip. "Where you been anyway? Why're you back now?"

"Lane got arrested."

His mouth twisted. "You didn't care what happened to her before."

"What *did* happen to her before?"

"Ain't talkin' about nothin' ain't my business. She hates you, you know."

"That's not going to stop me from trying to do what I can for her."

He glanced around the yard, like he suddenly thought he was being watched. "I just ain't comfortable talkin' about it, okay?" He tried to close the door again.

I pulled my foot out of the way and looked around, but I didn't see anything.

CHAPTER TEN

In theory, Charley should have known something, at the very least, about Lane's arrest, even if she'd had to consult with Ramona Wilkerson.

She was stable, physically. The nurses refused to pass judgment on her mental state, but she wasn't in the running for patient of the day.

I wasn't going to win anything, either. I turned her TV off.

"Hey! What'd you do that for?" She squinted at me. "Who are you anyway?"

I sat down on an orange plastic chair. "I hear they sedated you nicely, so maybe you won't stab me with anything."

She looked mildly apologetic. "I didn't do that. Don't be silly." She gave a tiny soap opera laugh. "Don't blame me for your problems. Not every little thing is my fault."

"Lane's pretty much fucked. Unless someone is completely overcome with guilt and confesses, I'd say you should count on visiting her in prison."

She burst into tears and I wondered if they were genuine or an act.

"Charley?" I waited as she reached a crescendo.

"I don't even know what you're talking about!" Definitely fake.

"I needed custody of Lane. You made me her guardian earlier today."

"Why?"

"Because they're going to say you're kind of nuts due to the whole trying to kill yourself thing and that's bad if it leaves her without a guardian when she goes on trial for murder. If she's a ward of the state, they'll find it much easier to just lock her up and throw away the key."

"Why would I give you my daughter? What are you talking about? Lanie's at home studying. I don't even know you."

I unbuttoned my jacket and laid it across the back of the chair. Rolled up the sleeves of my blouse and tried not to glance at the scars on my hand or think about the surgeries or the physical therapy or the lies.

I leaned forward, trying to figure out the best way to approach such an obvious departure from reality. "Do you remember Davis Groves?"

She shook her head. "Rotten bitch. Always in trouble. Man-stealing whore. Got herself killed."

I did? "When?"

She shrugged. "Hit by a car or something. Lane was supposed to take care of it." She looked at me and wrinkled her nose. "Why would you ask me such a thing? I don't like you."

I rubbed the scar under my ear and decided not to remind her that when I'd left, Lane had been twelve.

"Lane's not like her. Lane's a good girl. Home studying."

I stared at her.

"It's too bad no one could straighten Davis out. She was such a handful."

The smell of death and decay, the taste of mud and blood, hit me hard and fast. Panic coursed through me and it took several seconds of even breathing to push it away, along with the image of people from my past.

"Stupid girl."

I bit down on the last of my pain and let some of the anger out. "Get a grip, Charley. Lane was arrested Monday morning. You were notified not long after that." I crossed my arms. "You want to tell me why you waited until Tuesday afternoon to call me?"

"Why would I call you? They're kidding. It's not very funny. I mean, Lane?" She pooh-poohed that idea.

"You thought they were kidding? You thought the police department—in another town—routinely picked residences at random and told the parents their child was homicidal? For *kicks*?" My head hurt. More specifically, my sinuses hurt from holding back tears I refused to let her see.

"You wouldn't understand." She acted mildly incredulous.

"Because I'm not *high*! Charley, this isn't some stranger you're talking to here. Why didn't you call me sooner?" A sure sign I'd lost it: trying to reason with Charley.

"You? I don't even know you!"

I glanced at the scars on my hand. "You know, I need to make a phone call."

I left my jacket and closed the door behind me. I pulled my phone out of my purse and dialed Nik's number, double-checking the time.

She answered on the third ring. "What's wrong?"

"She thinks I'm dead."

"What? Who? Huh?"

"Charley. Our mother thinks I'm dead. She thinks I was hit by a car."

"You were." Her tone said she didn't like to think about it, much less talk about it.

"She thinks Lane's at home studying." Several people walked by, pretending not to eavesdrop.

"The nurse I talked to said she's going to be okay."

"Maybe the nurse doesn't know I'm not *dead*."

"Davis, you're not really upset about this. She's always said stuff like this."

"Stuff *like* this. Not this." I had my answer for why she hadn't been calling me by name. "She's happy I'm dead."

"Davis—"

"Look, I just…" I looked around at the people busy living their own lives.

"Davis, she didn't mean it."

"She meant it, Nik. And I know I should be okay with it because I know she's who she is." I felt a tear form and wiped it away with my thumb knuckle.

"I know." Her voice was soft, like when we were kids. Comforting. "You sure you don't need me?"

"No, you said it yourself. She's fine. Right?"

"Right." She didn't sound convinced.

I hung up and went back in the room, trying to block out all the stuff my brain was dredging up involuntarily. I stood at the end of her bed.

"I don't like you." Her voice became hard. "No one got killed. It's just a phase. Kids today. What do you expect?"

"Are you really *that* out of your mind? I mean, you've never had a great grasp on veracity, or Earth even, but dead is *not* a phase. Dead is dead. Dead is Daddy. Dead is Uncle Phil. Dead is Jackie, Ryan, William Guthrie. Dead is…" It suddenly occurred to me that I lost people like everyone else lost socks.

"You really think I'm so stupid I don't know what dead is?"

I hung my head. "Dead like you tried to make yourself this morning."

"I never did any such thing. People make mistakes. I'm fine. Everything's fine." The family mantra.

"Yeah. Right."

Her tone shifted. "And where's Lane? She should be out of school by now. She can't come see her mother in the hospital? What's wrong with her?"

I chose to ignore her outburst, as per our usual arrangement. "The police took her into custody for killing Billy Guthrie."

"Liar! I just saw him at the grocery store last week." She smiled. "He and Amber make a cute couple."

I wasn't sure what to do, so I picked at a sparring scab on my knuckle.

"She hates me." This time the tears were real. Maybe. "She's hated me since Davis died. She thinks I did it. Davis did it to herself. It's all her fault. She turned Lane against me."

I quietly watched her tantrum build.

"This is all her fault. Left me with this *mess*." She sobbed and smeared snot around her face. "Left me with this kid who hates me. Left me to do everything."

I pulled the scab off and watched the blood re-clot.

"Got what she deserved." She balled up her fists.

I rubbed my forehead and hung my head. I wondered what else she'd think I deserved if she only knew.

I picked up my head, asked, "Who's Ricky Gillikin?"

She smiled. "He's hot, right? Wait, you're not trying to steal my man, right?"

"No. I was just wondering. I heard he was friends with Lane."

"He's mine, honey." Her voice took on an edge.

I thought about the first man I supposedly stole. "Did you hate Davis in Virginia? The day you called the police on her? Told them you never wanted to see her again?"

"That never happened."

"She wasn't trying to steal your man, you know. She was stopping your john from raping Nik."

"Get out!"

I nodded and collected my jacket and purse. "I'll be back,

Charley."

"I hate you!"

"I know."

I stood outside the door finding my breath, pushing the past back into the spaces of my brain I tried not to visit. I shut my eyes. Reminded myself I'd made it out. Reminded myself Charley wasn't why I'd come back.

CHAPTER ELEVEN

I pulled into a gas station in Morehead and went inside for a soda and a bag of nuts or sunflower seeds. My head swam with possibilities, my eyes focused only on the goals of not running into anything and picking up something resembling calories. When a hand touched down on my right shoulder, my instincts kicked in.

I dropped the peanuts, put my left hand on his and spun, pulling him off balance onto the floor with his arm locked up, my foot ready to stomp the back of his neck.

The baby EMT yelped, dropped the hotdog he'd been holding and landed on it.

"Oh shit!" I pulled him back to his feet and reached for some napkins, even though the mustard-stained tee shirt was obviously a lost cause.

"What the…" He looked down at his shirt, at the hotdog, and up at me. "Craig said you were a little stressed. He didn't mention you were a damn ninja."

"Sorry. Reflexes." I gave up with the napkins and tossed the rest of the bunch back toward the rack. "I lived in some rough neighborhoods for a few years."

He cracked his neck and stared at me with a mixture of awe and terror.

I knew there was no way I was going to convince him I wasn't some sort of lunatic. Hell, maybe I was. I had totally blanked out, lost in my head. It wasn't like me not to be present, aware. "Look, I'm real sorry. Okay?"

He nodded. Backed away from me slightly.

"How 'bout I buy you another hot dog. Give you money for a new shirt."

"It's okay."

I reached in my pocket.

He backed away faster.

"Look. Take it." I held out a twenty. "I said I was sorry. I… I don't know how to explain what happened. I'm jumpy, I guess. Charley in the hospital, my sister in jail."

He took a step forward, but ignored the money. "Your sister is Lane?"

I nodded, confused that he hadn't put those two together already.

"Oh man, I'm sorry. I'd have said something earlier." He ran a hand through his scruffy blond hair then held it out to shake. "Scooter. From earlier. I feel like a real heel now."

I shook his hand, confused. "Davis."

"Lane and I went to school together. Over at the alternative place. You know it?" He didn't wait for a reply. "Can you believe I was a wild child back then? Smoking and all that?"

"You're older than her." He had to be, but to look at him, it didn't seem possible.

"Oh yeah, we were only actually there at the same time for maybe a few months. I graduated and she'd just gotten transferred in. She seemed like a good kid, I remember. Didn't seem like the kind to be over there, frankly. Made me wonder what'd happened. 'Course, she always seemed kinda quiet, sullen-like, so maybe she just did a lot of drugs I didn't know about."

I nodded like I understood.

"Listen, I don't know what happened. I heard the call, but I wasn't on that night and anyway, it was over in Beaufort. Not really my area unless they got something they need extra help with. But you know, all the calls come in on just a few channels and I heard it in my truck on my way to see my girlfriend. She lives over in Beaufort." He looked almost bashful for a moment and added, "I usually switch over to the Beaufort or Downeast channels whenever I head that way. Figure if something happens and they need an extra hand. Wouldn't hurt none, you know."

"So you heard the call?"

"Oh, yeah. Neighbors heard a shot. First responders were Murphy from the Sheriff's office and J.T. with the BPD. J.T. ran a little behind, sounded like. Murphy said he was nearby, but I think he just headed over 'cause it was Amber's boyfriend's place."

"He knows Amber?"

"Second cousin. On the mom's side. Used to do security down at

Wright's before he joined the Sheriff's department. Not a bad guy, just…
Well, let me not say nothing might get back to 'im."

"Oh, yeah, sure." I was only half listening to him.

"Yeah, so anyway. Sorry about Lane getting caught up like that. I
don't know what happened. Makes me almost wish I'd gotten to know
her a bit better, but she had her own crowd."

"You remember any of them?"

He rubbed his chin where a pair of hairs might have been trying to
make a beard. "A lot of them have died. Car accidents, some overdoses.
The ones that're left? Amber's still around. Rex was a few years older, like
Billy. Both of them were my grade, but they went to regular school." He
shrugged.

"Thanks." He reached out to shake my hand and I obliged. "And,
sorry, really."

"No worries." He grinned and went off to get himself another
hotdog.

I stood watching him, wondering if I'd fallen through one of those
sci-fi cracks in space-time and landed in a *Twilight Zone* episode.

CHAPTER TWELVE

Talking to Scooter led me to Lane's school, a former elementary school in a decaying part of what had once been a downtown. Sad old bricks full of students who walked by looking like they were older than the building. Among the trudging students, I found a bottom-heavy woman with dyed-yellow hair, teased and sprayed within an inch of its life. She sat on the old flat concrete platform that, based on the other side, had once held a proud concrete lion.

"You must be here about Lane." She took a drag on the cigarette clutched in her fingers like a joint. "You look like she used to."

I stopped, let the remaining few students pass.

"Lunch." She nodded after the sagging pants, too-tight skirts, and frayed jeans.

"You one of Lane's teachers?"

"Former. I'm Ellen. Haven't seen her in a few weeks. Figured she either dropped out on purpose or forgot how to find us. She's not the first. I've had kids show up the first day and don't come back until February. Want to know when they get their credits. And pot? Find me some kids these days who haven't smoked a little weed." She sucked up another healthy dose of pollution.

"You ever talk to Charley about it?"

"Look, I ain't gotta talk to you. You aren't the parent and you haven't passed through security or done the background check or whatever it is they do in the office these days."

I held up my hands. "Wasn't an accusation, just curious. Not like Charley would've remembered."

She relaxed and took another drag. "Only reason I'm talking to you is the resemblance and because I might as well since I'm not supposed to be smoking on school grounds either."

"You're retiring this year, huh?"

"Damn straight. I've been here since they opened. Early on, we had decent kids, just didn't like regular school. You know, the sitting in rows and turning to page thirty because it was Tuesday thing. Wanted to work at their own pace, get done on their own schedule.

"Last few years? Budgets tighter at other schools, legislature breathing down everyone's neck about test scores this and graduation rates that and where are all the STEM graduates and what are you doing for the kids with disabilities and other languages and…" She threw up her hands and went back to giving her cancer stick a blow job.

"Lane slip through a crack?"

"Lane? She had potential. Started out as one of those kids who needed her own pace. Freshman year she lit up a joint in the bathroom over at West Carteret. They suggested she come here." She tossed the butt, checked her watch and pulled out the pack for another. "She made some friends. Some of them the wrong kind. She'd have been okay anyway, but something happened."

"What?"

She inhaled. "That, I don't know." Exhaled. "You can ask her, but I don't think she'll tell you either. Never would talk to the school counselor. Wouldn't talk to me. Wrote some pretty good stuff in English class, but the themes changed somewhat. Wouldn't talk about that either except a snotty assertion it was fiction, imagination, and didn't I have one of those." She looked off at the semi-bare oaks. "Made you wonder just the same."

I agreed and wondered. I'd written a few of those myself.

"I thought she'd be one that got out."

"So she was into drugs before?"

"Just pot. After?" She sucked smoke. "Well, after, she picked up some other habits."

"Heroin?"

"Pills." Ellen took another desperate drag. The cherry burned down and charred the cotton. "Damn filters."

I watched her toss it into a bush.

"Something changed about a year after she came here. That's when she shaved her head, started getting tattoos—little girly heart on her wrist, a paw, stars down her leg, piercings all over—quoting old death metal from back when in her papers. Cry for help, I tell you."

"Anyone listen?"

"Several of us tried. We weren't the right ears."

"Who had the right ears?"

"You, maybe. You were her hero. You know that?"

I didn't believe it. Or, maybe I didn't want to. "I kind of got the impression that she hated me."

She checked her watch. "You saved her from something. She wrote a paper about it once. She was scared, but grateful. Then, you weren't there." She got up.

"I didn't mean to let her down."

"Neither did I."

CHAPTER THIRTEEN

Back in the car, I called Tom. "You still willing to help?"

"Mental health really isn't my field of expertise."

"Funny. Almost as funny as Charley. Like a sitcom a minute."

"That good, huh?"

I rehashed the highlights.

"Davis, why does your mother think you're dead?"

I sighed into the phone. "Because when she shot me, she did a shitty job? I don't know."

"She shot you?" His voice said this was news and he needed to know more.

I didn't feel like telling more. "Long time ago. Water went under that bridge and then we burned it down from both shores."

He was quiet for nearly a minute. "All right, what do you want to know?"

"I want to know what the hell Lane's been hiding, but I'd settle for anything on her friends or this Sheriff's deputy, Murphy."

"He have anything to do with this?"

"Maybe. If he does, I need to see him coming." I switched the phone to the other hand so I could stare at the scars that made up the left. "Look, whatever it costs, I'll pay you."

"You don't have to. You know that."

"The defense is going to need something to work with. Course, at the moment I can't even find a lawyer and I have too much money to use the public defender."

"So, you're thinking she did this?"

Outside the windshield, the sky was gray and the bank sign said the temperature was forty-three.

"I don't know what she did, Tom. I haven't seen her in years. We might not be able to force it, but people change. The Lane I knew could never have shot someone, but the Lane I knew? Maybe I never knew Lane. I don't think she wants me to know her now." And that worried me more than the murder charge, because it said she'd done things she was ashamed to talk about.

"Why did you leave?" His voice was soft, gentle.

"I thought I had to. I shouldn't have." It had been naive of me to assume Lane would be fine just because Nik and I had survived.

"What can I do?"

"What you do."

He sighed hard on his end and shuffled papers. "The mother. Looks like she's a nurse. Lives in Beaufort." He pronounced it like the one in South Carolina.

"Beaufort. Bow, like ribbon."

"Regardless." He rattled directions to an apartment. "Guthrie was twenty when he died. Just had a birthday last month. I'll have to call in a favor, see about the juvie stuff. Sally made just under thirty-eight thousand last year. Paid eight-sixty in rent on a two-one. William worked at Wright's Seafood in Harker's Island. He worked there three years, made nineteen thousand last year, a little less the other two, but only paid taxes on twelve."

"Is there anything you can't find out on people?"

"The things they keep in their heads." He sounded older than usual.

"Good to know."

"They recently came to own a boat."

"A boat?" I pictured the yachts outside Tom and Marilyn's house in the Las Olas Isles neighborhood. None of them seemed particularly useful in an aging fishing village, even if it had been reborn as a tourist destination.

"Forty-seven-foot fishing yacht with tuna towers. Inboard motor." He clicked something on his end. "The title transfer says they paid a dollar. Prior owner doesn't seem related."

"I don't believe in boat fairies."

"Yeah, doesn't look like the seller, James Martin, was doing well enough financially to give away a boat either." More clicks followed.

"Martin? He related to Amber and Brad?"

"Hmm…" He didn't say anything for a while, so I had to assume he was looking into it with one of the half-dozen databases he subscribed to. "Not immediate family. Could be a cousin."

I remembered what Scooter had said. "Like Murphy?"

"It's weird. James isn't the only name here. At first, I thought it was the title company, but it's a secondary seller. International WSD."

"Who owns that?"

More clicks. "Eric Wright."

"Well, that's a helluva thing."

"Yep. I'll call you right back." He hung up.

I started the car and headed toward Beaufort. My phone rang again on the causeway between there and Morehead.

"James Martin deposited a large sum of money right after selling the boat for a dollar."

"Could Billy have squirreled money away living with mom? Maybe they did it that way to avoid taxes?"

"My guess? Something on the side. But that's an ex–cop's hunch, not a fact."

CHAPTER FOURTEEN

Sally Guthrie lived in an older apartment complex that hadn't aged as well as the historic section of town. Its beige-yellow paint had collected dirt and a bit of mold and the blue on the doors looked faded.

Sally sagged like the privacy fence around the door. Her face had the suddenly aged look of someone dealing with loss and her clothes had the disheveled appearance of someone who'd been awake too long and didn't care.

"May I help you?" Her voice had a sigh built into it. Until she took a good look at my face, and her features shifted through confusion and hurt to anger. "What are you doing here?"

"My name is Davis Groves. I'm sorry for your loss."

"Lane shot my baby." She tried to slam the door.

I stuck my foot in the way. "I'm here because I want to know more about the relationship between Lane and Billy. I'm here because I don't understand and I want to."

"There's nothing to understand. She killed my boy."

"If you didn't see Lane shoot him, there's a possibility she didn't do it—or didn't do it alone. But, even if she did, don't you want to know why?"

"He was a good boy."

I nodded. "Last time I saw Lane, she was a good girl."

"You didn't see what she did. The mess. Took them two days to clean it. Still need new carpet."

"I'm sorry."

She stared at me. She smelled slightly boozy. Her hair matched the building and looked too sunny for her pallor.

"If this wasn't what it looks like on the surface, Amber could be in trouble, too." I gave her my most earnest attempt at concern and caring and sweetness.

"Amber's a nice girl."

"Lane used to be," I reminded.

She nodded. "Yeah, she always was." She opened the door a little wider. "I don't trust you, I just don't have anything left."

I wanted to tell her I knew how that felt, but also knew it would ring hollow.

The room reeked of bleach and paint. Carpet missing down to the concrete, a lone kitchen chair near a small television set on a folding table, the walls newly white.

"Lane shot him right here." She gestured at a spot of the concrete.

The cleaning crew had done a good job so far.

"There was blood everywhere. Bone. Brains."

I didn't know what to say to that. I couldn't imagine her living in that apartment.

She wrung her hands and looked around. "The detective gave me the number for a local crew. Probably still get evicted. I can't afford the new places."

"Sounds like it didn't take them long to clear the scene, though." I made a mental note to find out what the backlog at the state lab looked like and how hard the DA's office would likely push to get the stuff processed. Assuming they didn't just angle for a quick deal.

"I work nights, mostly. Gave him his privacy, you know. He was an adult. Just couldn't afford his own place yet." Her sadness hung off her like a blanket. "If I'd been here…"

If she'd been there, she might have ended up dead, too. "He seemed happy? No arguments with friends? With Lane?"

She shook her head. "The cops asked the same questions. He worked at a seafood plant. He coordinated work schedules and whatnot. How could that be trouble? How could that be dangerous?" She looked distraught, confused.

I had the same questions. "How'd he know Lane? She's supposed to be in high school."

Her face pinched at the sound of Lane's name. "They all met at some party over on the beach. Nothing too rowdy. Just kids being kids, you know. Not much to do around here. They used to go listen to music on the dunes, hang out at houses. He and Lane used to be so close. Like best friends back when he was in high school."

She headed for the stairs and motioned for me to follow her.

The upper floor consisted of a long narrow hallway with four doors. Two of the doors were closed. I guessed the one next to the open door of the bathroom was a closet.

The closest room had spilled the detritus of life through the open door. The bed, a simple mattress and box spring, had ended up tossed and sat lopsided, the sheets ripped and bunched.

She bent and picked up a photo album, still coated in remnants of black powder and handed it over.

"They left a mess, huh?" I fingered the lettering, wiped some of the black dust off and smeared it on my pants. "The locals did all this?"

She nodded nudged the piles with her foot until she unearthed a broken picture frame. She bent to pick up the photo. "They said it looked like someone was searching and he interrupted them." She handed me the picture. "Most of his friends had keys."

"Lane have a key?" I looked at the three boys in the photo. The one in the middle had to be Billy. I couldn't place the bookends.

"Her, the boys, probably Amber. He said he was gonna marry her. Don't know if he should've, but you can't talk sense into boys that age. Especially not when it comes to girls." She pointed at the picture. "Amber's brother, Brad."

He was slightly taller than Billy, with blond hair and a surfer's tan. His Wright's tee shirt hung loose like it had been well-worn. "They worked together?"

She nodded. "Off and on through high school, Brad's first year or two at the community college, before he went to Wilmington." Her face grew wistful. "Maybe Billy should've joined him. They were always so close in school. Thought he'd maybe go to school after the baby was older."

"Baby?"

"Amber. She wanted one."

"Amber's pregnant?" I asked.

She looked sadder, if that was possible. "Miscarriage. Billy was devastated."

I pointed at the other boy. "What happened to him?"

"Rex? Still works at Wright's from what I know." She took the album and flipped toward the back.

Rex had longish hair that wasn't quite red and wasn't quite brown. His face was dotted with freckles that bled into each other. The expression on his face, behind the smile of the moment, said he knew he was the dork of the group, the guy who caught the leftovers. He was pudgier than his buddies, in a doughy kind of way, and his posture exaggerated it. "What does Rex do?"

"Don't really know." She showed me a series of pictures. "This is him with Amber and Lane. They went out on the ferry to Cape Lookout that summer. Were gonna camp, but a storm came up. They borrowed a boat from his friend later that summer and went back."

Lane and Amber looked pretty happy. Neither looked terribly strung out or murderous. Amber's hair was wet and stringy, hanging past her shoulders as she gave a lopsided grin to the camera. Lane looked mischievous with her bad-girl spiky haircut, dyed hot pink.

"This was when?" I fingered the close-up of Lane. She looked connected, like she'd found the family she'd been looking for.

Sally scratched her neck and squinted at the photos. "I guess about two-three years ago. It was before Billy graduated. Right before his senior year, I guess." She touched the one of him and Amber hugging. "They'd just started dating. Brad hadn't been a huge fan of his baby sister going out with Billy at first. Billy took such good care of her." She looked up at me, pain raw on her face. "Don't let nobody tell you different either. He was there for her when her parents died."

"Their parents died?"

"Around the holidays. Car accident out in Newport, near Mill Creek. Roads were wet. It gets so dark."

I looked at the photos and flipped the page. Amber and Billy were celebrating a birthday with Brad, Rex, and Lane. They all looked happy and young and innocent.

I flipped again and it was Christmas. Billy looked concerned, even though he was by himself in front of a fine-looking tree. The picture under it was of a shy-looking Amber, eyes puffy, holding a narrow jewelry box.

"He gave her a real nice bracelet that year." Sally pointed at the box. "He picked it out months in advance, paid it off each week. It just wasn't the same after what happened." Her fingers drifted from the box to Amber's unkempt hair.

"I'm very sorry." I turned the page. "I don't suppose you'd have a number for Brad or Rex."

She shook her head. "The cops took his phone. Might be in the book."

I gave her the photos and shook her free hand. "Again, I'm so sorry for your loss. If there's anything…"

She nodded and looked on the verge of tears again.

CHAPTER FIFTEEN

Rex Whittman was indeed in the phone book. He lived in a small house down a street off Lenoxville Road in Beaufort, about three miles away from Sally Guthrie.

I had to pass an abandoned fish factory and the toxin-spewing veneer plant before coming to the turnoff leading to Rex's one-story clapboard. The first street was paved, but the second was mostly mud. My car slid and squished and threatened to get stuck before finally skidding to a stop on the Whittman front yard.

Rex stepped out onto the porch as I cut the engine, a cigarette dangling from his lips, shoeless feet on the bare wood. He took a drag and stared at me.

My phone buzzed another text from Matt. I still didn't know what to tell the guy, so I continued to ignore him. Part of me assumed he'd eventually give up, disappear.

I got out, left my purse behind and locked the door. "You Rex Whittman?"

He nodded and exhaled. He'd put on a few more pounds since the pictures at Guthrie's. He wore a Wright's tee shirt with stains and holes over a pair of dirty gray sweatpants.

"You used to be friends with William Guthrie, right?"

"Still would be if he weren't dead." He tossed the butt on the porch and ground it in with his bare foot. "Should I know you?"

I stood at the base of the porch steps and held out a hand. "I'm Davis Groves, Lane's sister."

"She didn't do it."

I didn't get my hopes up. Hope was for people who hadn't lived with Charley. "Who did?"

"Don't know." He ambled over and took my hand. "Comin' in?"

I followed him up the creaky wooden steps and through the screen door. The house smelled like cigarettes, cheap beer and mildew.

He fell into an orange-flowered couch and a cloud rose up around him in the late afternoon sun. "What 'choo want to know?" He shook a fresh cigarette out of the pack and stuck it in his mouth.

I looked around and perched on the edge of a recliner. "I wanted to know a little more about my sister. And about the guy they say she killed."

He lit the cigarette and took a deep drag. He waited and exhaled forcefully. "She hates you. Says she'd be better off with you dead."

I decided not to take an angry teenager personally, even if she was my little sister. "I get that a lot. But you're the first one who seems to know I'm not."

"Guess I've known her longer." His voice held resentment.

"You're an old friend of Lane's or an old friend of Billy's, then?"

"Billy and I went back to grade school." Rex sucked up smoke and snarled. "I think they went out a few times back before."

I watched his eyes. "You liked her?"

He made a face like he'd licked dog poop. "She was a prude and then she was a slut."

"She didn't like you back."

"Why would I want to date a slut?"

I raised an eyebrow. "Based on experience, I'd say for sex."

His eyes said even "slutty" Lane had rejected him. "That mean you're a slut, too?"

I smiled, coy. "If they were friends, why would she kill him?"

"She didn't." He stabbed the ashtray with the smoldering filter.

"Then who did?"

He lit another cigarette. "Don't know."

"Would you tell me if you did?"

He shrugged and exhaled.

I tried a different track. "You work for Wright long?"

"Few years. Pay's okay. Why?"

"Used to know him is all."

"He's got some fancy place over on the beach. Don't ask how he paid for that thing. Used to be hoity-toity types bought there back when I was a kid. Ain't no fucking locals be caught dead over there now. All dingbatters and ditdots; don't know not to build in the storm-tide line."

Colorful. "How do you fit into this? Or do you?"

He shook his head. "I don't get to play their reindeer games. I'm just the grunt they take with them when they trawl for ladies.

Somebody's gotta look innocent, right?" He got up and went to the next room. I heard the fridge open. "You want a Bud Light?"

"If you're willing to give one up."

He rounded the corner with a couple of cans and tossed one my way.

I caught it. "How much did you want in on the reindeer games?"

He smiled and cracked open the beer. "Not enough to kill anyone."

I tapped the top of the can with my keys, opened my beer. "Billy into drugs?"

"You know your mother uses, right?" He drained his beer and set the empty on the scarred coffee table.

I sipped. "That's not really new. Lane using the same stuff Charley is?"

"Couldn't say about that. Lane didn't really talk about mommy dearest too much. Seemed a sore subject. She's smoked the whole time I've known her. Says it chills her out. She used to take it to school, smoke it in the bathroom between classes." He lit up. "Wasn't like she was the only one."

"Charley does more than smoke a little weed."

"So I heard."

I took a stab at an idea forming in the back of my head. "Wright imports more than fish, doesn't he?"

"Wright?" He snorted and stood. "Think I'll get myself another beer."

I followed him down the musty hallway.

He opened the fridge, took out another can. A shotgun sat on the counter. He made no move for it, just opened the beer and drank.

"You always keep shotguns in the kitchen?"

He glanced at the gun. "Can get dangerous around these parts."

"Uh huh." I sipped my beer. "Come on, you've worked at Wright's for years. You telling me they never let you in on the big secret?"

He reached for the gun. "Who'd you say you were again?"

I moved in close, much too close for him to use a long-barreled gun, and angled up so his belly touched mine. "I don't give two shits about your stupid dope sales. What I do give two shits about is figuring out why my little sister might have shot your friend in the head." I put my hand on the barrel of the gun, which he'd left sitting on the counter.

He glared at me. "I could kill you."

"Look, you and I both know they're up to no good. You said, yourself, they aren't letting you in on it. All I'm saying is if you change your mind about spilling some beans, give me a call." I winked at him and drained my beer.

"You're just playing me."

"Maybe."

"I been played by better."

I ran the index finger I'd had on the beer down the curve of his jaw. It was cold and left his stubble damp. I purred in his ear. "Oh, I doubt that."

He stiffened below. "I could be wrong."

I lowered my lids and kissed him on his scratchy cheek. "I'll slip a business card in the screen on my way out."

Driving away, I wondered if I still had it, that magic touch that had once parted men so easily from their money, and if it would work on secrets, too.

CHAPTER SIXTEEN

Driving back toward Newport, across the high-rise bridge separating Beaufort and Morehead City, I realized how exhausted I was. My shoulder hurt. My back hurt. My hand ached in the cold. And I hadn't eaten since I'd scared the hell out of Scooter, which explained why my brain felt like it was eating itself.

I looked down at my outfit when I stopped at a traffic light downtown. It was probably the most acceptable thing I'd brought with me and, despite the bruise on my cheekbone, I looked presentable enough. A pub-like restaurant sat across the railroad tracks, so I did a U-turn and parked at the curb.

Wednesday night, it was quiet inside. A few families at tables by the windows, a couple of guys drinking beer at the bar. The hostess looked around me, almost hopeful. "Just one?"

I nodded and followed her to a booth near the bar. Basketball on the big screen, the sound turned low. The guys added their own commentary, peppered by occasional shouts or boos. I slipped in on the side facing the door and pushed myself back against the wall, one foot propped on the bench. A neon ad for Fat Tire beer caught my eye so I ordered one, along with a water.

The menu featured an assortment of fried meats and seafood, burgers and fries. The sort of stuff people ate while drinking beer and watching basketball. I wasn't sure what kind of food went with mulling over thoughts of murder and suicide, so I ordered a side of mixed vegetables and some fries.

I wanted to call Tom, listen to a reassuring voice tell me things would be okay and nothing was as bad as I suspected. I wanted to go back to the days when Nik and I could fix anything together. I wanted to believe there was no way Lane had shot William Guthrie in his mother's apartment. I wanted to be the kind of woman who didn't sit with her back to the wall, eyeballing the place to make sure no one jumped her.

Instead, I nibbled garlicky broccoli and wondered what to do next.

It seemed somewhat obvious that I needed to find Brad and Amber, but I had a nagging feeling Eric Wright – and by extension Vince Zellner – were involved and old fears made me want to get them before they could get me.

Jackie had fallen for Eric hard, as hard as Charley had ever fallen for a man, and the results had been as disastrous.

"I think Eric's selling drugs," she told me one night, standing in front of a muted TV and holding a bowl of ice cream.

I was studying on the coffee table in the apartment we shared and looked up at her, not sure whether to take her seriously or not.

She sensed my hesitation. "You don't believe me."

I put down my highlighter. "What makes you think he sells drugs?"

"He buys me things. Nice things. We argue sometimes and I guess he wants to make sure I forgive him, but sometimes he just buys things to be nice." She put the bowl on the top of the TV, shoving the rabbit ears to the edge to make room. The picture turned fuzzy, but she didn't seem to notice. "I saw one of the purses at the mall today."

"You hate the mall."

"My *mom* hates the mall. Thinks the devil can get me through cheap sweaters that show too much."

"Don't forget how she feels about jewelry without crosses."

"I was thinking of getting a part-time job. Something a few days a week while he's at practice, you know. He doesn't really think it's a good idea, says he can buy me anything I want, but, I don't know. You have a job."

"You don't want my kind of job."

"No, I could never do that." She turned pink, then downright red. "I don't know how you do that." She shivered and made a face. "I have a hard time just taking my clothes off around Eric. He says it's okay, but I always think of my mom. Oh, gosh, that sounds wrong." She found a way to turn redder.

"He doesn't make you do things you don't want to, does he?"

She shook her head a little too vehemently. "No, nothing like that. And I mean, we don't do *it*. Just, it feels wrong. I don't know. I'm not like you. Maybe he's right, though. Maybe I don't need a job. Most of them wanted me to work more hours than I wanted. I wouldn't be around when he needed me."

"You said you saw a purse?" I still had three hours worth of studying to do in the two hours before work. I didn't have time for her insecurities.

"Oh, yeah. It was in one of the stores that offered to hire me. She was nice. You know the green one, with the funny letters on it?"

"Gucci?"

She wrinkled her nose. "Doesn't look like much to me, but the lady at the store said it was real nice. Cost four hundred dollars."

"Is it real?"

She looked puzzled.

"Real. Is the one Eric gave you real or counterfeit?"

"I don't know. Why would someone counterfeit purses?"

"Oh, honey, sometimes you're adorable."

She smiled. "Eric says the same thing. He says he's gonna show me the world."

"Uh huh. Look, a lot of the strippers I work with like designer bags. Makes them feel like they're getting something for the money. I don't know. Guess they don't have surgeries to pay off. At any rate, some of them buy fake bags downtown. They come in on ships at the port and look pretty much like the ones you saw today, except maybe the G looks like a C or the lining's the wrong color. From a distance they look okay."

"I don't get it. Why would you pay for a fake purse?"

"Honey, if you aren't the kind of person to want the real one, you aren't going to understand the fake ones."

I picked up my beer and stared at the excess butter congealing around my limp asparagus spears. I remembered seeing several handbags in Lane's room when I was looking for towels to clean up Charley's mess. At the time, I'd thought nothing of it, but suddenly the patterns and clasps stood out in my mind. Lane shouldn't have been able to afford Fendi and Coach. And she certainly shouldn't have been able to have several of them scattered around like dime store castoffs.

I pictured the connections between Billy and Eric, between Lane and Billy. I thought about boat fairies and how Vince had worked at the port when we were in college. How he and Eric spent a lot of time together, but had seemingly nothing in common. How Lane might have met Vince as easily as she'd met Billy in such a small town.

CHAPTER SEVENTEEN

Charley's oversized, dilapidated house and the old Hathaway place sat slightly opposite each other at the end of a long dead-end dirt road in the middle of nowhere. Mrs. Hathaway had died six years before in her living room, and even then the house had been old and not exactly structurally sound so her family could never sell it and the yard eventually took over.

In other words, there was no reason for a brand new Mustang to be sitting on the overgrown, dried-up lawn in front of a dilapidated house in the last remnants of dusk.

I parked next to the Mustang, walked up to the door of the house and knocked. It fell off the hinges.

From the Hathaway porch, I could see most of Charley's house, the rest obscured by trees. My phone buzzed in my pocket. Tom.

"I think someone's at Charley's. We'll talk later."

"No way. You call the cops."

"Sheriff's department. Charley's outside town limits." I tried the doors on the Mustang, hoping to get lucky. None were open, but I couldn't find any trace of an alarm either. I went back to my car and popped the trunk.

"Davis?"

"Huh?" I wrapped my scarred hand around the tire iron.

"Why does it sound like you're about to do something stupid?"

"What do you even hear me doing?"

"I can't hear you doing much of anything. That's what worries me."

"Quit being a cop." I hit the mute button and smashed the passenger window of the Mustang. I reached in, opened the glove box, and pulled out the registration card. "Shit."

When I didn't get a response, I remembered to unmute.

"Davis?"

I stuck the paper in my pocket and went back to my car. "I might be in trouble here." I got back into my car and stared at the steering wheel.

"Because you just broke the window out of a car?"

"I muted the phone, Tom."

"I know you."

"Oh."

"And?"

"It belongs to one of the scariest people I've ever met." Vince Zellner. What he'd done, what I'd let him get away with through my own cowardice, was unconscionable. The pain left in my shoulder couldn't rival the pain in my heart, but at least the shoulder could be iced.

Outside Charley's house would've been bad enough. Across the street made him seem like he was trying to hide. Trying to hide implied he was trying to sneak up on one of us. If he knew Lane was in jail that left Charley and me.

"I really have had too many people try to kill me."

"What?"

"Nothing. I wasn't his intended target last time."

I groped in my purse and pulled out a Swiss Army knife. Not quite as good as the tire iron but easier to conceal, what with my gun being at home, where it belonged, and Phil's being in a cardboard box, where they didn't belong.

"Davis."

"I'll call you back." I stuck the phone in my pocket with the knife.

I'd never been good with following rules—Nik's, especially—so I'd spent a fair amount of school sneaking out my bedroom window. Charley was as good a homeowner as she was mother, so the lock was still broken. I slipped in, left my shoes and purse on the bed, and tiptoed down the hall.

I found a tattooed teenage girl in Nik's old room, pulling apart a plastic trophy for no apparent reason other than spite. A discarded trail of broken knick-knacks littered the floor from dresser to desk to shelf.

I leaned on the doorway. "What'cha looking for?"

She jumped, composed herself, and growled.

"So the dog collar's not just a fashion statement?"

"Who the fuck are you?"

"Davis. And you?"

"Davis is dead. Who the fuck are you for real?"

"This is getting old."

"Whatever, bitch." She went back to her petty destruction, dismembering a Barbie that might have been Lane's.

"So, how 'bout if I guess you're one of Lane's friends. You have a name or do I just call you Fido?"

She turned and rolled her eyes at me the way only a well-trained teenager could. "Who the fuck is Fido?"

"Really?"

Nothing.

"That your Mustang outside?"

"So what if it is?" She asked.

"Because I was wondering if I should call and report it stolen."

"Fuck you, bitch. He lets me drive it." She tilted her head. "What's it to you?"

I stared back at her. "He's what? Ten years older than you?"

She shrugged. "Didn't stop Lane."

"She dating him or just getting drugs off him?"

She looked me up and down. "Fuck you."

"Right." I fought the urge to punch her. "How'd she meet him?"

"Says you introduced them."

I squinted at her.

She smirked. "What'cho gonna do if I pull a knife?"

I let out a sigh. "Well, shooting you would make a helluva mess, but I already got cut dealing with a glass-wielding nutjob today so I might be feeling lazy."

She chewed her lip. "You can't be serious."

"Quite. Try me."

"Lane said you was dead, bitch."

"Yeah, I heard that one already."

"She wants you to be bad enough, she can make it happen. Vinny will do anything for her."

I tilted my head. "Really?" If I had to guess, I'd have said that power flowed the other way. "That what happened to Guthrie?"

She ignored me. "Lane wants you gone?" She snapped her fingers. "Poof. No one ever finds you again."

I felt a chill but ignored it.

"You're out of your league, bitch."

"So, who are you anyway?"

She stood taller, like it was a dare. "Sylvia. What's it to you?"

"Great. Get out."

"Lane told me to meet her here tonight."

"Lane's in jail," I said.

"For reals? No shit?"

She sounded way too excited about the idea. I raised an eyebrow at her. "For reals."

"Shit."

"Yeah. So, how come you didn't know that?"

"Look, don't go getting into my business. Lane ain't here, she ain't here." She pulled out a phone and typed a string of messages like I wasn't there. When she was done, she looked up and grinned. "You better watch your back."

Something dark welled up in me. I turned to look out the window at the dark sky. The aches in my muscles suddenly couldn't compete with the ones in my soul, my subconscious, whatever part of me couldn't just let the fuck go. "Why does Lane hate me?"

"You don't know?" She snorted like it should be common knowledge.

I had a guess. I hoped I was wrong.

"She said you were a drama queen. Said you got what you deserved."

I watched her walk past and didn't bother stopping her.

"You don't get to tell me what I deserve. Neither does Lane." I caught sight of myself reflected in a picture frame. I looked like shit—not even warmed-over shit, but smeared off a shoe onto a cheap motel carpet shit.

"Fuck you!" It echoed down the hallway, followed moments later by a door slam.

I went down to my old bedroom, surveyed the mess and the memories. The revolver I'd shot as a kid sat on the dresser. I picked it up and thumbed rounds into the chamber before going back down the hall. I knew it was more talisman than anything else. I wasn't sure I'd use it. I still felt safer with it.

Lane's room was messier than it had been earlier in the day, but it was hard to say what had been moved and what hadn't. I found the purses easily enough since they'd been relocated to a pile on the bed. I picked one up and opened it. The lining felt cheap, confirmed by several tears where it attached to the seams. Outside, it was too clean to have been used much, the interwoven letters a little too irregular and the leather a little too plastic-smelling, like Payless shoes or gas station wallets.

I took out my phone and snapped pictures of a few of them with some close-ups of the lining and logos and texted them to Tom's wife. Tom knew criminals. His wife—the only daughter of a successful Cuban immigrant who'd come over long before the Mariel boatlift and established himself as a real estate developer back when there was still land to develop—would know the real thing if she saw it, and she'd also know which season these were supposed to be mimicking.

Every purse but one had a torn lining and they were all full of receipts for gas and food, a few for motels, up and down the coast. The one that didn't advertise its knockoff status was heavier than the others and smelled better. It had been not so much part of the pile, but tangled in the bed sheets, and I'd almost missed it.

I sat on her bed and stared at it. "What have you been doing, Lane?"

CHAPTER EIGHTEEN

I needed a shower and maybe some coffee. The aspirin I'd taken that morning had worn off hours before. My stab wounds throbbed, my head ached, and my emotions were stretched and frayed. The bathroom grout still had blood visible in it. I ignored it and dropped my pants.

The hot water stung my cuts but massaged my muscles. I let it beat my forehead until it ran cold.

I hadn't closed the bathroom door and the cold air from the rest of the house broke through the steam to leave gooseflesh along my arms and shoulders as I toweled dry. I caught sight of old scars in the mirror patched with condensation.

The back stairs creaked.

I froze.

Light footsteps, like someone in heavy boots tiptoeing, left the stairs and moved down the hallway.

I'd left the gun on Charley's bed with my purse.

I slipped through the open doorway to her room and grabbed the gun. An old pair of sweatpants and a tee shirt topped the pile of laundry on the bed. I squirmed into them one-handed and picked up my bag slowly so the contents wouldn't jostle together.

A shadow on the wall of the hallway arrived before he did.

I stepped back toward the window, gun in hand, purse slung across my chest like a too-tight messenger bag where I could hold the contents steady with my free arm.

"Police. Got a call about a burglar."

Something about the voice was off.

"Be a shame if I had to shoot you. Probably should just come out with your hands up."

I turned, smacked the window lock with the butt of the gun and shoved the window up.

A man in jeans and a flannel shirt took a Weaver stance in the doorway.

I tumbled through the window as a bullet shattered a pane above my head. My foot hit a patch of pine needles and slid until I hit shingles again.

I crawled to the edge and lowered myself, gripping the rusty, clogged drain hard enough to open the scab on my hand. I tapped my toes against the house, found purchase on the window trim and shifted sideways until I was over the overgrown grass.

A bullet hit the gutter next to my hand and barely missed me when it exited. Swampy water polluted by rotten leaves drained out of the hole onto the sweatpants.

I dropped, landing for a second time in one day in a squat on the dead lawn.

Above me, the mystery man fired three more times, tearing holes in the overhang of the house, each one hitting the ground a foot to my left.

I took off for the woods at the edge of the property, zigzagging until I was surrounded by trees, pine cones puncturing my feet. When I felt entombed in the forest, I stopped. The sweat on my forehead chilled in the evening air and I wrapped my arms close.

The man had been in shadows, but he hadn't been who I'd expected. That was a voice I knew. And I worried his stance meant he really was with law enforcement. If someone had paid off a cop, Lane's chances at a fair trial fell even further.

CHAPTER NINETEEN

I came out of the trees at the edge of a field surrounded by a grayed split-wood fence. In the middle sat a single-wide trailer older than Lane with fading green paint. Wind blew across the open space and through my thin shirt.

The gun I shoved in my purse, and noticed a hole in the baggy sweatpants, too circular to be a rip from a tree branch. Looking at it made old wounds ache harder and I rubbed the base of my skull to quiet the fear and hurt.

I pulled out my phone and dialed Tom as I ducked under the fence and started across the lawn toward the trailer.

"Hello?"

"A cop just broke into Charley's and shot at me." The sound of the words leaving my mouth suddenly hit me hard. My knees almost buckled under me and I stopped in my tracks.

"Davis?"

"I'm fine."

"That's good. I had kind of assumed since you called me instead of an ambulance."

I didn't say anything.

"Davis?"

"Stop saying my name like that." I felt on edge, and stupid for feeling that way.

I looked up to see a shaggy-bearded man on the cinderblock steps of the trailer. He held an over-under shotgun pointed at my chest.

"Tom, I gotta go." I hung up the phone and held up my hands.

"What are you doing on my property?"

"Lost? I was running in the woods. My mother lives next door."

"Girl, you ain't got no damn shoes on and the crazy woman lives a half mile away ain't got but one kid. Runs wilder'n the deer."

I mashed my lips together.

"Don't go making no shit up. Talk, girl."

"Davis," I said. "My name's Davis."

"The one the crazy bat said was dead?"

I threw my hands up further and let them drop. "Really? Is there anyone she hasn't mailed my obituary to?"

"Musta done something pretty terrible for your own momma to disown you."

He didn't know the half of it. I sighed because I couldn't think of anything else to do and couldn't work up the effort necessary to explain any further, even if he was still pointing a shotgun at me.

"Get on up here and tell me what's what."

I took a few steps closer, my brain scrambling for some version of a story that was truth-y enough and left out almost everything.

"Who you running from?"

"No one. Ex–boyfriend."

"He the one shooting at you?"

I stopped.

He lowered the shotgun slightly. "I been living out here for forty years. I know the sound of a rifle and I know the sound of a handgun. Someone out that way was shooting a pistol, and you don't hunt with no damn pistol. 'Sides, ain't season."

"He's—"

"Why isn't he dead? You had that revolver." He gestured at my purse.

"You were watching me?" I glanced over my shoulder and saw the fence line illuminated.

"I do that. Old man. Heard shots."

"Dad was a Marine. He died in Beirut. The gun's his. He never got a chance to teach me to use it." As usual, lies were easier than the truth.

"Don't go running around with guns you can't shoot. Good way to shoot yourself or get someone else to do it for you."

"Yes, sir."

"Why are you here if your momma thinks you're dead?"

"She had an accident. Looking after the place for a few days."

"And the younger one?"

I hung my head like I was embarrassed. "Jail."

"Come on in, princess. I was just fixin' to have some tea."

He turned and went inside. I looked for more surprises. When nothing else materialized, I walked up and waited on the top step.

"Rug ain't clean no way."

The interior of his modest trailer was dark and decorated with musty doilies and doodads I envisioned having been carefully placed by a long-dead wife.

I expected iced tea sweetened with so much sugar it would sting my teeth. Instead, he poured water from a cast-iron kettle into china I suspected had also been chosen by the doily owner. He spiked the tea with Jim Beam. "You sure you okay?"

I nodded and sipped.

He disappeared down the hall. I picked at my feet, trying to dig one or two of the pinecone thorns out of my calluses.

When he returned, he handed me a washcloth and a bottle of alcohol so old the label was discolored and peeling. "You want to tell Bob what happened to you?"

I cocked my head and tried to figure out if he meant himself or the large mutt that had suddenly begun licking my left foot.

"Where you from?" He chewed his lip behind the bushy gray beard.

I gave him sheepish. "Florida."

"Used to have a cousin went off up there. Never did have a lick of sense, that one. Got arrested in no time trying to sell dope to the cops."

Up? "I don't sell dope."

"Don't you go lettin' no guy mess you up. My momma's aunt Shirley had one a'them. Beat her before church."

I said nothing.

He sipped some more rocket fuel tea. "That how you got all those other scars?"

I started to get up. "This has been real nice of you and all—"

"Sit down. Old Bob don't get much comp'ny. You don't want to talk about it, we won't talk about it."

I sat.

"Gets mighty lonely out here since my wife died. Been thinkin' about going to church again, but I don't know. I might be too old to get religion."

I dumped some alcohol on the washcloth and held it in my bloody palm.

"You got religion?"

I wasn't sure what the right answer was, but I was confident the truth wasn't it.

"You can say no. It's okay. Just wonderin's all."

I shook my head. "My mother was never much for churches."

"And your dad? Most military men I know believe in God."

My biological father had been a musician in San Francisco. My "uncle," the Marine, had suffered a falling out with God somewhere between his sexuality and his survivor's guilt. "Not so much, sir."

"Then it weren't God holding you back from shootin' that man."

I started to remind him of my lie.

"Don't give me that. Everyone watches enough TV to pull a trigger. Might not have any aim, but they can squeeze."

I set the washcloth on the table. "I think I should go."

"Feel free to stop back by."

The dog hauled itself to its feet and ambled after me. The man held out a hand. "I'm Bob."

That cleared that up. "Thanks."

CHAPTER TWENTY

I walked back toward Charley's house via the road. I kept a lookout, but didn't see anyone. As I rounded the corner I saw the Mustang was gone. I noticed my Toyota was gone, too.

I decided to deal with that later and entered Charley's cautiously. The inside was dim and I let my eyes adjust before I moved too deep into the domiciliary abomination.

I called Tom from the living room. "Sorry."

"What the hell, Davis? I thought you were dead by now."

"Sorry."

"You don't get it, do you?"

"Yes, you think I'm your daughter and you care, but I'm not. You care too much, Tom."

"No such thing."

"The only one who ever gave a damn about me before was Nik. But we're adults now."

"Being an adult doesn't mean your loved ones stop loving you."

I had no answer to that.

"Davis?"

"I'm here."

"It's okay. For people to care." His voice sounded warm, grandfatherly.

"I guess I still don't know why you do."

"Frankly, I don't know either except by now I've known you long enough I feel invested in the project." He sighed into the phone. "Guess that's not so funny. Truth is, you have a good heart and a warrior spirit and I appreciate that. Not too many like that."

I didn't know what to say so I shook the warm fuzzies free. "Did Charley own a car?"

His tone turned businesslike. "Wouldn't you know that?"

I made a face he couldn't see into the phone.

"Right." Clicking followed. "Chevy Impala. A ninety-five. In blue."

"Then where is it?"

"That, I don't know," he said. "What's going on, Davis?"

"I don't know, but I have an overwhelming hunch that Lane's paying for my mistakes."

"Davis?"

"Eric Wright owns the company Billy Guthrie worked for. Lane was friends with Billy and his girlfriend. According to the dog-collar-wearing Sylvia, Lane is also friends with Vince Zellner. Zellner used to be friends with Wright. Super-close friends. Like the kind that are always together. Even when Eric was dating Jackie, Vince always seemed to be, I don't know, lurking. Like they'd be in the bedroom making out and Vince would be sitting on our couch, staring at me like he was waiting for them to be done. It was creepy. Weird."

"That doesn't mean they had anything to do with Guthrie's death."

"He didn't go to the college. Worked the port." I touched the scar behind my ear. "And now he's some kind of manager at Wright's."

"Makes sense."

"Except, what's he doing hanging out with teenage girls?"

"I know you can remember girls in high school chasing after college boys. Wright's twenty-five. Zellner's only a year older. Small town like that? Not that weird."

I knew he was right. Billy and Amber had been a few years apart, enough that in some states he could've been arrested, but I also knew most high school boys were impossibly immature. "It just feels wrong."

Silence on his end told me he knew I'd done far worse than date a guy a few years older.

"If I give you some dates, can you see what you can dig up?"

"Yes. Anyone in particular I should look for?"

"Me." I told him the dates I'd lived in Boone.

"Are you sure you're okay?"

"I'm sure I'm not, but it won't stop me from lying about it."

The house was a mess, but no more so than it had been before. In my old bedroom, I counted the guns. All the boxes were there, but another one felt light. I picked it up and shut my eyes as I opened it. When I looked, all that was left was the outline of a SIG Sauer P226 pistol. Another handgun floating around in the hands of either a teenager or a sociopath.

"Fuck."

Two hours later, I'd methodically searched the house. I'd found, among other things: Charley's stash and Lane's address book; three bongs and seventeen pipes of various sizes; five burnt spoons; a pile of used lighters; several empty bottles of cheap booze; more than a dozen pill bottles; and Lane's journal, which appeared to be little more than a wire-bound notebook covered in faux Satanic symbols and pot leaf doodles. I flipped through it, but the last entry was three years old.

I rummaged through the four dressers until I found a pair of jeans that fit and a long-sleeve shirt I'd last seen when I was a high school junior. In my duffel bag, I shoved Lane's journal along with my dwindling supply of clean clothes.

When I finally checked my phone, I discovered it was getting close to midnight. The thought made me consider raiding Charley's stash for an upper before common sense kicked in.

If I wanted my brain to work right, I had to feed it and not do Charley-esque things to it.

On the other hand, I had no car and I had at least one person who wanted me dead.

"Double fuck."

I called the Sheriff's department and asked who was on duty before reporting my car stolen. It wasn't the elusive Murphy, so I decided to take my chances. While I waited, I dug out Lane's journal and read through her days of hating English and gym and a girl she called Bucktooth Becky.

The man who showed up drove a pickup with the Sheriff's department logo, but without light bars or other signs it belonged to the office. He wore brown polyester pants, a tan shirt, and a belt with entirely too much stuff on it, like he'd increased his girth just to accommodate a few extra gadgets.

"You called about a stolen car?"

"Yeah. It was parked over there. Two hours later, it was gone."

"Isn't that the old Hathaway place? Why'd you park there?"

I checked his face for wrinkles, but only found small creases around his eyes. If he spent much time on the water they'd be deeper, even at his young age. "Someone was in the driveway here. Didn't want to block the car in."

"Who was here?"

"Friend of my sister's."

"You own this place?"

"Belongs to my mother. Not sure what that has to do with my missing car."

"Missing? Or stolen?"

"Well, if it's missing and I don't know who has it, stands to reason it was stolen. You need the registration information?" I opened the door more so he could come in while I went to the couch to dig my wallet out of my purse.

"I'm not sure sarcasm is in your best interest, Ms... Groves?"

"Davis Groves." I handed over the registration, my license and insurance card.

"I heard you were dead."

"I'm not dead."

"I can see that. Just tellin' you what I heard."

"I guess I'm Mark Twain." I waited for him to write down the information in his report.

"Huh?"

"The report of my death was an exaggeration... Never mind."

"Oh." He finished writing and handed back my papers. "Why are you here if you're from Florida?"

"Visiting my mother."

"She's in the hospital, right?"

Small-town gossip traveled so fast, I was a little surprised I had to tell him my car had vanished. To avoid sarcasm, I simply nodded.

"I hear she's..." he lowered his voice and even ducked his head slightly, "not well."

"You mean she's a jolly drug addict with a suicidal streak? Yeah, that's Charley."

He turned red.

"You arrested her for soliciting yet?"

He turned redder.

"Don't worry, I'm sure you will. How do I get a copy of that for my insurance company?"

"Stop by the station later today." His tanned skin slowly fought back the embarrassment.

I shifted my bag on my shoulder and cut through the woods to

Bob's.

His lights were out, but when I got about a foot from the porch his hound went crazy and every light in the trailer suddenly blazed like Christmas at the Griswolds'.

He came banging out the door with his shotgun, dog yapping at his heels. "Who's there?"

"Davis."

"Davis?"

"We met earlier. Do you think you could point that shotgun somewhere else?"

"Not 'til I knows who you are!"

"Redhead from Florida."

He lowered the gun. "Why didn't you say so? What's up?"

"Car disappeared."

"You been gone hours." He scratched his head, scratched the dog's head, and held the door open for me to come in.

I nodded as I came up the steps. "Yeah, it was there. And then it wasn't."

"Weird."

"I agree."

"You look like you got something else on your mind."

"I do. You have any old newspapers?"

"Sure. Come on in, girl. You want a fried egg?"

My stomach nodded enthusiastically. My mouth watered. I shook my head. "I don't want to impose too much. I just need to look something up and the library's closed."

"Ain't you got a computer or something? Thought all the kids your age were like robots by now." He led me into the living room, where he had a stack of *Carteret New Times* on the cushion under the window.

"I left my computer at home." I smiled, pretending I was warm and friendly. "Who steals a beat-up Corolla anyway?"

He got a cast iron pan off the dish rack and set it on top of an ancient stovetop. "Kids'll do anything these days. Breakin' inta places ain't got no place to be in. Doin' drugs at the schoolhouse. And that's just the stuff makes the papers."

I picked up a couple from the stack of papers and followed him to the kitchen, watched him pour oil in the pan and crack an egg on the side.

"Shouldn't you be getting some sleep? You can borra the couch if'n you want." He stared at me while waiting for the toaster to pop. "Butter?"

"No thanks."

He handed me the dry toast with a look that said he suspected it wasn't really food without butter.

I looked at the paper I'd picked up. "Know anything about this Wright's Seafood place?"

"Other people think he's great. His grandpa was okay. Younger one's kind of a mixed bag. I mean, what I hear, he treats them workers okay. Didn't make such a bad commissioner. Can't keep a woman, though."

I flipped through the latest paper while he plated the egg. Aside from the story about Billy's death, there was no other mention of violence.

He set the egg in front of me. "Eat. You look thin. And scared."

"That obvious?"

He nodded and sat opposite me.

"I'm not." I sat up straighter. "Not really. I'm pissed. I'm… resigned."

"You need some rest."

I put down the paper and picked up another. "It's not right of me to burden you with all this. It's my baggage. I need to carry it."

He got up and poured himself a finger of amber liquor out of a Mason jar. "You talk like a soldier. You ain't." His voice got faraway and I wondered where he'd gone in his head.

I left him to his memories and scoured a few articles.

He eventually patted me on the shoulder and wandered down the hall. I heard his bed creak and then the sort of wall-rattling snoring that would probably kill him one night.

The idea of dying in my sleep sounded better than any of the ways I'd nearly been killed so far. Certainly sounded better than Uncle Phil's prediction that I'd die violently, painfully. I had a feeling he'd been right, but at the time I'd wondered what had possessed him to tell a teenager that. I knew what had possessed Charley to tell me the same thing.

CHAPTER TWENTY-ONE
Thursday, February 9

The smell of rot permeated the air in the dimly-lit trailer. The curtains covered the boarded-up front windows, smashed or shot by something long before us. We'd been there two weeks. Long enough to call it home. Not long enough to think we'd stay.

We dropped our bags and books, called Charley's name, and set out in our predetermined directions. Nik headed toward our bedrooms. I headed past the kitchen to Charley's. Lane stood in the doorway, holding a stuffed monkey, waiting for us to make sure her mother was still alive, still present, still out of jail.

I found her first. Charley. Sprawled across her bed, leopard panties bunched around her knees, pink bra with broken straps, aspirin bottle spilled on the floor, half empty bottle of Ruskova on the nightstand next to a couple of quarters. I checked her neck for a pulse. When I found one, I went to her dresser, to the top drawer, the one that was always closed and currently sat ajar. I knew, feared, what I'd find when I opened it. My throat fell to my stomach as I stared at the underwear, shoved aside to reveal the cardboard cigar box, once full of twenties and tens, now empty except for a school photo of Nik, still stamped with the photographer's logo.

I turned to Charley. Fear and revulsion waged war in my head. I knew in my gut, just looking at her, what had happened. I knew I wasn't supposed to resent her. But I did. I wanted to turn her over and slap her until I'd transferred all the pain inside me to her.

I heard Nik coming back down the hall and yanked Charley's panties up as best I could, pulled the corner of the sheet across her still-bare ass.

Nik ran in and her eyes raked the room. Stopped on the dresser and then again on Charley. "No."

I knew her tone. I heard the same sadness, the understanding. I shoved my anger further down. "She's a hooker." Apparently not far enough down.

Nik delivered a slap so hard I tasted copper. "That's not an excuse. It's never an excuse. And she's our mother." Tears welled and spilled on her face.

I focused on the copper. I ignored being thirteen and knowing as much about hooking and its disadvantages as Charley.

"I'm going to make coffee. Find some crackers."

"She needs an ambulance," I said.

"No one will believe us. Her. They'll lock her up again." She pulled back the sheet, all business. Some part of her walled off after that slap, as if she'd hit herself.

I grabbed Nik's wrist. "That's destroying evidence. That makes us accomplices."

She pulled me into a hug before giving me her sternest mom look. "We can't let Lane see her like this."

I looked over her shoulder at Charley and hated her as much as myself.

I woke up with my face stuck to a damp newspaper and an urgent need to pee. The stove clock said it was nearly four. I pushed the dream, memory, out of my head. No one knew who'd attacked her then, maybe not even her. Because of Nik and me, no one bothered trying to find out.

Time hadn't removed the sick feeling I got when I thought about it.

I glanced at the notes I'd made. I needed to get out of there.

I grabbed a tee shirt out of my bag and padded down the hall to Bob's bathroom. I wanted a shower, but I didn't want to wake Bob or the dog. Instead I peed and stared at myself in the mirror. The person I saw looking back at me had newsprint on her face, a crease on her cheek, twigs still in her hair, scratches on her forehead. She looked sad and tired, the guilt almost visible on her shoulders.

Something wasn't right about Billy's death, but less was right with everything else.

I knew Tom would tell me I was focused on the wrong thing. That I needed to find Lane an attorney and get Charley some help. Except, something was pulling me down a rabbit hole.

Lane.

I'd read in her journal the night before, but it wasn't helpful. She'd started it when we'd moved to NC. She'd been eight, had little girl problems. Why didn't Samantha invite her to a birthday party? She didn't want to eat meat after her class read *Charlotte's Web*.

How did a little girl that concerned with Wilbur grow up to shoot a guy in the face?

But then, she'd had our problems, too. Why did Charley have so many boyfriends? Why didn't Santa come to our house like he did Samantha's? Why were we teaching her how to check for track marks between Charley's toes?

Eventually, the differences grew, drove a wedge between her and the girls she wanted to be, left her feeling alone.

Nik and I had been largely blind to Lane's isolation. We'd known about her acting out here and there, but we hadn't understood. Even when we'd hid things from each other, she'd been there. She'd known things she shouldn't.

When we'd left, we'd thought we'd set her up with a pretty good life—better than what we'd had. Except, I'd been selfish, lost in my own world.

And then I'd almost died. And she'd been sent to the hospital with Jackie's mother. And she'd met Vince in the lobby, waiting around. And he'd made her feel special. Even though, at twenty-one, he was too old to be making a kid feel anything.

I thought about the first time I'd left. I'd gone to college in Wilmington because I'd thought Jackie needed my help, my protection. Her mother, obsessive and overprotective, had filled her with worry— and the mission to find a Christian husband.

At first Jackie had appreciated my watching her back, but then she'd felt smothered. I hadn't seen it for a long time. Because I'd been suspicious of Eric when they'd met, I'd missed the signs that I was doing the same thing.

When I saw it, I had to walk away. I had to let her grow up. I had to let her make her own mistakes.

Lane had been a casualty. I thought I was helping her grow up. But I'd walked away too soon. And I'd left her with none of the skills Nik and I had hard-won.

"Dammit, Lane. Why didn't you tell me?"

I collected my purse and snuck out the front door. From there, I stared out into the darkness and remembered Mabel, the senile neighbor who'd lived near Charley since we'd bought the place. She had an old car. Not only did it seem like a safety hazard for Mabel to have a car— and by extension, my stealing it would be a matter of public safety—but I was pretty sure it was old enough for my limited hot-wiring skills to apply.

I remembered Tom as I walked down the street.

He answered, equal parts groggy and grumpy.

"I got sidetracked." I filled him in on my reading.

A light came on. I decided that if my gut said stealing the car was the best idea, it probably wasn't, given the way yesterday had gone. Instead, I walked up the driveway with renewed purpose.

"A lot of teenagers seem to die around here of overdoses and car accidents. Like way more percentage-wise than any of the schools in South Florida. But they don't make the news, just the obits."

I knocked on Mabel's door and waited.

He yawned. "Most small towns have their fair share of teens drinking and driving, doing drugs, driving dangerously."

"Yeah, the usual jackassery. The key phrase there, Tom, is 'fair share.'" I knocked again and listened for the sound of Mabel shuffling toward the door. "In the past year, there have been five ODs and seven car crashes involving dead kids just at Lane's school. There were another three overdoses, two more car accidents and a terminal illness at the main high school on this end of the county. At the other end of the county, they had a car accident that killed three and a suicide, not to mention six ODs. That's a lot considering these schools only have about five-six hundred students, tops."

"Bored, small-town kids do *a lot* of drugs, Davis."

Mabel flung open the door and stared at me. "Hi."

I stuck out my hand. "Miss Mabel? Can I borrow your car?"

"Sure thing, Nik." She beamed at me. "Just get it back to me by Monday. I have a doctor's appointment." Nik? Really? We looked a lot alike if you discounted my being a foot taller, but I was inclined to believe that part would be memorable.

"Stealing an old woman's car, Davis?"

"I have a hunch I need to check out in Wilmington. And I don't know where the hell mine went. Besides, I'm not stealing."

"Uh huh." He didn't sound convinced.

CHAPTER TWENTY-TWO

My hunch was born out of memory and I wasn't sure it could be trusted. I had little evidence to prove the things I remembered happening had actually taken place. We'd moved too often to leave a permanent mark anywhere and it had left me feeling shifty, as though at any moment I might drift away and become nothingness. Even in Florida where I had a few friends, where I owned property, where I'd assembled a resume based on actual jobs in a semblance of a career, I knew it was far too easy to slip into the night and be forgotten.

Perhaps that's why I felt at home in Florida. We'd lived the longest in North Carolina of any of the places we'd alighted after leaving California, but the Carolinas – even in the tourist areas – held a sense of heritage. People were plentiful who'd been rooted there for generations, sometimes even next door to each other.

Florida, especially south of the St. Lucie-Palm Beach county border, was as transient as my family. People came and went with the seasons, the tides, the rental agreements, the hurricanes and the semesters. The idea of "locals" existed on a continuum, with the few people actually born in the area on one end and the person with the longest residency on the other end.

For its quirks and its seedy underbelly and its shiny impermanence, I felt at home in Florida. So many bad things had happened in North Carolina (and Kentucky and Texas and Montana and a dozen other states), it was a wonder I hadn't ended up in Key West drinking myself stupid.

Despite Tom's insistence that bad memories could grow and change with time and fear and pain, I knew any shifting mine had done was from my attempts to erase them, to diminish them, to downplay and ignore.

Four cups of coffee and three hours later, I pulled into the lot of my old campus library. It felt familiar and familiarity stirred memory.

Tom called me as I parked.

"I need your authorization to use my tech guru."

"You mean your hacker?"

"You lack subtlety, Davis."

"Yeah. Do what you have to do. Just send me the invoice when you're done."

"I won't."

He didn't hang up, like he knew I had other things on my mind.

I stared at the building I'd once felt most at home in. The place I'd gone when Jackie and Eric's drama had become too much, when the static in my head was too loud to concentrate anywhere else. When I'd needed to feel the oppressive silence of the research stacks or the chatty nonchalance of the café. When I'd needed to feel as close to normal as I could get.

"Nik wanted us to pretend. She wanted us to strive, I should say, to be like everyone else. She made me read everything she could find on how families were supposed to act, on the kinds of 'problems' normal people had. She must've made me read stacks of books on kids upset by divorce or a lost dog or regular bullies." I thought about the Judy Blumes and Cynthia Voigts. "It sounds pretentious to say it now – and I used to get looks and taunts then – but I preferred the stuff with meat: *The Odyssey, Beowulf, Hamlet, Antigone, Lysistrata.*"

"Your sister did what she thought was best."

"I know." Nik's insistence that I do homework and read and study no matter what was the thing that had gotten me into college in the first place. It was the thing that allowed me to juggle stripping and calculus. But it separated me from both worlds. It left me alone with all the things I couldn't tell Nik. "What if this is all our fault?"

"It's not."

I hung up before he could argue further.

The local newspapers were stored in piles until converted to microfilm. What I was looking for was about five years old, which meant it had already been microfilmed and stored in the back of a cabinet to be forgotten. There were plans to digitize the microfilm, but it hadn't been done. On the back of my notes, I had written a few vague dates I'd wanted to check out. Not having kept a journal or possessing a meticulously ordered brain like Nik, I had to rely on seasonal clues like weather, holidays and midterms.

Around the time the coffee wore off, I found myself staring at a headline under a date two days off from the one I'd written on my paper: Local Woman Found Murdered. A waitress at a bar a mile from our dorm had been found in the alley near her car. She'd been beaten and possibly raped, the contents of her purse dumped, but police weren't saying anything else.

Two days later, police confirmed that the woman had been sexually assaulted and her wallet and keys were found beside her. The paper ran a yearbook-style photo of the young woman. My memory told me she looked familiar because she'd often waited on Jackie and me at the bar. I'd forgotten the murder because I'd been mostly hiding in my dorm desperately studying physics at the time.

I stared at my list of dates. I felt like I had a broken TV in my head that kept playing snippets of shows, flipping channels, and occasionally going to static. The dates triggered little bits of my past and I felt guilty I hadn't noticed sooner.

In my memory, Jackie and Eric had started a ridiculous fight that had gotten out of control, more verbal than physical, and the fight had escalated to Jackie telling Eric she never wanted to see him again.

The following day, I'd had a huge philosophy exam.

Around that time, a cocktail waitress had died.

My gut told me it was more than coincidence, but the police had never suspected Eric. They had no reason to. He was only a jerk in my head. The victim's boyfriend was arrested two days later.

I followed the story through the rolls of microfilm. In the photos, she looked cheery and innocent. I knew too well how she'd felt at the end and that feeling left an ache in my chest.

I followed the trial of the boyfriend to his acquittal and the photos of sobbing parents and the relieved defendant. Not guilty wasn't the same as innocent.

I looked him up on the library computer and found he'd committed suicide a year after the trial. Comments in forums still blamed him for her death and called the jury morons.

I wondered.

CHAPTER TWENTY-THREE

By the time I left, the sun still hung high overhead but had already started its descent. Tom had tried to call three times. I finally answered as I stood on the steps in the relative warmth, a fistful of copies in my purse. My stomach growled and my eyes felt blurry and dry.

"Where are you?"

"Hi, Tom. How's it going?" Great. I sounded like Nik bitching about phone pleasantries.

"Yeah, where?"

"Wilmington, why?"

"Perfect. You're right near Charley's car. It's in an impound lot on the edge of town."

"Why is Charley's car impounded in Wilmington?" As far as I knew, she'd never even been here.

"A group of teenagers were driving it. Hit a deer. Turned out to be a bunch of runaways from all over three states. The youngest claimed not to speak English. Got an interpreter and she tried to hang herself with her sheets. She's still in the hospital. The other four? Two went to foster care, one went to a youth camp. One's back home with her parents."

"Runaways?"

"One from Charleston, one from Danville in southern Virginia, another just outside Raleigh, a town outside Charlotte, and no one knows where the other one came from. She just says she doesn't want to go back. Not sure if that means with the other girls, to her home, or to Mexico."

"You assume she's Mexican?"

"Translator assumed it, based on word choice, accent."

"Huh."

"I talked to some buddies. Looks like they may have been prostitutes. The oldest was sixteen, acted like the leader until they got her alone. Then she turned innocent."

I took a deep breath. "Yeah, I know that game."

"Not at that age, though." He sounded hopeful even though he knew damn well what I'd been up to in Miami a few years back.

I let go of a sigh. "Younger."

"You ever have a pimp?" His voice sagged on the line.

"No. Everything I did? That was on me. My idea. My choice. No one owns me."

He didn't answer for a long time. "You think that's what these girls were up to?"

"I have no idea."

He fell silent again.

"Tom, I've gone a lot of years without telling anyone these things."

"Davis, you can tell me anything. If I haven't heard it already, I've heard pretty close."

"Keeping things inside is a hard habit to break, even if it's done more harm than good."

I hung up and steered Mabel's car to the warehouse edge of town, thankful I'd had the foresight to get power-of-attorney papers out of Dick and that I hadn't left my purse behind when I'd run from Charley's.

I pulled up in front of Port City Transport and Towing with a cup of Port City Java and my forgeries already in hand.

Perhaps the skinniest Southerner I'd ever met held out a grease-stained hand to shake and hitched his green work pants as he led me to the lot. "It's not a bad Impala. You looking to sell it? I know a few guys who could flip it if you don't need it anymore."

I still hadn't even seen it. "What gave you that idea?"

He shrugged. "Been here almost a month."

"Really?"

He stopped in front of a blue mid-90s Impala. "I can get you maybe five hundred for it."

I suspected it was worth a little more, but couldn't see how. The driver's side headlight had been smashed in, the windshield cracked, and the hood had a deer-shaped dent running diagonally from the headlight to the spider-webbed glass. "So, it still runs?"

He looked sheepish. "Yeah."

"Eight hundred and it's yours. I just need to get some stuff out of it."

"Like what?" He looked nervous.

"Paperwork."

"Oh." He smiled like he'd gotten the better deal. "I'll go write it up."

I watched him leave and pulled my sleeve down over my hand to open the car door. Any car had plenty of hiding spots and over the years Nik and I had tried most of them. The slot in the door, center console, and glove box were obvious and I started with those. By the time the grease monkey had returned, I'd found about two dozen motel receipts from up and down the coast, including several from Myrtle Beach. I shoved them all in my purse to sort later. Shoved under the seats, I found several used condoms, food wrappers, a couple of half-empty soda bottles and a wad of gum.

The trunk yielded a bag of spandex outfits suitable for clubbing, a bag of randomly-sized pills and a couple bags of brownish-white powder.

The grease monkey's eyes went straight to the bag before he recovered. "Got everything, ma'am?"

"The police never checked out this car?"

He shook his head. "Car accident. Seemed pretty straightforward."

I wondered about that, given the occupants. "But you went through it."

He shifted from one foot to the other. "Not at first, ma'am. It's just, it didn't look like nobody was coming back for it."

"Tell me what you want out of here?" I hefted the bag slightly.

He rubbed his beard. "Well, there was some merchandise and I was thinking I could unload."

"That why you wanted to buy the car?"

He shrugged.

I set the bag on the trunk, heard the click of the cheap clasp on the metal. I unzipped it and tossed him the drugs. "You need the hoochie clothes, too?"

He smirked. "I'm good."

I signed the papers and threw the bag of clothes in Mabel's trunk on the off chance one of the girls had stuffed something in a pocket.

CHAPTER TWENTY-FOUR

My phone rang again as I pulled up in front of a pizza joint. Tom. I answered and yawned. "What now?"

"You asked me to dig."

"I did."

"You sure you want to know what I found?"

I stared at the neon pizza slice in the window. "Sure."

"Your roommate died in a car accident two days after your friend, Jackie, was hit by a car in a parking lot. Your apartment building burned to nothing but a cement shell the night your roommate, Ryan Winston, died."

I said nothing. Listed out like that, it sounded like a bad Lifetime movie. It didn't sound real.

"You were in the hospital."

"Ryan's boyfriend found me in the snow in the woods next to the parking lot. He and a girl from his anthropology class. They were laughing. And then they weren't."

"You nearly died."

"Maybe I was supposed to."

"Don't give me that. What the hell happened?"

"I failed. I told Jackie I'd keep her safe. I promised. I lied."

"You thought you could keep a car from hitting her?"

"I thought I could keep the guy driving it from hurting her. I was wrong."

"Davis, it says you were treated for multiple gunshot wounds."

I swallowed hard. "That came after the car."

"The car that hit you two? It belonged to Eric Wright. He reported it stolen that morning from in front of his apartment in Wilmington. Police found it that night in a strip mall lot ten miles outside Boone. Inside wiped clean. Your blood, your friend's blood still in the grill. Your hair caught in the broken glass of the windshield. Bits of her skin were still stuck to the undercarriage. Case is still open."

I wrapped my arms around myself, but the cold that had seeped into my bones that night wouldn't subside.

"Someone tried to kill you, Davis. Why the hell didn't you ever tell me this?"

"It was my fault."

"What?"

"I left her. Her mother loved Eric. She hated me. Even knowing none of my past, she called me a whore. But that's not why I left."

"You think he did it?"

"Not directly." His wasn't the voice I'd heard that night.

"The car that hit your roommate…?"

"Ryan," I said. "He loved me, you know. Not romantically, but…"

"You didn't kill him."

"But I didn't stop it either."

"You were in a fucking coma, Davis. Someone stole a car a town over, bumped him, not even hard. The roads were icy."

"He was driving my car, Tom. The one with the balding tires I didn't have the money to replace. He was coming to see me. I might as well have killed him myself."

"Davis!"

"No, Tom. You don't understand." My breath caught in my chest. I felt like I'd been punched by a giant. I'd known what he'd find, but I hadn't been prepared to relive how I'd felt.

His voice soothing, he asked, "What don't I understand?"

I sucked up snot and tears, dug my fingernails into the cut on my palm and let the blood flow again. "He was there. When I was raped."

"Davis, what—?"

"It took me a long time to say that word. Until then, it never felt like it fit."

"Davis—"

"No, let me say this. I thought it was over. Stupid, I know. It just sounds silly, crazy maybe. But growing up, if I wasn't screwing someone for money, I was doing it to prove I was in control or I was doing it because someone was holding me down. It all blurred together at some point into just the way things were. And I don't mean to say that for pity. I never wanted any and I still don't. It *was*. Some kids get cancer. Some kids go deaf, get paralyzed. Where I came from, kids talked about it like it just happened. Just life. And I never saw myself as a victim. Not really. I made my choices. Even when all the options sucked.

"But I stupidly thought that was over when I was an adult. I thought since I lived on my own, that since I had a job and a car and *control*, that I could try dating. Not hooking. Dating. I thought I could go out with guys who seemed nice. I thought if I followed all the rules, that if I ate something light, didn't drink alcohol, didn't do any drugs, didn't stay out too late, didn't wear the wrong thing, didn't lead him on… I thought…" I stopped. I was breathing heavily, like I'd been sparring, and I wondered what the hell Tom was thinking on the other end of the line.

"It wasn't your fault," he said in his old cop voice.

"That's what I'm telling you. Don't go treating me like one of your old victims. It's not like that."

"I know that."

"Then say it. Say it's stupid. That it was a dumb idea. That there shouldn't need to be rules. That I never did anything wrong. That it was the one time I didn't deserve it and wasn't asking for it."

"Davis—"

"I know what I was before, Tom. I know the speeches and I know…" I panted until the urge to break passed.

"You think taking responsibility makes you—"

"He drugged me, Tom. I drank too much damn water with dinner and I had to pee. He ordered us coffee. Coffee, Tom. And I was stupid enough to drink the damn coffee. So, the girl who gave blow jobs to a sheriff to keep her mom out of jail at thirteen? She got raped by the Ken doll-looking frat boy with the fucking dimples."

I could hear his breathing on the other end, but he said nothing.

I swallowed. "And Ryan took care of me when the asshole dropped me off, groggy and confused. Ryan took me to the clinic that Friday morning."

"I'm so sorry, Davis."

"Don't give me that shit. Ever. You know as well as I do the person who bumped my car did it because it was mine. It wasn't an accident. Ryan lost control of that car because I couldn't afford new tires. And he drowned in an icy drainage ditch because of me. That's how I repaid him. That's how I proved my friendship to him. Three days after he took me to the clinic. I never pressed charges against the frat boy. I never found Ryan's killer."

"He died less than two days after you were hit. Are you telling me all this happened in one week? In one weekend?"

"I had to work Friday night. My head still hurt. By Monday night, everything, everyone, was gone."

"And you blame yourself for not knowing how to handle it?" He sounded mad, incredulous. "Are you kidding me, Davis? Who the hell would know how to handle that?"

"I should have. Isn't that what my whole fucking childhood should've been training for? If I couldn't handle it, who the hell could have?"

"No one, Davis."

I was shaking. Tears streaked my face and my nose was clogged with snot and self-hate. "I ran, Tom. I ran from Jackie and her problems followed me. I ran when Charley… We always ran. I woke up and Ryan was dead. I was missing a big patch of hair. I was stuck in casts. Doctors were talking rehab and therapy. There was a news story around that time about tourists getting killed in Miami."

"I remember that."

"I owned nothing, so I stole a wallet. And I ran. I went to Miami because I wanted someone to finish the job. I wanted to be the next lost, dead tourist. And I couldn't even manage that."

"Davis—"

"I abandoned Lane. I thought because she had a roof, because we sent money, that it'd be okay. How stupid could I be?"

"Are you going to let me help?"

"You are."

"Why did you have me dig this up? Why didn't you just tell me?"

"Would you have believed me?"

"Of course, Davis."

I shook my head into the phone. "No, you wouldn't. Not really. Who would? I know what I heard that night. If Eric reported that car stolen in Wilmington that morning, he didn't drive the car that night."

Tom waited.

"Lane met Vince Zellner at the hospital that week." I looked around the car like it might have an escape hatch I hadn't noticed before. "He's the voice I heard. In the woods, next to the parking lot. He's the one who killed Jackie."

"And you never said anything." It wasn't an accusation, just a statement, but I heard the weight of all my guilt in it.

"I need you to tell me the truth. Did I screw up Lane worse by running?"

"I can't answer that."

"Did I make it worse by not telling anyone what happened? Would anyone have even believed me? Fuck, I barely believe me."

I hung up and rested my head on the steering wheel of Mabel's old Buick. On the seat next to me sat copies of newspaper reports, receipts, and a sack of clothes designed to make little girls look like twenty-somethings. I pulled out the receipts and laid them out by date, let a map form in my head. Every few days they passed through Newport and stayed at the Hostess House on an account registered to Allister Connolly.

I stared at the name and called Nik.

"Hang on a sec, sis."

I stared at the dash. "I think I fucked up with Lane."

"What are you talking about?"

"Remember before I moved to Florida? How I lived in Boone for a while? And then I didn't?"

"Yeah." Her voice sounded strained and distant.

"What if William Guthrie is dead because I didn't die five years ago?"

"What the hell are you talking about, Davis?"

"I don't know." It was possible I was losing it.

"Then at least explain what you just said."

"I kept too many things locked up in my head for too long, and I'm afraid now that I need them they're all false or fabricated or rearranged. And if I can't figure it out, I can't make things right."

"When was the last time you slept?"

"Last night."

"For how long, Davis?"

"I don't know. An hour or two."

"And the night before?"

"I drove."

I could almost hear facial expression through the phone. "Okay, let's start over now that I know why you aren't making any sense."

"I'm pretty sure the man who shot me the night Jackie died lives here now."

"If you knew who shot you, why the hell didn't you ever tell anyone?"

"I couldn't talk for days. And then I didn't know what to say anymore. It sounded too crazy. It still does. No one could have believed me. No one ever did."

She was silent, probably remembering how I didn't call her for two years after that night, how I'd refused to talk about it.

"Nik, I'm sorry. I shoulda-coulda-woulda, but how do I fix it now?"

"How do you go back in time and get yourself killed?"

I could picture the exasperated look on her face. The one mixed with sadness because she was trying to come to terms with the inevitable. The one I'd caused too often.

"Because what you're telling me is that the solution to everyone's problem is a time machine and a magic bullet."

"Less-magic bullet, if you want to go with the doctor's theory."

"Call me when you've had some sleep." She sighed and hung up. Nik's version of tough love.

I stared at the phone and thought about the name on the receipt. I'd have to get Nik's opinion when she didn't think I'd gone Charley.

CHAPTER TWENTY-FIVE

Nik was right. I needed sleep.

I also needed clothes, so I stopped at an outlet on the edge of town and picked up some jeans, shirts and more running gear. Back on the road, I got as far as Jacksonville before my eyes glazed over. Thoughts of a decent shower started winning out. Jacksonville had quite a few crappy motel choices, since few upscale tourists decided to visit a Marine base or its surrounding strip clubs, pawn shops, used car lots, and chain stores. I found a place that charged by the night or hour and, for the most part, looked like the kind of place nice, respectable young women would avoid. It was nicer than my first apartment in Miami, and probably safer, so I paid for the night with cash.

The man at the desk didn't seem concerned. Neither did the guy puking on his shoes next to the door of my room. The second guy did, however, offer me some of his cheap whiskey. I declined.

The bed smelled like mildew and stale sweat but most of me didn't care that much. I put my gun in the nightstand drawer with the Bible. Dirt and decay drifted through my memory. I shivered and put that thought back in its box.

After I showered, I cleaned up my scrapes and bruises. I didn't do as good a job with the bandages as Craig. Basically, I wrapped everything in medical tape and toilet paper. When I caught myself staring at my old scars, I went to find a shirt.

I needed to call Craig and try to make amends, but it seemed too late for apologies. It wasn't too late to call my supposed boyfriend Matt. His long hours and lack of imagination were as attractive as his boyish nerdy looks.

He answered in good spirits. Restaurant noises were apparent in the background, despite it being almost eleven. "I won a huge case today, Davis."

"Sounds great." It didn't, really. The normal me I'd tried so hard to be had peeled away, like a costume left on the floor after a night of Halloween partying.

"I was going to take you to dinner but you weren't here."

"Did you take Chloe?" His paralegal did a tremendous amount of research for less pay than I knew she could get from someone like Dick. Then again, she didn't have to work with Dick. For his flaws, Matt certainly wasn't as volatile as Dick.

"I'll take her to lunch tomorrow. Where are you anyway?"

I gave him the abbreviated, G-rated version of my past few days.

"Did you want to talk about it?"

I thought about what I could say about my family that someone like Matt would understand. The conversation, the *tinking* of glasses and silverware, the laughing all seemed like artifacts from some other time and place I'd been. "No. Not really."

"I miss you."

"Same here." Another of my lies. I found I missed the person I'd been with him more than I missed him. And yet, he hadn't just been another john. I'd tried. Just, not hard enough. Or maybe it wasn't a skill I could learn.

I hung up stared at the wall. I should have been sleepy, but I suddenly wasn't.

I went to my bag and pulled out some gym clothes. After I warmed up, I worked on some combinations, fighting opponents in my head, my memory. When I finally stopped and sat on the bed again, exhausted, my head felt clearer.

I wiped sweat off my brow and emptied the faux Coach tote I'd found in Charley's car. Most of the clothes were short skirts and dresses. Nothing stuffed in a bra. Everything smelled like sex and sweat and cheap deodorant.

Memories of strange men in small rooms, backseats, truck cabs, alleys. My breath caught and I threw the clothes across the room.

At the bottom of the bag, another receipt caught my eye. The Summer Winds Motel in North Myrtle Beach. Dated in late November, the low price wasn't shocking, but still brought me back to the days spent scraping together enough for another night in some cheap, out of season, bad neighborhood, rundown, bullshit place we'd landed only to leave town in days or weeks in search of another. Places that smelled like the one I stood in. Places that smelled like despair and home.

I looked at the signature. Allister Connolly.

My watch said it was just after eleven. That meant it was still early enough in Phoenix. I plugged in my phone to charge it and called Nik back.

"Don't tell me you slept."

"What does the name Allister Connolly mean to you?"

"It doesn't." She sounded annoyed. "Wait, Allister?"

"I found it on a bunch of receipts in Charley's car."

"As in Charley Allister?"

"And Kenneth Connolly Groves." I said.

"I'm sure it's a coincidence."

"Really, Nik?"

"You know, Lane asked me about three years ago about our family tree. For a school project of some kind."

"So you think it's Lane?" I didn't want it to be true.

"Charley isn't that sly or clever."

"What'd you tell her? About us?"

"What I knew. The Allisters disowned Charley when she married Ken. Edith Connolly kept in touch for a few years. Burt Groves, we never knew."

I hadn't thought about those names in years, more than a decade. "Do you think…Would she…?" I told her what I'd found. The car, the drugs, the clothes, the runaways, the receipts. I tried to keep it factual, to lay it all out and let her smarter-than-me brain connect the dots.

When I ran out of words, her silence filled the airways.

"Nik?"

"She used to call me Nikki. I used to call her Lanie. Sweetie. Bug. She always smiled when I called her Bug."

"What happened, Nik?"

"I don't know."

"I didn't mean to leave. I didn't want to. You know that. Right?" She sighed. "I'm not Lane."

"We left her the house. I sent her money. Always. Even when I had none left for me. I never wanted you two…" The words stalled on my tongue.

"I'm flying out there."

"No."

"It wasn't a question, Davis. The reason we survived our childhood is because we worked as a team. I have to wrap some things up here, but then I'm on a plane. Give me a day or two."

"Nik, I still don't know what's going on. If anything happened to you, I couldn't forgive myself. Especially not after everything else."

"Whatever Lane's been doing, it's not your fault. And I'll see you soon." She hung up before I could argue again.

CHAPTER TWENTY-SIX
Friday, February 10

I slept fitfully and woke just after three, sweaty and panting.

I sat up and turned on the light. The dim bulb only illuminated the ugliness. I noticed the bloodstains on the hotel sheets and touched my shoulder. Red blood, white sheets.

Red on white. White, like snow.

I shut my eyes tight, but the after-images remained.

Jackie was crying. Her thin fingers covered her battered face. "He's going to kill me. I know it. I just know it."

I needed a run. I needed a mind-clearing, soul-reviving run. I needed to run until my legs gave out and my brain shut down.

Snow clung to her hair as I cradled her blond head in my arms, afraid to ask, but knowing the gist of it anyway. She sobbed and choked. Her bony shoulders shook.

I shook the image from my head, put on a hooded sweatshirt, and zipped the room key into the pocket of my capris. In the cold darkness of Jacksonville, nothing was open, but a few pawnshops still had neon dollar or gun-shaped signs lit in the windows. I took off at a slow jog north toward the creek.

Her body heaved against me, wrapped in a papery shirt, and I held her tighter, not sure what to say. Bruises and cuts were visible around her wrists, her collarbone, her face.

I picked up speed.

"It'll be okay. I'll keep you safe." My words echoed in my ears.

But it wasn't okay. It never got close again.

He was waiting for us even as I promised it.

I ran faster, jaw set, tears streaming in the cold.

I thought I knew what she would tell me if she could find the words. She never did. Even across the miles we drove from her friend's dorm to mine.

I drew in cold air. Dark buildings and asphalt looked on,

unconcerned.

She sat in my car, head in her hands. When he pulled up, she screamed, got out and ran across the parking lot toward the trees at the edge of the property, blond hair streaming behind her. I jumped out and ran after her. Snow fluttered around us. I noticed her limping.

I crossed the bridge and followed the road to the intersection of 24 and 17. Few streetlights and few cars. Just me and the dark and the cold.

He revved the engine of Eric's Monte Carlo. Tires squealed and the smell of burning rubber mingled with wood smoke from nearby chimneys.

I followed Highway 24, panting from effort and emotion and the kind of exhaustion that could almost, but not quite, mask the pain or dull the memories.

She crested a hill at the end of the parking lot, slipped on an icy patch and fell.

The Monte Carlo bore down on us, aimed at her.

My feet navigated the cracked sidewalks, my legs exhausted but moving. Always. Still.

She tried to get up but she'd hurt her ankle, slipped on the ice, fell again. I was almost there. Almost.

She stood again and glanced behind her. Her features froze.

My lungs burned in the chilly air. I pushed harder as though that could change things. It never did.

I leapt, pushed her out of the way. Her light frame crumpled into a snow bank.

The Monte Carlo's grill collided with my thigh. Pain. Blurred vision. Crunching metal, breaking glass, cracking bones. Helplessness. Flight.

A car passed on the opposite side of the street, near a closed-up steak joint. Three Marines hooted drunkenly from inside.

They were too young to be drunk legally. They were too drunk to be driving.

I landed several yards from her. It might as well have been miles. Pain and blood surrounded me. I tried to get up, but my limbs failed me. Blackness ringed my vision.

I turned at the next intersection and followed faint lights blindly.

She got to her feet again and tried to run, limping, crying. She glanced at me with a look that said she hoped I could still save her, that said I'd promised to save her. I wasn't able.

The Monte Carlo hit her going maybe fifty or sixty, slid on the ice and took the bumper off a Ford.

I ran faster until I could no longer feel my legs. I bit my lip until I tasted blood and tried to slow my pace.

She was thinner, bonier, shorter. The impact broke her back, her pelvis, ribs. Her shirt caught on the bent grill. Dragged her. Blood. Snow. Red on white.

I crawled, moving myself forward with the few unbroken parts that remained able. I clawed at pavement under the snow. I shoved with my toes. I left a streak of dirty snow leading into the woods that bordered the parking lot.

There was nothing I could do. I knew if he found me, he'd kill me. I wasn't sure I cared, but my body worked on reflex. Instinct.

The car carrying the Marines turned sharply and followed. Their catcalls turned ugly and their car screeched to a stop in a driveway ahead.

I forced myself back to the present. Didn't seem like much of a fight, three trained killers against a glorified secretary.

And yet, my body was still convinced of its own survival. It would do what it had to until it couldn't anymore. Like it had done before.

I could see him through the foliage. He stepped out and glanced at the damage to the car. He played with the slide on his gun the way he'd seen guys do on TV. I knew he did it to bolster himself and scare me. It still worked.

I pushed myself off the trail and rolled down a small embankment into the dried branches.

The driver put down his window. Leered.

I stopped. Waited.

In the car, the backseat passenger argued with the driver. He got out, dragged the driver out of the car. "What the hell are you doing?"

"You think she's gonna report us? Get real. She's out here, same as us."

I was easy prey. Familiar territory. A place I'd taken myself too many times.

I rolled myself behind a rotting log, just past the reach of the high beams. I'd left a trail. If he looked, he'd find me. And I was in no shape to keep moving. The adrenaline had run out and the queasy pain had moved in.

He hung at the edge of the bushes, the wooded area between the buildings and parking lots. He had on the wrong shoes for the steep path in the snow. "If you come out now, I'll make it fast."

"Come on, we just want to talk." The driver staggered a little.

I shook my head. "I got nothing to say."

I kept myself quiet. Still.

He fired blindly, halfway through his rounds before one finally found me.

My legs shifted, hands crossing my chest in a concealed combat stance, intending to just look cold in the night air. Adrenaline automatically solved my exhaustion problem, but I knew that would be short-lived and then I'd crash hard.

The driver laughed. "Scared, tough girl?"

When the gun clicked dry, I lay behind a rotting log, bullets in my thigh and the base of my skull, not far from my ear—the last of which had passed through copious amounts of twisted arm and broken shoulder and part of a tree. Burning inside. Cold outside, creeping in.

"What do you want?" I glared at him without losing sight of the other two.

"What do you think?"

"Come on, man." The passenger tried to pull him back to the car. The guy in the front seat appeared to have passed out.

"Let's not do this. You're drunk. You should go home." I kept my voice even.

"Think you're so tough." He lunged a few steps and threw up. Beer and Jägermeister from the smell of it.

I glanced at the other one; the taller, more sober one. "Take him home."

"It's not safe out here alone." He smiled.

"Is that why you travel in packs?"

"For what's it's worth, I'm sorry. We're not all like that. You can report him, you know. If your CO has questions…" He shrugged.

I wondered what made him think I was one of them.

After they'd driven away, I made it another block before the adrenaline crash and exhaustion merged into a wall of aches and nausea. I threw up bile and walked the half-mile back to the motel where I sat on the bed and pulled off my smelly shoes and checked for blisters.

I'd done worse.

CHAPTER TWENTY-SEVEN

The sun shone through the cracks in the curtains. My wounds had turned shades of purple and blue and brown and most of my muscles were on strike. I dry swallowed a couple of aspirin from the bottle I'd bought the day before and evaluated my options. After another shower, I pulled on a pair of dark jeans, a long-sleeve knit top with scooped neck that hid none of the scar on my collarbone, and my leather jacket. With a pair of small earrings and black boots, I looked nearly normal, which was as good as I was going to get.

I traded Mabel's car for a rental at the airport and wiped hers clean.

On the way back, I called Craig's father's A/C repair shop. Craig's smooth voice answered. As soon as he heard my voice, he said, "Look, Davis, maybe you're right. Maybe old times should be left where they are."

"Craig, I'm, well, I'm sorry."

"You're dying, right? This is a prank."

"I deserve that."

"Oh, wow. You're serious."

"You're right. I shouldn't have said that. I shouldn't have kept so many secrets."

"Davis, what happened?"

I was quiet for a long time. "I have to learn to stop running. I have to start telling. And I should have started years ago."

"Okay?" He still sounded like he thought I'd lost it. At least he didn't think I was dead.

"Do you want to meet for dinner tonight?"

"Uh, what? Okay." He cleared his throat. "Look, I have a job down to Harker's Island this afternoon, so how 'bout we meet at Clawson's around eight. You know it? Probably not. Beaufort waterfront. It's quaint. Tourists like it. Locals like it."

"Sounds good. See you there."

Oh, if only if were that easy.

The phone rang as I slipped it in the front of my purse. Tom. I started to pull off the road before I answered. Up ahead I saw a sign for a coffee shop. Perfect.

"Got a guy I want you to talk to."

"Okay." I parked and jogged across the street.

"Retired officer. Lives in Morehead."

"Morehead?"

"Down from Raleigh. Staying at his sister's."

"And you know him because…?"

"He called me."

"You know the person who shot at me claimed to be a cop."

"Wasn't this guy. Rubelli worked a task force with his CO about ten years back. Says the guy's good people." He rattled off an address that I dutifully copied on a stray receipt as I leaned on the stair railing. "Told him you'd stop by early afternoon. Don't make me a liar."

As he hung up, another call came through. A local number, but one that didn't look familiar. "Hello?"

"Is this Davis Groves?" He spoke low, his voice altered by the connection, but I still recognized it.

"Eric Wright."

"Sh, not so loud. What if someone hears you?"

I tilted my head at the phone like I often did with Charley. "What's going on?"

"I can't talk on the phone. Just stop calling me. Leave me alone."

He hung up and left me staring out at the shrimp boats at the end of the street. "What the ever-loving hell?"

Everyone else at the coffee shop had sense to stay inside where it was cozy and warm. I wanted privacy so I retreated to the porch.

I knew from going through Lane's papers that most of her friends were dead, except the mystery runaways. Overdoses, car accidents, suicide. Since I had to assume the police had her phone, I had no way of figuring out whom else she'd talked to unless Tom's hacker buddy could get her call list. Besides Sylvia and Rex, the only three left were Amber, her brother, Brad, and a Kelly. Amber had an address just east of Cape Carteret.

I called Amber's number and waited while it rang six times before a bored-sounding teenager told me to leave a message. I hung up and redialed. On the third attempt, the bored teen actually answered.

"I don't want any." She hung up.

I called back and immediately got voicemail.

"Amber, my name is Davis Groves. I'm Lane's sister. We need to talk."

I sat down at a picnic table outside the shop to sip my brew.

After a few minutes I tried again. The chill in the air rapidly cooled my coffee. By the time it reached tepid, she answered again.

"Hi, Amber."

"Who are you? Really?" Her voice was somewhere between tough and cautious. I recognized the tone and the false bravado.

"Davis Groves."

"She's dead. Try again."

That was getting old. "Amber, tell me about Allister Connolly."

"Go away." She hung up.

I finished my coffee in a long swig and wondered where Amber had been when Charley's car hit a deer.

CHAPTER TWENTY-EIGHT

I found myself at the stoplight in Cape Carteret, specifically in the far right lane even though the fastest way to Newport would have been going straight. I'd turned on the blinker without thinking about it. I told myself it was because I missed the ocean, but that was a lie. It wasn't like I'd grown up near the water, though I did find something like peace in my daily runs along Fort Lauderdale beach.

No, I knew Atlantic Beach and Eric's "dingbatter" house sat at the other end of Bogue Banks and that was exactly the direction I'd pointed the rental sedan.

When faced with other people's problems, I was perfectly capable of being methodical and reasonable and quietly researching answers until everything was solved. When facing my own problems, however, I had a lifelong tendency to behave irrationally, violently, and ridiculously. Lane's problem felt too much like my own.

I was running on too little sleep and too many bad memories. So, of course, I was primed to do something stupendously asinine, incredibly stupid, probably uncalled for, potentially illegal, and in all likelihood dangerous.

Eric and I had developed a mutual respect and hatred of each other that I had a difficult time figuring out, let alone explaining. He hadn't gone to high school with Jackie and me. He'd lived on the other end of the county so he'd gone to the other Carteret, with their blue and gold and us in our red and blue. Jackie had met him in English 101 and had been smitten from the beginning. He had that effect and he knew it. He used it. They'd become an easy item if an uneasy couple.

From the first time I'd met him, I'd known he was damaged. I never knew how, but somewhere in his eyes was the same pain I kept buried in mine and his efforts to play the regular guy seemed as forced as mine.

He was a baseball player, good-looking, always surrounded by superficial friends and his shadow, Vince. Her mother loved him from day one. He was like that. Such a charmer he even knew the right words to say to a housebound zealot. Jackie'd accused me of being jealous: of her, of him, of what they had. Maybe a little. Mostly, I worried no one else saw the wolf in the snappy clothing, but maybe more so I was worried I was imagining things that weren't there.

I tried to enjoy the scenery.

Emerald Isle, Salter Path, Pine Knoll Shores – all beautiful little beach towns in summer, full of tourists with sunburned skin carrying lawn chairs and skim boards. In winter, the beach houses sat quiet, some still boarded up from hurricane season. Clouds hung heavy. A misty rain started just east of the Emerald Isle high-rise bridge and shrouded me until Pine Knoll Shores. Occasional glimpses of the ocean between houses and dunes revealed it angry, a dull grayish green dotted with white caps. Certainly not the flat turquoise water I'd grown used to further south.

I rolled passed Eric's house like I belonged. It was a three-story wooden structure on stilts that sat midway the street about a sixteenth of a mile from the ocean. There weren't any cars in his driveway, and since there was no carport, it seemed likely no one was home. Most of the houses on his street looked abandoned for the season.

I scoped the neighbors for signs of life – cars, open curtains, soccer moms, minivans, balls left in the yard, footprints. My thievery as a kid had never really extended to breaking into houses for monetary gain, but that didn't mean we hadn't done it for other reasons. I'd also met enough criminals only too happy to share their thoughts on target casing.

I found little evidence of life forms inhabiting most of the houses on his street aside from a sign proclaiming the house next door as Ned and Nancy's Vacation Paradise, where the lawn was littered with Little Tyke cars and plastic animals. A silver minivan was parked in the driveway, cartoons visible on the TV through the front window. Didn't look much like paradise to me.

I drove around to the street behind his, where none of the houses looked inhabited. I parked in the public-access beach lot at the end of the street and walked back, hands in pockets, hood up like I was just a cold local out for a walk. No one tried to stop me as I slipped along the fence line separating Eric's property from Vacation Paradise. His yard was mostly sand and sparsely populated with half-dead yucca and sea oats.

Wooden stairs, a minor upgrade from a loft ladder in a camp cabin, led up to the second-floor door. Too long and high for me to sneak up. I glanced around again before walking across the yard and up the stairs as if I belonged. My lock picks were at home where they belonged, assuming one had a reason to own such a thing other than having a cat burglar neighbor who kept trying to teach me his former trade.

Eric apparently wasn't afraid of break-ins, though, because his back door didn't even have a deadbolt and the lock popped easily with a little finesse and a pair of safety pins from the tags on my new clothes. Okay, I may have hip-checked it, too.

The back door opened into a laundry room. Aside from the fact Eric seemed to own no soap or fabric softener, it was fairly standard, with an inexpensive washer and dryer. No muddy axes. No piles of suspiciously bloody clothes. No written confessions. No vats of acid or body parts. Just rarely used appliances.

Inside, I found the air still cold enough to need my jacket. From where I stood, I could see straight through the kitchen pass-through to the living room. A lamp near the front window was still on, but otherwise the place looked and felt deserted. A large TV surrounded by electronics and whatnot took up one wall. No books, no movies, nothing personal. Like the place was for show. The fridge held a sack of condiments and a bottle of fifteen-dollar Chardonnay. I pulled the cork out and sniffed, got a nose full of vinegar. Two glasses still sat on the counter, the residue at the bottom no longer even syrupy.

Off the living room I found a staircase, carpeted in the sort of mind-numbing beige common to new construction. The kind that caught dirt easily and still had enough pile to show impressions. What looked like a pair of large boot prints had tamped the carpet down on their way out; I used the impressions to go up.

The hallway upstairs looked more like a suburban house than a beach cottage, with narrow drywall hallways and closed doors. Windows had been placed at either end, facing the street in the front and the back of another house to the rear. Everything white with just a hint of beige.

All the rooms had windows designed to take advantage of ocean views on one side and Intracoastal views on the other. On the right sat an office, a bathroom, and a small bedroom furnished with a cheap futon. On the left, a master bedroom with its own bathroom, a closet full of linens, and a spiral staircase up to the final floor, which housed nothing but cardboard boxes and stacks of old, dirty campaign signs.

I headed back down to the office. My phone vibrated as I checked out the credenza, wall shelves, and desktop as best I could in my winter gloves.

I flipped it open. "Yeah?"

"If you have to whisper, I know you're up to no good." Tom.

"Just a bit of recon."

"You broke in."

I didn't answer because I was busy trying to figure out his screensaver password. If Tom hadn't been on the line, I had almost just enough chutzpah to call Eric and ask for it.

Password. Wright. Eric. Seahawks. Baseball. Menhaden. Jackie.

The screen came to life and I found myself staring a photo of a dead teenager.

"When you're done breaking the law, I have something you might find interesting."

I hung up and stuck the phone back in my pocket, feeling queasy.

She had been laid out on black sheets in a small wooden space without windows. A nearby shelf, like the kind in a cabin, was covered with powders and needles, but the thing that stuck out, literally, was the knife protruding from the center of her small, naked chest, right under a large tattoo obscured by blood.

I forced myself to look closer, but I saw none of the signs that the drugs had been her idea. No tell-tell tracks, no skin-popping marks, no dust in the blood around her nose. What she did have was considerable bruising around her upper arms, on the inside of her thighs, across her face. The kind of bruising I not only recognized, but knew from the color was at least a day older than the fatal knife wound.

I shivered and fought the urge to run out of the house, and out of the state.

Instead, I took a deep breath and looked at the rest of the screen. Email. He'd opened an attachment and found this. The email had been sent through a web-based service from an igotyou465. No name, nothing to identify it. Had I been savvier, I might have still gotten to the sender. As it was, my only clue was the subject line: MISTAKE.

I pulled out my phone and recalled the number Eric had called me from. After three rings, a gruff-voiced woman answered. "Capt'n's

Table."

"Is Eric Wright still there?"

She sighed into the phone before taking it away from her face. "Hon, this is for you. You think I'm your receptionist? You ain't commissioner no more, you know." Seconds went by and her voice softened, in tone and volume. "I do appreciate you givin' my nephew a job, though."

Eric's voice replaced hers. "Hello?"

"What the hell, Eric?"

"Davis?" He whispered my name. "How did you find me here?"

"I called you back. Seriously, what the hell? There's a dead girl in your email and it doesn't look like you've been home in days." My anger did a fine job of masking my fear as usual, but I also knew eventually that'd run out.

"Sh… Wait. You're at my house?"

I waited.

"You can't be there. It's not safe. Look, I have to go."

"Eric, no, what the hell is going on?"

"Get out of there. Please." He hung up without further explanation. If I remembered right, the Captain's Table was a dive in Morehead, which, if I were a crow, wasn't too many miles away yet still far enough he'd be gone by the time I got there.

I stared at the screen again. The open email was nearly a week old. Another email with the MISTAKE subject line had appeared, and been left unopened, a day ago. When I clicked it, a naked blonde appeared. She squinted in what looked like a boat compartment. The flash, too bright against her milky skin, barely illuminated the cubbyholes. I saw no evidence of drugs, but she'd been handcuffed to a rail attached to the paneling. A note came with the photo this time: Your choice.

The rest of his email folder was related to Wright's, his last campaign, or the sort of spammy ads that filled my inbox. Nothing had been opened since the first photo, which had arrived the day before Billy Guthrie died.

I called Tom back. "What's your hacker's email address? The one he uses for stuff he doesn't want getting back to you?"

"Why?"

When I didn't answer, he rattled off a random series of letters and numbers as I typed them in to forward the two photos.

"You gonna answer me?"

I hung up and turned to the desk and started with the bottom drawer, where I found a lockbox with a cheap lock. I popped it and found myself staring at a stack of deeds and titles. I picked up a Post-it and scribbled down the names and addresses. From what I could gather, Eric somehow had the deeds or titles for twelve houses, his seafood company, a menhaden fish factory, and twenty-one boats. Most of the boats and properties had been acquired in the past two years. The seafood company he'd owned for almost six. Where the money had come from wasn't explained.

I turned around to the fax machine on the credenza behind me and made copies.

While they were scanning, I checked out the other two desk drawers.

One was a junk drawer of sorts: a couple of jewel cases for rap artists, a half-used roll of shipping tape, a semi-melted roll of duct tape, some more cheap pens, a swatch of bubble wrap, push pins, a computer mouse without the scroll wheel, some batteries and more paperclips.

In the other, I found six spindles of blank DVDs and a bunch of stray paperclips. I pulled out the top three discs from the closest spindle, flipped them over and held them at an angle to see if there was a change in the silver rings. The discs underneath were either blank or full, but the top one only had about three gigs on it. It just wasn't labeled.

I stuck the disc in the drive and waited for it to load some software and play.

Homemade porn. Low-quality homemade porn.

I started to turn it off before I realized I recognized the actress. Then I stared, dumbfounded.

Jackie. Little church girl Jackie, who'd been dead for years.

Jackie. His password.

I looked at the surroundings in the video. The walls were an older brick, with sheets hung up over the loft windows, and cheap futons. Eric's old Wilmington apartment.

And then I noticed something else. Jackie wasn't acting. She seemed completely unaware of the camera, but she didn't look happy either.

The guy stayed back to the camera, hair and face in shadow, but as he finished, the lamplight caught a tattoo of a tiger on his shoulder.

I searched my brain until I found the image I needed: Eric pulling his shirt over his head after baseball practice one day, turning to pick up another shirt off the bench so that his whole, ink-free back was visible.

Before I could eject the DVD, another video started. This time it was Eric, not Jackie. He smiled at the tiger tattooed man, who leaned down and kissed him.

CHAPTER TWENTY-NINE

I passed an abandoned amusement park and pulled off at the first gas station. The place stunk of spilled fuel. They had a sign that claimed clean restrooms but it was the pay phone between them that caught my eye.

The only security camera I saw was pointed at the cashier. I pulled my hat low on my head and ducked out into the chilly wind. The weather gave me a good reason to be wearing gloves, and the sun gave me a reason to be wearing the massive shades I usually wore around South Florida.

I dialed 911 and waited for a dispatcher, then told her I thought I'd heard screams and gave her Eric's addresses. When she asked for a name, I gave her Sandra Lewis and hung up.

The address Lane had for Amber turned out to be a trailer park next to an old campground. There were no adult-sized tricycles or golf carts in front of Retreat signs. No palms or citrus trees and no shuffleboard tournament signs. Instead, it was the sort of dilapidated, rusty place that epitomized rural white poverty, and except for the massive Confederate flag in the window, it could have been half a dozen of Charley's nicer homes.

I parked behind a dinged pickup truck that might have been older than its driver. I felt terribly overdressed next to the patch of dead lawn festooned with beer cans. The porch didn't look like it really wanted to support me, but it did, and once near the door the smell of marijuana leaked out of a nearby window.

I knocked hard, rattling the bent screen, and waited.

Amber answered in an oversize tee shirt, holding a large pink plastic cup, a mostly-spent cigarette between her fingers. "What the fuck do you want?" Her brown hair hung to her shoulders, mussed and full of split ends. She looked older than her years, maybe even older than mine.

"We need to talk about Lane."

"I don't got shit to say to you." She tried to slam the door, but I stuck my boot in the way.

"Why would Lane want to kill Billy Guthrie? *Your* Billy."

"Fuck you, bitch." She stomped my foot, but she was wearing flip-flops.

I pushed against the door. "Look, you were dating Billy, right? So, I'd guess you're angry at Lane."

"You don't know shit." She gave up on the door and stumbled into her living room, spilling what looked like Kool-Aid and smelled like Boone's Farm on the linoleum.

I followed.

"Lane's had no family around for as long as I've known her. Go back to whatever hole you crawled out of." Amber flopped on a seventies-era orange flowered couch and got out another cigarette. She had the shaky look of someone on the edge and her face wore a kind of pain I recognized in my nervous system. I was torn between the urge to punch her and hug her.

I tried again. "I'm Davis. I'm not dead. You were friends with Lane."

She glared, her fingers twitchy as she took a drag. "And now I ain't. What's it to you?"

"I want to know what happened."

"Lane is a bitch. A nosy-ass bitch. And you are a dead woman."

"How was Lane nosy?"

"Just like you. All up in someone else's business."

"Can I be frank?"

"You can be Fred for all I give a fuck." She ground the butt out on her flip-flop. "Fuck Billy. Fuck Lane, too."

I gestured at the light-brown bruise poking out of her tee shirt collar. "Billy ever hurt you?"

"Fuck you and fuck Lane. Ain't none of your business. Ain't none of her business. Billy loved me. Billy cared about me. And that bitch killed him." She gulped the rest of her drink.

"Why?"

She looked annoyed in that way that only teenagers, who think they're worldly because they do things no adult in her right mind would do, can actually pull off. I knew it well. "Look, Billy was a do-gooder.

Couldn't keep his mouth shut. I ain't that dumb."

"Doing the right thing is dumb?"

"Please. Like you ever did what you shoulda." She sat up. "Look, you gotta go. You ain't worth me risking what I got going on."

I stood my ground. "What you have here is a shithole. I grew up in dumps like this. If you're lucky, you're going to turn into Charley."

"A girl can dream." She gave me a wry smile and lurched toward the avocado-colored fridge. "Lane says there's no such thing as friends. Family either. You have what you take. You use who you can until they run out on you or die."

"Interesting philosophy. I can't say I'd have argued with you about that when I was your age." I sensed more to the story.

"We were going to be happy. We were going to be a family." She slammed the fridge and opened the cabinet. "Doesn't matter." She poured several blue pills from a bottle and downed them dry.

I watched her, but only saw Charley.

"Why'd you leave?"

I shook myself back. "Had to. I thought they'd be better off."

"Lane says you were a pussy. Selfish." She opened a drawer and crushed a couple of pills on the counter with a spoon.

"Maybe she's right."

She snorted the powder with a cut-off straw. "Vince says he killed you."

"He tried."

"He says he killed your friend."

I nodded, held my anger and sadness under the shell. "Who'd Billy talk to that got him killed?"

She rubbed her belly like she was pregnant, but it was much too flat. "Lane."

"You lost the baby?"

"It wasn't the dope." She shrugged. She was just like a dozen other young junkies I'd known. She wanted love. She found everything but.

I knew she'd never be clean. I could see her future mapped out in shades of Charley's, in the faces of the strippers I'd worked with.

"It was supposed to be okay." She scratched her arm until she drew blood, but didn't seem to notice.

I walked over to her. "What'd you take just now?"

"Just a few bars." She clawed harder. "I really wish I had some heroin. Opiates are the best. They just make you feel so warm and safe. Like you're sleeping in clean laundry with a puppy." She slid down the cabinet and sat on the floor. "You don't have any, do you?"

I shook my head slowly. Watched her head loll and her eyes turn glassy.

I pulled her into a standing position. "With me. Now."

"Why? I'm fine."

She didn't look fine. She looked like Charley right before she passed out and we had to decide between ambulances and pumping her full of uppers. "We'll go get pancakes. Jell-O shots."

She smiled and walked to the door with me, a sure sign she'd lost control of her own thoughts.

At the ER, I parked illegally and half filled out some admission forms before slipping out the way I'd come in. We'd dumped and run on Charley a couple of times. The scariest part was wondering if she'd be there when we came back.

I looked back at the brick building behind me. Somewhere in there, Charley was watching TV or sleeping.

My phone rang as I unlocked the car. Dick.

I picked up, hopeful.

"I made an appointment for you with a friend of mine for three. I don't know why he's practicing up in that Podunk state after paying good money to Miami, but if you're late, don't bother calling me." He hung up before I could say anything.

CHAPTER THIRTY

Former Detective Lawrence Jacobs's sister lived in a nice, quiet neighborhood in Morehead where kids could still play in their yard and dogs could still hang out near the street. Since it was Friday, I should have been cleaning up after my pre–lunchtime kickboxing class and getting ready to spend the afternoon making up excuses for Dick's clients while he got a massage from his girlfriend. Instead, I was traipsing around town playing detective. Poorly.

Jacobs was a huge man with deep brown skin and short, salt and pepper hair, dressed in jeans and a black tee shirt. He offered me coffee and a seat on the sofa. Then he told me I looked like crap. Or maybe he said hell.

I touched my face self-consciously.

He grinned, his teeth proportioned to match the rest of him. "Don't worry about it. You don't look that bad for someone got the crap beat out of her." Maybe it had been crap.

"I can take care of myself." I smiled and tried to look like I believed my own press.

"Uh huh."

"You know something about my sister's arrest? Lane Groves."

He scratched his chin. "Interesting names. Especially for such pretty little girls."

He reminded me of Tom.

"Don't suppose your mother would be the lady they hauled off to Carteret General on Wednesday?"

I gave him one of those damn-you-caught-me looks. "Charley named us after the members of the band she was in back when we lived in San Francisco. At least she had the sense not to name me Chuck."

He offered to refill my untouched coffee.

"You told Tom you knew something?"

"You realize this is way off the record. Based on a chat I had with Detective Huber over coffee down at the shop yesterday."

I nodded.

"Detective Huber and I have known each other a while. Used to see each other at conferences, those little mandatory classes, up at the state lab. He heard I retired in the area, he gave me a call."

"But you can tell me things he can't. Things he thinks are hinky, but can't divulge."

He put a finger to his nose and leaned back in his recliner. "Neighbors heard a gunshot and called it in. Sheriff's deputies pulled in first. First one, then the other. One neighbor thought she saw a couple leave in an old car wearing one of the Sheriff's jackets. Later, she said it was dark and she didn't see nothing but the lights flashing on a cruiser."

"One of those deputies Murphy?"

He rolled his lips like a girl distributing lip gloss. "Doesn't matter. Unverifiable. Besides, state lab will still confirm it was Lane's gun that shot Guthrie."

I noted the future tense. "Any idea how it got to the scene, the gun?"

He shifted and sipped. "She was unconscious when Huber arrived."

"Like she passed out? Fainted?"

"Got herself knocked out from the looks of it. Knot on the back of her head, but she wouldn't talk."

"Did she fall? Was she on something?"

"Lotsa stuff's possible, but the area was carpeted, swelling on upper back of her head... Nobody did a tox screen that I heard about. She did, however, land *after* the shooting. Found fluids under her."

"If she and the victim were the only ones there, how'd she get knocked out?"

"Huber found a void pattern nearby." He sipped, let that sink in.

"Someone standing? Or something disappeared?"

"If anyone else had been there, there should've been some footprints at least. She threw up all over the floor, and unless you've seen the back of someone's head blown off, it's hard to imagine the mess." He looked over at me to see how I took that.

I held my mug and thought. I'd seen that before. So had Lane. I wasn't sure if she remembered it. Probably better if she hadn't. It had been well over ten years. "No other fingerprints, footprints?"

"Void on the floor seemed foot-shaped. On the wall?" He

shrugged. "Huber played that angle close. My guess? Somebody was behind Guthrie, but the size of the void would point toward who."

"How badly did they mess up the floor responding?"

"Huber didn't see obvious footprints leading out if that's what you're asking. But remember, the deputies got there first. Supposedly secured the scene."

I wondered how much that "supposedly" had to do with bickering departments and how much had to do with actually suspicious behavior. "Guthrie boy was stabbed from behind before he died. Shortly before, according to the coroner."

"I thought he was shot."

He nodded. "Stabbed. Then shot."

"How'd Lane do that? And who left the voids?"

He spread his hands and I noticed how worn they looked.

"It's possible the stabber moved before the gun went off. Did the body end up where the stabber would have been standing?"

He nodded. "Blood drops in the void look like they came from the stab wound."

"What about the gun? I was told she had powder residue on her hands. It couldn't have been much. Phil always kept those guns in pristine working order. It wasn't like some Saturday night special."

He eyed me. "It's possible you read too much. 'Cause you're not a cop."

"I used to shoot competitively."

"Huber said the powder was a little strange. Not much, you're right. Traces of metal, same kind as the barrel. That much fits. But most of the powder was on her finger, like the rest of her hand was wrapped in something. Huber noticed because he to swab three times before he came up with anything."

"So, what's all that mean?"

"A gun grip doesn't hold fingerprints very well but the metals do, including brass."

Brass. The cartridges. "So, whose fingerprints were on those?"

"Guthrie's." He leaned back while I absorbed.

"Billy killed himself?"

He shook his head. "Huber thinks he tried to stop her. His hands had the same traces of metal and powder."

"Why'd he load the gun?"

He turned up his hands like he thought I might know and want to tell him. "They couldn't find a thing that didn't belong to your sister, the mother, or the victim."

"But, of course, you're talking the big, obvious stuff. Hairs, fibers, all that takes time and money. If someone says this case is a slam dunk, none of that stuff gets processed."

"This isn't exactly *CSI*, but then, neither is Vegas." He gave me a look that said I should know that.

I did.

"The state backlog is into years, so yeah, unless the prosecutor really wants it, it sits in storage."

"The deputies showing up? That normal?"

He shrugged. "Normal enough. They cover some of the smaller towns Downeast. Beaufort's got ten officers. They claimed to have been visiting friends in the apartments behind Maxway."

"You sound like you don't buy it."

"Just saying it was a big coincidence."

"And cops don't tend to like those." I grinned.

"What is it you said you do?"

"Paralegal. My closest friend used to be a sergeant down in Florida."

He nodded. Taking it in. "Your friend, MacQuayde?"

"He tries to keep me out of trouble."

He gave me a look that said he wasn't sure Tom was trying hard enough.

"He has his work cut out for him. I know." I tucked stray hair behind my ear and fought the urge to linger on the scar. "Do you think she did it? Really?"

He looked at the floor for a full minute. "Based on what I could dig up from other places you guys lived, she was a good kid for the most part. Until recently."

"She was."

"You, on the other hand… And while we're being frank—or mostly frank—I'd have to guess from *your* record that you'd been sexually and/or physically abused. That juvenile warrant in Texas weren't no joke. Arrested not a year later for prostitution?"

I suddenly felt naked, and not getting paid for it. I studied the knee of my jeans before answering. "Officially, it never happened. On paper, I'm just a bad seed."

"My guess would be Lane never reported anything either."

I bit the inside of my lower lip. "That doesn't make her a killer."

"You either." He looked at me pointedly.

I set my cup on the table, stood. "Thanks for your help."

"That girl's scared of something and it's not prison. Go talk to her Sunday."

"Yes, sir."

"Keep yourself out of trouble. I've seen too many people in the morgue thought they could take care of themselves."

CHAPTER THIRTY-ONE

I had some time to kill before I had to meet Dick's lawyer friend so I stopped at a chain restaurant on the west end of town. Too many years of eating irregularly had made my diet sparse, erratic, bouncing between nutritious and empty, cheap calories. While I waited for soup, I flipped through Lane's address book. Most of the names had been crossed out. Several I remembered seeing in the newspaper. Lost children who'd died young.

Besides Amber, the next most promising number yielded a woman when I called.

"Kelly? No one's asked for her in almost a year." Her voice was old and tired. "She was a bit of a handful, but I'd hoped she'd turn out better than her mother."

"I'm sorry."

"Ain't your fault. Mind if I ask who's calling?"

"Oh, sorry. I'm Davis Groves, Lane's sister. Kelly was in her address book."

"I heard Lane's been in a bit of trouble herself."

"Yeah." I tried not to sound as dejected as she had.

"They'll break your heart. Kelly, she got pregnant at thirteen. Said it was her boyfriend's. I hadn't even known she had one. She was so quiet, so sweet. Lane started hanging out with Kelly at the alternative school. They'd go on trips together."

"Trips?"

"Little road trips. Just the girls. I didn't want to pry. Didn't want to let her down. I learned my lesson with Kelly's mom. Seemed like a fun bonding experience." Something crashed in the background and a toddler cried. She put the phone down to soothe.

The waitress dropped off my soup and refilled my water. She looked vaguely familiar, but neither of us decided to figure out why.

"Sorry about that," she said. Her voice sounded wistful. "Never thought I'd be playing mom again. Too old for this, you know. But, you do what you have to."

"Yes," I agreed. "We do." I blew on a spoonful of soup.

"She came back after one of those trips all upset. I just thought it was the usual girl stuff. You know how girls can be."

I did, but not in the way she thought.

"Not long after, Kelly died—killed herself, the cops told me. There was a hose in the tailpipe, but I saw her before I called them. Her head was bloody."

My chest tightened. I knew about carbon monoxide poisoning. Charley had tried once, but we'd come home earlier than she'd expected. Found her drunk on the front seat of a rusty hatchback, garden hose not quite long enough, limp on the ground under the tailpipe. Equally drunk john or "date" passed out in front of daytime soaps on the couch.

I snapped back to the present. "Blood?"

"Exactly. I had a great cousin accidentally killed hisself with a generator after Floyd. He didn't end up bloody. Sure as hell smelled ripe after a couple days in the heat. Underside of him downright nasty when his mama found him, but he weren't bloody."

"Someone hit her?"

"That's what I always thought. Cop told me I was just crazy. Hysterical, he said." She snorted. "I ain't lived all this long, seen all this much, go crazy over that. Sad, yes. Crazy, no."

"Mind if I ask who the cop was?"

"Stockley Lamar. Always hanging out with that Murphy character down to Harker's Island like a couple of knuckleheads."

"And you're sure she didn't do it alone?"

"Honey, I ain't stupid."

"I'm so sorry."

"Ain't your fault. Hope things work out with your sister." She hung up as the toddler wailed again.

The waitress reappeared with my check. "Now I remember you. Used to go to West Carteret. My boyfriend back then worked at Cherry Point. Saw you at the titty club in Havelock."

"You still with him?"

She snorted. "Caught him banging one of them titty girls."

I left her some cash and called Tom on my way out.

"You need me to come up there?" he asked after I gave him the rundown.

I wanted more than anything for someone else to help. And I knew I couldn't have that. "I'll be fine."

"Uh huh." He didn't believe me either.

CHAPTER THIRTY-TWO

Dick's friend was in New Bern. Why I had to go all the way to New Bern for a lawyer, I wasn't sure, but when I tried calling Dick to find out he sent back a text that simply said: DON'T ASK.

New Bern was about a boring half hour's drive west on Highway 70, which ended up taking me northish through Croatan National Forest and Havelock, an apparent monument to seventies strip malls. Most of the traffic I left Morehead with stuck with me, except for the vehicles heading to Cherry Point MCAS, and given the time of day, there weren't many of those.

Robert Lawson's office was tucked into a second-floor corner overlooking an alley near the river in an area that might have been gentrifying or falling into disrepair. The elevator looked broken, but I preferred stairs anyway. The flakey, industrial green paint had a certain charm that reminded me of an old middle school I'd attended in a humid part of the deep South where dank was the county smell.

His name on the door was too modern—the font too sans-serif, the color too black—for the building or the door. Beyond the door, his receptionist desk sat empty and his office door was flung open.

"Come on in."

I crossed the entry room and leaned around the doorframe. "You're Robert Lawson?"

"Rob, if it's the same to you." He got up to shake my hand. Jeans on the bottom, white dress shirt and navy blazer on top. Converse sneakers when he came around from behind the desk.

"Are you even old enough to practice law?"

He grinned. "You must be Dick's friend. Come on in."

"Coworker." I studied the walls, his degrees, the lack of pictures. "Why New Bern?"

"Parents live up here. They're getting older. Wanted to be able to spend some time with them before the inevitable. You know." He gestured at his guest chairs and plopped back into his own.

"No, I don't." I handed over the guardianship papers Dick had drawn up. "Why'd you agree to do this?"

"Dick kind of insisted. Not really my thing, actually. Mostly focused on tax law, but I know enough. Little like doctors, you know. Have to know how all the systems work even if we generally spend our time with one."

"That's not exactly reassuring."

"I already looked into this a little. Dick told me I was doing it."

I slipped my phone out of my pocket and replied to Dick's text: What the hell?

"Here's how I see it: You've got a teenager killing a guy about the age of a boyfriend. It's not related to Wright's. Not really. But the place employs a good number of people on that end of the county. And the guy used to be a commissioner. Don't discount small town politics."

"What the hell does the one thing have to do with the other?"

"You got a lotta lawyers see themselves in politics eventually. Maybe they never do anything about it."

"And you?"

He snorted. "Look, I ain't Dick. I'm doing this 'cause I'm horrible at math and my parents were the 'doctor or lawyer' types."

"Didn't you just say you do tax law?"

"Tax law's easy. I mean the kind of math you have to do to get into med school. This? This is ninety percent plugging income into software for the three and a half months leading up to April fifteenth, creating shell companies, and reading legislation that'll cause a coma right fast."

"I'm gonna kill Dick." I stood.

"No, wait, look, I told you. I looked into this. I can do this."

"Oh, well, *that* instills confidence."

"Just sit a minute. Jeez. I got this."

I sat. "She did it. I don't know why, but Lane shot Billy Guthrie."

"Oh." His expression fell and he leaned back. "Dick said that might be the case, but, whoa."

"Your parents paid for law school, didn't they?"

"Well, yeah."

"And they set you up in this office with the understanding that you'd sit here and do people's taxes and not do anything to embarrass them, right?"

He looked left at his UM coffee mug.

"And this stunt is your way of suddenly deciding you're going to be your own person and do what you want. Am I warm? That Dick called you because he knew this is what you wanted to do and knew your parents didn't want you doing it and it'd be the perfect chance to thumb your not-quite-Princeton nose at them." I rubbed my temples.

"Look, look. It's not like that. Well, it's kind of like that. My mom thinks criminal law is dangerous." He gave me a look that was supposed to engender sympathy.

It didn't.

"My father thinks it's slumming unless you're angling for a judgeship, and he assured me I don't have the kind of face he can put on a billboard."

I wanted to ask what the hell was wrong with his face. Seemed like a perfectly white-bread, well-moneyed face to me. Thin lips, lotta freckles, pudgy cheeks, but still… About thirty and no sign of real strife or struggle. No deformed features or weird growths. Not even a broken nose.

Instead, I held out my hand. "It's been nice meeting you and all, but I need a real attorney. I don't come from the kind of family that gets a good life handed to it."

He held onto my hand too long. "Please. Don't go. I can do this. I swear."

I didn't yank my hand free, but I didn't encourage him either.

"This is my little sister's life. Not some game you're playing with your parents."

"I know. Look, I hate taxes. I really did look into this. Those two deputies who showed up. They were off duty. And they didn't show up together. Lamar and Murphy. Only Murphy was still there when BPD got there. The ballistics? Not done yet. Everyone assumes it was the gun at the scene that shot the victim, but they haven't proven it, yet."

I disentangled my digits and sat.

"And the initial fingerprints? He loaded the gun that killed him. Not the shooter."

"Where'd you hear all this?"

He looked back and forth like a spy might be hiding in his potted plastic rubber plant and opened his desk. He studied my face and pulled out a photo. "That's my father."

I looked at the picture. A white-haired man shaking hands with a salt-and-pepper-haired man. White Hair wore a suit. Salt-and-Pepper wore judge's robes.

"He doesn't want me following in his footsteps because he thinks I'm a screwup. He's grooming my brother. That doesn't mean I can't get access to information. It doesn't mean I can't read between the lines. I passed law school. I passed the bar in three states. I just didn't go to Harvard like my brother and I didn't get a perfect MCAT score like my sister."

"I'm not exactly the family angel either."

"But you've never killed anyone."

"Not yet. Doesn't mean I never wanted to. Doesn't mean I shouldn't have."

He bit his lip. "That's not bad, actually. There's more than one reason to kill a guy. Especially one you thought was a friend." He tapped his chin.

"Tell a convincing enough story, you might persuade a jury of reasonable doubt. Trouble is, you're not in South Florida anymore. Reasonable doubt in the Bible Belt is a different animal."

He smiled. "Luckily, I grew up in these parts. I know all about the word of God and how to spin a good ol' Southern yarn."

I pulled a piece of paper and scribbled Tom's contact information on it. "This is an investigator friend of mine. He has friends and connections of his own. If you need something, call him."

"He's in Broward?"

"He's the best I know of. He also probably knows as much about your new client's family as anyone outside of it, so he's a good resource if you start thinking Lane's a product of her environment."

"You seem sad. You were angry before." He tilted his head. "You said she did it. Why?"

I gave him a sly smile. "You have some paperwork you need me to sign?"

The outer door of the office opened as I stood.

Lawson looked startled. I took that to mean he wasn't expecting anyone. When the kid walked in, gun in his right hand, I was already beside the doorframe. I grabbed his wrist with my left and elbowed him in the throat with my right, twisted the gun away and put it to his temple.

"Who are you?"

The teen delinquent pissed himself. "Bu-bu-bu Buddy."

"Sit."

"I don't want that on my upholstery!"

"Then I'll buy you a new chair, Lawson. I don't want him standing." I grabbed the kid's collar and dragged him to the chair. He fell into it heavily before he realized what had happened.

Lawson sighed and sat back in his own chair. "What the hell?"

I stuck the kid's gun in my purse. "I was thinking of asking you the same thing."

He held up his hands like he wasn't sure what had happened and wasn't sure what to make of it.

I folded my arms across my chest and looked at the kid with the wet spot. Chubby, with limp hair and a line of greasy acne running from his chin to his forehead like a mountain range. He looked like a kid I'd known when I was thirteen. That one had paid me a hundred dollars of saved-up allowance and summer mowing money to lose his virginity. Told me he had been saving up for a car, but I was cheaper.

"What the hell, kid?"

He shook his head.

"Really? You show up with a gun and you can't explain why?"

"I wasn't gonna shoot anyone." He stuck his bottom lip out slightly, so I couldn't tell if it was a pout or just his resting face. "I was supposed to follow you."

"I've been here," I glanced at my watch, "fifteen minutes."

Buddy hung his head. "I couldn't find parking."

Oh, right, because that made sense. "How'd you get here?"

Sheepish. His chest rattled like he might cry. "I borrowed my dad's truck."

"He know you borrowed it?"

He stared at his crotch. "No."

"So, you stole it? Classmates put you up to this? Some sort of punk-the-ugly-kid thing?"

A couple of tears joined the urine on the front of his pants. "No."

"Then what the ever-loving hell?"

Lawson picked up his phone. "I'm calling the cops."

"No!" The kid raised his head, panicky and snorting mucus.

I motioned for Lawson to put the receiver down.

He didn't look happy about it.

"You. Can't. My dad'll kill me."

I leaned closer and tried not to take deep breaths. "Who put you up to this?"

He swiveled his head between us, eyes wide and puffy. "I can't tell. You won't understand."

"Try me." My expression was maybe harder than it should've been. No one's ever accused me of being good with kids. That was always Nik's thing.

"Mr. Jackson. Tanner."

"Who the hell is Tanner Jackson?"

Lawson answered by shoving a folder my way. I stared at the legalese until I figured out why he'd handed it to me. "You mean Rayford Jackson?"

Buddy blinked at me.

"This guy a lawyer?"

He nodded, then shook his head.

"Tanner's the son," Lawson said. "Rayford's the lawyer who handles all Wright's Seafood business. He's made a pretty fair penny off that operation, especially considering the seafood market these days."

"What's wrong with the seafood market?"

"Increased competition, increased pollution, questionable imports, decreased stock."

I turned back to Buddy, who had a look on his face like he knew more than he was letting on. "Spill it."

He mashed his lips together.

"This Tanner dick? He give you the gun?"

"Borrowed. From my dad. I wasn't gonna use it. I swear."

"Where do you live?" I asked.

"Mill Creek?"

"You aren't sure?"

He stared, wide-eyed.

An address I'd seen on deeds at Eric's stood out in my head. "Your dad have a boat?"

"Had. Had to sell it. Mr. Wright still lets him use it, though, for charters. He just has to work some nights."

"Doing what?"

He looked at the floor. "Dad told me not to tell anyone. He said we'd get in trouble."

"You pulled a gun on a lawyer five minutes ago."

"He doesn't *want* to. They make him. It's like part of the deal."

I waited. Lawson showed restraint.

"It's just seafood. I don't know where the heck it comes from, but it comes in on a ship and they load it onto little fishing boats and charters. My dad took me with him once to help him load, but Tanner told him not to do that again."

I glanced at Lawson. "This make any sense to you?"

"Maybe. Appearances are everything. Imported fish might be cheaper, but a lot of locals would shun Wright's."

I looked from Lawson to Buddy. "For real?"

Buddy's lower lip trembled. "I was just trying to get my dad's boat back." He studied his shoes. "Tanner told me my dad had screwed up too many times. He didn't trust us. That I had to follow you and get this guy to not help you."

"That's it?"

Buddy nodded.

I looked over at Lawson. "I'm taking him with me."

Lawson didn't look happy with that plan. Neither did Buddy for that matter.

I glared at Lawson. "I'll deal with this."

"How do you plan to do that? Dick said you weren't even all that good as a secretary."

The kid started to stand. I put my hand on his head and shoved him back down. "You do that again, I punch you. That don't work, I shoot you. No one told you to move, kid."

Lawson jumped up. "You cannot shoot someone in my office!"

"He and I are going to go talk to his father." I pulled out my wallet, threw several hundreds at him. "Go get a cheap motel room, go stay at your daddy's mountain cabin. Something. Just keep your head down and figure out how to get Lane off."

"Lane? That slutty kid at the alternative school?"

I looked at Buddy. "You know her?"

"Didn't she kill that guy? My dad said he was okay. Could be kind of a jerk, but okay."

I took a deep breath and splayed my fingers to keep from balling them into a fist.

Lawson looked at the kid like he'd suddenly figured out something he wasn't sharing.

I grabbed Buddy by the ear. "Like I said. You still have objections?"

Lawson sat and shook his head.

CHAPTER THIRTY-THREE

Somewhere between New Bern and Havelock, Dick called. "I do you a simple favor and you try to get my frat brother killed?"

"No."

"Then what the hell, Davis?"

"Still trying to figure that out."

"Figure it out faster." He hung up.

I stared at the road. "Where's Mill Creek?"

Buddy pointed straight ahead. "You okay, lady?"

"How old are you?"

"Fifteen."

He looked older. I'd looked older. Felt older, too. "Kids shouldn't have adult problems."

"I'm not a kid."

I swallowed the imaginary taste of blood and bile that had risen in my throat.

Buddy's mood became increasingly darker, damper, like I was sitting next to a gray cloud. Then again, maybe he felt the same way.

"My dad's gonna kill me."

I doubted that.

Mill Creek, situated between Newport and Core Creek, had a couple of churches, an abandoned gas station and a smattering of houses.

He stared out the window. "Turn here."

I turned down a lane bordered by forest. "You think you let your dad down. That's why you don't want to face him."

I glanced over and caught a slight nod.

"This is pretty secluded. You trying to lead me into a trap?"

He sighed the kind of heavy, bloated sigh only teenagers could pull off. "No. I guess that means you know that Martin guy—Brad—has a house around here." He snorted. "Trailer, really. I've never been there. I've heard about kids going there. I'm not like that. They're all losers and drug addicts. Whores."

"Like Lane?"

He made a face. "She does drugs. Sleeps around."

"Runs in the family."

The house was a modest brick in a ranch style popular in the seventies. A rusty truck sat in the driveway, a large boat trailer parked, empty, on the lawn.

An older man with a leathery tan, Guy Harvey knockoff shirt, old jeans, and worn boat shoes shuffled out onto the porch. The family resemblance was unmistakable, though it was largely in the nose and neck. He wore an expression that was a mixture of confusion, anger and sadness.

The father stopped us on the porch. "Who are you?"

I gestured at his son. "I brought this home. You should be happy he's not in jail."

Buddy's father looked at me with a mostly blank stare. Finally, he glared at Buddy instead. "What the hell did you do?"

Buddy shuffled his feet and tried to hide behind me.

"He tried to shoot my lawyer. Well, my sister's lawyer."

His head swiveled back to me. "Who are you, exactly?"

"Davis Groves, sir."

His mouth opened, shut, opened, and shut again.

"Sir, we need to talk."

He looked at me and shifted to Buddy. "Boy, where's my truck?"

"Sir—"

"Didn't ask you."

"Do you beat your son?"

"What?" He turned, anger overriding annoyance. "No. Who sent you here?"

"He's trembling." I could feel him nearby, vibrating out of his skin beside me.

His dad scowled. "Look, I don't know who put you up to this, but me and Buddy here are fine." His words and expression didn't match his body language.

"I find that difficult to believe, sir. What's your name?"

"John Taylor. Why are you asking?"

"What do you know about Tanner Jackson?"

He eyed me suspiciously. "Why *are* you here?"

"Because I'm trying to keep your son out of trouble. You want to help?" I scowled at him just long enough for his shoulders to sag, like Buddy's. "Tanner Jackson put him up to following me. You know anything about this?"

He turned and went back inside, leaving the door open behind him.

"He's gonna kill me," Buddy said.

I pushed him ahead of me up the steps.

The living room of the house was filled with frumpy, overstuffed denim couches and a china cabinet full of knickknacks and memories. We sat under the watchful eye of the blank television, which was probably at least as old as Buddy and had sticky rings on its surface.

John sat heavily on the couch. Little puffs of dust billowed up and settled again. "Boy, what were you thinking?"

Buddy stood next to him, looked at the floor. "I wanted to help."

"By getting yourself arrested? I already lost my wife."

"It wasn't supposed to be like that. I just wanted to scare him."

"Son…" John lowered his head, rubbed his thumbs together.

"What happened, sir?"

He gestured at a framed photo of a brunette posed in a traditional Olan Mills shot with a younger Buddy. "She had complications with her second pregnancy."

I waited, but he seemed to sink back into his internal melancholia, his lips disappearing behind his mustache and the wrinkles around his eyes becoming chasms.

Buddy studied his shoes as though the teenage scribbles on the rubber parts were a secret code with all the answers. "Mom wouldn't want you doing this."

His father glanced over at me, then watched his thumb rub the calluses on his forefinger.

Buddy took a step closer, but held back.

"Never had insurance. Thought we'd just get by like everyone else, but we couldn't." He looked up at me. His gaze was steady but there was a subtle sheen to his eyes.

"I heard from one of the guys that some had sold their boats to Wright, that they'd worked out a leasing deal where they could still charter and fish but they got quick cash." He suddenly looked ashamed.

"Things that sound too good to be true, right?" He reached out and touched Buddy's hand and I realized Buddy had been crying silently next to us.

He swallowed hard and looked at the sandy hair on his son's head. "The manager handles everything, but Wright has the deeds."

"The manager? Guthrie?"

"Zellner." He looked up, defiant. "This ain't being a fisherman. This isn't what I want to be doing. I just can't walk away."

"You consider going to the cops?"

"Tell 'em what? I don't know anything besides them skirting FDA inspections. Lying to consumers."

I watched the two and felt a sudden wave of jealousy I hadn't known I was capable of. I swallowed the lump in my throat. "Look, I've done things I wasn't proud of in the name of family. How 'bout I drop you two back at your truck if you can keep from killing off my sister's lawyer?"

John looked at Buddy.

Buddy tried to make himself smaller. "Tanner said he wanted Lane to lose."

John looked back to me. "What makes you think I should trust you when everything else is dirty?"

I looked into his lemony-hazel eyes. "I'm not here because I'm a good person. I'm just tired of watching people die."

In the car, bouncing down the driveway, Buddy leaned up through the seats. "Her sister shot Billy Guthrie."

"I don't know if she did or she didn't and I had nothing to do with it either way." I pulled out my phone and dialed Craig's number to cut off more discussion. "Can we meet at eight-thirty instead? I have to take care of something first and I swear I'm not trying to stand you up."

He sighed the sigh of a man who was used to being let down. "Fine, Davis. Whatever."

I ignored the sarcasm and guilt trip. "Great. See you at then." I glanced at the clock again and floored the pedal.

"You know we have a lot of speed traps around here, right?"

I eased off and watched the lights of Havelock disappear in the rearview. Darkness filled the car. "You should go somewhere. Hope this blows over."

"Where? I don't have any money. That's how I got into this situation. This is our home."

"Coastal motels are cheap in winter. Places along the interstate, too. Something's coming to a head up here. Something's wrong with their operation. Someone's gotten squirrelly. You don't want to be around for that."

He didn't say anything, but he took Dick's card with my number on the back when I dropped them off.

CHAPTER THIRTY-FOUR

I found Craig at the bar, nursing a beer. He held up a pink squeak toy that sort of resembled Q*bert and pointed at a monitor behind the bartender. "We're supposed to watch for this to be seated." He gestured at the empty bar stools. "Guess the dinner rush is over now."

I gave him my best innocent kitten face with a Miami-style hug and peck on the cheeks.

He didn't bother hiding his displeasure. "Should I ask?"

I smiled brightly. "How was your day?"

He didn't smile back.

I looked from him to his beer to the TV, which displayed a purple and green zebra. "Look, can we start over? Can we just pretend I'm close to on time and I don't look awful and that Charley doesn't think I'm dead and her security system—which consists largely of disorganization and a funky smell—isn't a complete failure?" I smiled and tried not to look creepy or crazy. "Can we pretend we're just normal old high school friends having a drink and some food?"

"So, your idea of apology for lying is to fake it?" He didn't look happy.

I ran a hand through my hair and realized it was matted to my head. "I don't think I can be who you want me to be, Craig."

He gestured at the picture of the pink Q*bert on the TV. "I'll go get us a table."

I plopped on the barstool and noticed I had dried blood under a couple of fingernails. I watched him and wondered how long that had been there.

The hostess brought us to an old-style wooden booth. Craig slid in across from me and handed the hostess his empty beer bottle.

"You want another one, hon?"

He nodded.

I ordered my own.

He glanced at the menu, exhaled heavily, and tossed it aside. "I'm pretending as hard as I can, but what are we doing here? If I ask you anything, you lie, avoid, accuse me of caring…" He threw up his hands and slumped in the booth.

"That sounds like a first date, doesn't it?"

"This isn't a first date, Davis."

"I'm sorry." I stared at the menu, but I wasn't reading it. "I never meant to hurt you."

The waitress showed up with beer and a pair of water glasses. "What can I get you two? I'd tell you about the specials, but we done sold out of one and the other," she lowered her voice, "wha'nt so good, y'all."

I smiled at her and mimicked her sweet, Southern drawl. "It all just looks so yum, but I'm afraid it'd just wreck my stomach. Can I just get a plain baked potato and a cup of the garbanzo beans you put on the Sherman salad?"

"Oh, I don't think I can ring up the beans separately." She looked distraught about it.

"Just charge me for the whole salad if you have to. I just don't want anything but the beans."

She scribbled it down and glanced at Craig. "And for you, Shug?"

He glanced at me, then the menu he'd tossed aside. "The spinach and crab dip and a calamari app. I'm not that hungry either."

She faked a smile, collected the menus and floated off.

"See, it's performances like that leave me wond'rin' if I can believe anything you say." He took a deep draw of the beer and watched me.

"Is this why Hollywood marriages always fail?"

"You're more grifter than actress." He took another sip of beer.

"Have some water, Craig." I took my own advice and drained my water glass.

He crossed his arms and stared at me.

"How about this: if it sounds awful and too horrible to possibly be true, it probably is, and if it sounds all happy and light and average and fine, it's probably some crazy bullshit I tell people so they'll sleep better than I do." I slid across the booth and started to get up.

"Don't leave."

"I don't follow commands very well." I reached into my purse and pulled out my wallet.

"Please." He reached out and grabbed my wrist.

I glared at him. "I'd break your hand if I didn't count you as a friend."

He let go and leaned back. "Haven't I earned some version of the truth?"

I sat. And stared into his caramel brown eyes.

"You probably don't want to hear this, but I've cared about you since the first time we met. Maybe yeah, at first, I wanted to rescue you. Maybe later I gave up on that. I still loved you. Maybe never stopped. Maybe it wrecked my marriage. Certainly what my ex claims anyway."

I sipped my beer. "I don't deserve that."

He swallowed hard and met my eyes. "How can you say that?"

"I'm not the girl people fall for, Craig. I'm not supposed to be."

He turned my hand over and traced the lines from my multiple surgeries. "You lied that night. Over and over. To police, nurses, doctors, me. You told a detective he might as well arrest you if he didn't believe you."

"It was my fault. I had a gun registered to a dead guy. It was all I had, at the time, of my uncle's. I'd been shooting in the woods behind the house. I just, that one time, left it out. Left the ammo out."

"You told everyone it was an accident, that you were cleaning it. No one seemed to believe you, but you told that story so many times, I saw the point when you started believing it yourself."

I watched his perfect fingertips trace the lines across my ruined palm. "You asked how I couldn't see the seriousness of a few stitches. I'm too damaged to notice. That's the truth, Craig. I have aches and pains most days. I live in the tropics like an old lady. I'm missing a chunk of lung. And don't ask what I do to metal detectors. I have more pins and plates and screws holding me together than a car. But that's not what keeps me up at night. It's not what wakes me from a dead sleep. Even that? Easier than the guilt." I laughed the sort of laugh that wasn't. "Good thing I have all that metal to support the extra weight of the guilt, huh?"

The waitress came by, refilled our waters, and left the appetizers.

He stroked the exit wound, the dent between the robot bones of my hand. "Tell me."

"I can't take it back." I was trying to tell him this would alter the course of our friendship, but his face said it already had.

"Tell me."

CHAPTER THIRTY-FIVE

I picked up a plain chip and examined it. "About Wednesday, it was wrong to say what I said the way I said it."

"Who really shot you? Your mom or the boyfriend?"

The waitress dropped off another beer and he nodded thanks at her without warmth.

"She didn't…who am I kidding? There was a moment when I thought she was coming to save me. And then I realized her anger wasn't for him. It was for me. She didn't mean to shoot me where she did. She meant to kill me. And in some ways, she did."

He stared at me for what felt like a long time. "Your mother shot you?"

"She was high. They were freebasing. She can't handle her uppers like that."

"Why?"

I felt myself shrink at the question, felt the words *Nothing, I'm fine* form on my tongue automatically. "He didn't handle his uppers well either. He hit her one too many times. I tried to stop him. He turned on me." I swallowed only to find a desert in my mouth. "He raped me."

His expression darkened, his eyes shiny.

I put my finger to his lips. "It wasn't… It shouldn't have… You don't know everything about me. What hurt that night was Charley's betrayal. I'd been pretending so hard I was like you; I forgot I wasn't."

"Why didn't you tell someone?"

"To protect Charley. Because I didn't want you to know."

"What? Why? What about him? Why not tell on him?"

I put my hand on his. "I got my licks in. It would've been his word against mine. My record works against me. There's no sense pushing for a case, if you're the one who goes on trial."

He covered my scars with his hand.

"At the time it didn't matter, and now it only matters because I let him get away with it."

"How could it not matter?"

The waitress dumped off my potato and a cup of beans. I stabbed a bean with a fork and ate it. Salty.

"You don't understand. Your parents lived together. You had your grandmother. Who cooked family meals on Sunday after church. My dead father's one-time lover willed me a box of guns and shot himself. My mother's a washed up singer, painter, whore, and addict. You were in the Boy Scouts and spent summers at camp. I once lived in an abandoned car. My mother almost got us all killed in a bar shootout, of all things. I've been arrested. More than once. I've been a prostitute. A girl like me wasn't supposed to be in a relationship with a guy like you. Nowhere in your childhood is there any frame of reference for mine."

He took my other hand in his and ran his thumb along my new cuts and scrapes.

I jerked it free. "I don't know how to explain this. I don't know how to explain how numb—"

"It's okay."

"Cut the platitudes. Remember when we first had sex and you told me you were a virgin and I told you I was, too? One of us was lying."

"We both were."

"Who?"

He looked sheepish. "Becky Sanderson. We went out the year you moved to town. She kind of talked me into it."

"That's it?"

He nodded, embarrassed.

I leaned back and pointed, for some reason, at the calamari. "See, that's why."

He glanced at the plate.

"High school girls, they're either virgins or sluts. Don't ask me why. I didn't make the stupid rules. But there's a reason you went out with Becky and everyone in school knew what it was."

He turned pink.

"We were supposed to be permanent here. We were supposed to be different. And you were different. And I was trying to be. I wanted to be."

"So you weren't a virgin eight years ago. So what?"

"I've been a lot of guys' Becky Sanderson." I looked from him to the table and back. I thought about draining my beer, but I wasn't hungry and I had to drive. "I first had sex when I was eleven."

He dropped the chip he'd picked up and leaned back. His mouth worked a little, but no sound came out.

"Yeah, see, that's why I don't tell people that." I rubbed my triceps, felt the muscle under my too-thin shirt. It felt too strong to be part of me.

"Davis, it wasn't your fault."

"You don't know that."

"You were eleven. It couldn't have been."

I picked up the abandoned chip and examined its edges. Jagged. Raw. I bounced it off the far end of the table and watched it skid under an empty table.

"Davis?"

"We were foster kids for a few months, at the time. Charley in jail for prostitution. There was an older brother. Sixteen. Kept sneaking into our room at night, looking to fool around. I cut a deal with him to leave Nik and Lane alone. *I* did that."

His jaw worked independently of the rest of his face, like it was stoking the fires in his brain.

"So, no, legally, I couldn't make that choice. But I did." I looked at the brick wall beside me. It wasn't any help. "Except he took it too far a couple of times. And I never knew how to draw the line between what was okay and what wasn't. What I *agreed* to and what I didn't."

"Davis…" He let his mouth open, but couldn't seem to find any more words.

"It's so much easier for people outside to label everything, to just throw it all in one box and say 'here's your rape collection.'" I gave him a smile that didn't quite make it all the way to my lips. "But those people didn't spend four days in juvie with me that month. Those people can't understand how I walked out of there feeling lucky. And trapped. Those people never agreed to be Becky Sanderson for a group of high school nerds so they'd have enough money to get out of town."

He stared at me.

"Two of those kids were seniors. Eighteen. Wanted to get laid before they went to college. The law says they were in the wrong, but I took their money." I picked up a garbanzo bean. "Law says I was wrong, too."

He looked pale. "You never told anyone?"

"Who would I tell, Craig? The law doesn't protect people like me. And it sure as hell wasn't protecting any of the girls I met in juvie. The girls do the time while the johns walk free." I took a sip of beer and realized it was warm and nearly gone.

"But—"

"Don't give me that. Please. Don't." I flexed my nostrils and tried not to cry because it wasn't worth it. "Don't think I haven't second-guessed myself and pictured every other person he may have hurt because I didn't stop him. I was eleven. I had no one to turn to but my twelve-year-old sister and I didn't want her to know."

He reached for my hand and I jerked it away. "I'm sorry?"

I finished my beer and sat the bottle at the end of the table. "I fucked up."

"You can't blame yourself."

"Don't tell me who I can blame either. I made my bed." I rolled my eyes, partly at my words, but mostly to try to keep the tears in. "I played my part. And I wasn't old enough. And I didn't want to. But I did. We needed money. And I got us money."

"I've never—"

"No. You never. That's what I've trying to tell you." I put my forehead in my palms and wracked my suddenly tipsy brain for a way to explain, to describe. All that came were tears I thought I'd run out of. I watched them drop soundlessly onto the hardwood table. Squinted my eyes shut trying to make them stop.

He put his hand near my elbow but didn't touch me.

I looked at him, glared, trying to find the me that had put all this shit in a box with Phil and Jackie and Daddy and a dozen other things. "You know, in some neighborhoods, it's almost a rite of passage. Which is fucked the fuck up. Cause you know what sucks more than your own pain and fear and shame and blame? Sharing a room, locked in the dark, with a twelve-year-old who's had a train run on her. Who wakes up in the night screaming and tearing her hair out at the root. Who gets *laughed at* by the other girls from her 'hood cause it's already happened to them or a friend and it's all they know anymore."

He stared at me with just enough self-control not to let his jaw hang open.

I swallowed hard and thought about draining his beer too. "And you know, that normalizes it. For all of us. And it becomes a sliding scale of 'at least not that.' 'At least he didn't do that.' 'At least it wasn't my uncle.' 'Or my dad.' 'At least it was just the once.' 'At least I didn't get pregnant.'" I smiled my deranged smile. "And you realize most of the older girls are hooking to support drug habits to dull the pain, to forget. They're being pimped out by people who're supposed to love them. Or they've attached themselves to some abusive guy who feeds into their little 'at least' world. And 'at least' was that I called my own shots. Even if it meant a few times I found a knife at my neck or a gun in my mouth and my money walking out the door without me."

"I had no idea."

"I know."

The waitress picked up my empty bottle and left a full one, avoiding eye contact.

"Look, I know you want to tell me the special episode lines or reassure me, but it's not so easy. It doesn't all fit in one box. Not for me. Except, I say that, it takes away from other victims. It implies blame I don't intend. Implies apologies I'm not offering to people who've done terrible things. To say that I exploited my own abuse makes it seem like I'm diminishing the abuse of others. It lessens the hurt for me to admit my part, even when my choices were very limited. But I fear it takes away legitimacy from people who need justice to move on."

"You've put a lot of thought into this."

"It's something I do in those small hours of the night when other people are sleeping." I looked at the garbanzo beans for help, but they just sat there. "I don't want to cry about this shit anymore. I don't want to have to keep lying to myself, because the older I get the more I know better."

"Crying is okay, Davis."

"No. It's not." Stray tears fell from my eyes. "Because it means I regret things I can't regret."

"We all have regrets, Davis."

"We had what we needed. I paid our way when Charley lost or spent all our money." I looked down and realized I'd pulled the hem out of the napkin. I didn't remember doing it. I pushed myself to the end of the booth. "I can't do this. I can't look at you looking at me like that."

"Please. I'm trying."

"I don't know how to make you understand." I leaned across the table and lowered my voice. "I was a prostitute for more than three years before I met you. For two more later."

He reached for my hand, but I slid it away. "It's expensive to be poor. Unbelievably so."

"Couldn't you guys get food stamps or something? Subsidized housing? Isn't that what that stuff's for?"

"We had trouble staying put long enough to get approved. And even the cheapest rental wants a deposit. We usually took off when that ran out. Probably lived three or four days every month in the car.

"Something snapped in Charley when our dad died, like she'd been hoping for a year he'd quit the 'gay thing' as she called it and come back. They used to play in a club in San Francisco. Hit the road a few years before Lane. She'd sell brightly colored paintings of instruments and people dancing at fairs and those trendy little galleries. They'd sing in bars and clubs. And then they weren't *they*. Just her. And she started to fall apart."

"She paints?"

"Not in years."

He reached out a hand. "Your dad died when you were ten, right?"

I took his hand, squeezed.

"Does Nik even know what you did?"

"I never told her." I glanced at the condensation dripping off my water glass. "She knows enough. She's probably guessed the rest. Every hit I've taken is one she didn't have to. Which is maybe why I can't talk to her about it."

He looked sad. Heartbroken. "I keep picturing my daughters at that age."

"I wasn't your daughter. I thought I had it all figured out." I grabbed the napkin off the table and twisted it. "Nik survived our childhood untouched, *untainted* by the things I did. Most days, that's enough."

He ran his fingers softly over the whorls on my left palm. The smooth scarred flesh vibrated under the skin, where damaged nerves tried to make sense of what they felt.

He kept his eyes on my hand. "Who burned you?"

I shrugged and didn't fight the urge to wince. "Random asshole. I got my licks in on him, too."

He sat quietly a moment and fingered the edge of his plate, rubbing a grease spot around the edge. "Are you okay? I mean, really?"

I almost told him I was fine. Instead, I took a deep breath and winced. "I try to be. Most days. It's a lot of years of crap. A lot of it bleeds together." I looked at the scars on my hand. Fingered the one at my collarbone. "Even in the years since I last saw you. But, hey, you got married and had a couple kids."

"Three." He ran a finger down the edge of his beer glass. Wouldn't look at me.

"I did my best to keep them safe. And then I left. And I fucked it all up. And it might get Lane killed." And I wasn't sure I could live with that.

"I…"

I glanced at him, the worry etched on his face, and felt my whole day collapse under my feet. "I did everything I knew to do." I came out as a whisper. "It wasn't enough."

CHAPTER THIRTY-SIX

Once we had steaming cups of coffee from a shop around the corner, he asked, "How did you and Jackie ever end up friends?"

"She was getting hassled. We started talking. Got along."

"I got the impression her mother was real religious."

"I think she was at church more than the preacher. She once found out I'd tried cigarettes…" I raised an eyebrow and gave him a grin.

"How could you be best friends with someone who didn't know you?"

"There's more to you than a divorce, right? Look, by the time I met you guys, I was a different person. Or I thought I was. Wanted to be."

"She never figured it out?"

Jackie had known more than Craig, but maybe that had been her undoing. Not directly, but in some small way, I tainted everyone I touched. "She knew I was a stripper in college."

"Her mother said she died in a car accident."

"It wasn't an accident." I sipped my coffee. "I'd moved to Boone. She called in a panic. Wanted me to come get her. Said she knew a girl going to meet her boyfriend in Raleigh. That she'd meet me there. Somebody'd beat her up. She wouldn't talk about it." I told him the rest.

"It wasn't your fault."

"It'll always feel like it was." I left out Ryan and the frat boy and the fire. There was only so much I could handle reliving in one night and I was well past that point.

He put an arm around my waist and guided me as if I were a regular date. I let him, basking for a moment in the fantasy.

We were the only ones on the sidewalk and only about half the streetlights had bothered to stay lit for us. I could feel the wind on my cuts and scrapes through the shirt. "I've had a good time tonight, so you know."

He said nothing.

"I have to be stronger than this."

"No one should have to be, Davis." He rubbed my shoulder near the stitches.

"The pain? It never goes away. It's better when it's something I can put a bandage on."

He held me without comment. I let him, too tired not to.

"Every time I try to get away… "

He pulled me closer, shielding me from the cold outside. "It boggles my mind how you keep going when anyone else would give up."

"It's all I know." I stared behind him. "Truth is, the times I wanted to die most never coincided with the times people most wanted me dead."

We crossed the street to the parking lot where I'd left my car. Aside from the light from a stray sailboat and a string of half-lit Christmas lights on the patio of the Dock House, we were alone in the dark. The water slapped the pilings of the boardwalk and the wind rattled the lines in the sailboat cleats.

"They say my father drowned." I glanced over my shoulder at the black waters between us and Carrot Island. Other people were at home, snuggled into their beds watching TV, reading, or spooning loved ones. "They never found him. Phil, they found." I looked back at him. "The dead can do all sorts of talking to the right person. The missing never say a thing."

"You said you had a good time. This is your idea of a good time?"

I breathed him in and felt safe and warm for the moment. "Yeah. I guess it is."

CHAPTER THIRTY-SEVEN

When I opened the front door I could see that someone had downgraded Charley's craptastic decorating scheme with destruction and spray paint. It was less than awesome.

Craig leaned over. "Why does the wall say 'die bitch'?"

"Because my life sucks."

Something crashed upstairs in Charley's room. Footsteps ran down the length of the hallway toward my old room.

I let loose the kind of sigh only possible after everything that could possibly go wrong had been followed up by an asteroid in the living room.

"Go back to the car, Craig. Don't get yourself shot or stabbed." I took off toward the front staircase. Craig followed me. I stared at him. He stared back. I gave up. "Fine, stay behind me. And stay quiet."

He nodded. "Maybe we should call the police."

"Rural area. Sheriff. It'll take forever. Sh!" I didn't mention they might already be there.

I kept my footsteps light. Craig tiptoed like one of the Scooby-Doo gang. At the top of the stairs, I turned into the hallway and sighed at the broken glass glinting in the moonlight.

"You didn't fix that?" Craig whispered.

"I did." Now the glass was mostly inside instead of out.

Someone moved in the shadows near my old room. I caught a glimpse of metal in the faint moonlight. It moved closer and I slipped my hand behind me to pull out the gun I'd stuffed in my waistband when I got out of the car. Apparently I figured if I shot my own ass, no one else would do it for me.

"Now I get it."

I ignored him and watched the shadow. It didn't move. Just waited. I felt bored with waiting.

A cloud moved and moonlight lit the shadow and I could see it wasn't a gun he had but a hunting knife. The face belonged to a teenager

I'd yet to meet.

I handed the gun to Craig. "Don't shoot me." To the teenager, I said, "Don't stab me."

He didn't answer. He lunged forward like he'd seen one too many drunken Civil War reenactments.

I shoved Craig backward and sidestepped the attack, deflecting the knife and catching his wrist. Drove a knee into his ribs and twisted his wrist until I heard the clatter of the knife on the wood floor.

I kicked his legs out from under him and landed with one knee in his back. With the hand that wasn't still holding his wrist behind him, I grabbed an ear and yanked his head an inch off the floor. "What are you doing in here?"

"Fuck you." He meant to sound tough. It came out whiny.

"Spill it." I hadn't really hurt him yet. But I would.

"Man, that bitch ain't worth this."

I waited.

"Sylvia. She said if I hurt you, she'd sleep with me. That girl likes it rough."

I bounced his face off the hardwood. "About that rough?"

"Man, fuck you. She said Lane was still holding. That she had a stash before she got popped."

I hauled him to his feet and shoved him toward the stairs. Craig trained the gun on him inexpertly until he'd rounded the corner. Thirty seconds later we heard the front door slam.

Craig crumpled against the wall and let the gun hang at his side. "What the hell are you?"

I rubbed a kink out of my neck and rolled my shoulder. "Pissed. Think you can fix whatever I've fucked up?"

He followed me downstairs, looked at my shoulder and walked toward the door.

"Hey, what'd I say?"

"I'm going to get my gear."

"Oh."

I watched him walk out the door and felt stupid. It wasn't like me to ask for help. Or accept help. It wasn't like me to find people other than Nik gluing and sewing me back together unless circumstances were dire. Or to care if stitches had come loose.

It wasn't like me to forget the douchebag who'd just run out the front door. The douchebag with nowhere to go, who probably still wanted a fix.

I ran out the door too fast. Dumb move. Amateur.

The first thing I saw was Craig lying prone next to his truck, the door open, light on. The next thing I saw was a fist coming at my face.

I dodged too late, taking the hit on the side of my head instead of the nose. I immediately turned defensive to block a second incoming blow, head still a little full of starbursts. Getting my bearings on the fight, I blocked a third hit with my left arm and brought an uppercut into his ribs with my right, then rolled my elbow into his neck. Hard.

He wasn't a fighter by training, just a guy playing tough like he'd done on a schoolyard. I had more experience there. By which, I mean I should have just knocked the asshole out, but I was pissed. I wanted to hurt him. I wanted him to hurt me, balance out the mess in my head.

He caught himself on the rusty railing, kept from landing on his ass or his head. Instead, he swung himself onto the patch of mud and dead leaves Charley called a yard. I swung myself over the railing, planting my feet in his ear.

He went down to his knees. I landed on one of mine, but quickly recovered.

He came low, a small black survival knife clenched in his fist. He swung the point at my knees.

I spun out of his arc and thrust-kicked his shoulder.

On the driveway, Craig stirred and sat up, rubbing the back of his head.

The teenager ran toward Craig.

I ran after him.

Craig stood, slowly, not noticing us in the darkness. We were out of the range of the truck's glow and beneath too many trees for the moon to reach us. He heard the movement and turned as the teenager swung the knife for his midsection.

I was behind him, about seven feet away. I bent my knees and sprang, colliding with the kid's left hip. I jammed my shoulder into his kidney and caught his wrist mid-swing.

His head hit the edge of the truck's doorframe with a horrible crack and he went limp. We landed in a heap. Blood was smeared down the side of the truck, visible in the light from the dome inside.

"Ow."

I disentangled myself and stumbled backward, glancing over at the "ow."

Craig sat, leaning against the side of the truck, feet splayed, on the other side of the door. Through the window I could see him holding his stomach. He looked stunned and pale.

"Fuck." I reached down and checked the teenager's pulse. He still had one. "Craig, you okay?"

I shoved the kid out of the way and closed the truck door enough that I could keep my eye on the teenager while I checked on Craig.

"Craig?"

He looked up at me and smiled. "Damn."

I bent and put my hand over his. "How bad is it?"

"Just a scratch."

"If you move the hand, will anything fall out?"

"Just blood."

"Where's your box?"

"You think I'm a wuss."

"Not now, Craig. Where's the box?"

He looked sullen. "It fell under the truck."

I crawled under after it, scooped up what I could see had fallen out, and shimmied back out.

"Can you walk?"

He nodded. "I'm not dead."

"Good to know." I jerked my head at the teenager. "I'll meet you at the door."

CHAPTER THIRTY-EIGHT

I dumped the kid on the couch. He'd split his lip and knocked out a tooth. I rolled him over, pulled his shirt over his head, and used the sleeves to tie his arms behind his back. Having him run off again didn't seem like a good idea, so I pulled off my pants and used the legs to tie his together.

Craig perched himself on the arm of the loveseat, clutching his tackle box of medical supplies and his abs. "You don't have rope?"

"Have you seen how Charley keeps house?"

"I'd forgotten how beautiful your body is."

I glanced down, realized my shirt was bloody, muddy, and ripped. "He hit you that hard?" I yanked the shirt off and threw it at the kid.

Craig shrugged and winced.

"Sit down. Get comfortable." I motioned for him to put his ass on a seat cushion and pulled his shirt over his head, balling it up over the cut. I dug a flashlight out of the purse I'd dropped on the loveseat when we'd first walked in. "Look at me." I checked his pupils.

"You do that often?"

"More Nik's thing, actually." I opened his tackle box and pawed around for a gauze pad to use on his scraped chin.

He traced a scar on my upper arm. "This one wasn't here when we were kids."

I found a packet of alcohol swabs and opened one. "I kind of got hit by a car." I dabbed his chin.

He tried not to wince.

Once clean, the scrape didn't look too big, so I dug around for a Band-Aid and ointment.

"Let me see the back of your head." I got up and pointed the flashlight at the knot. "It's stopped bleeding."

He touched the scar that ran halfway my thigh.

I pulled his hand away from his belly and stared at the cut. It was long, but not deep. "Probably leave a nasty scar." I reached over with my right hand and rummaged for sutures or glue.

When I looked back I caught him staring at my right hand.

I glanced at it like it wasn't part of me and nodded. "I lost some fine motor skills, but I was never going to be a surgeon anyway. It might work better if I'd quit punching things with it." I took out some gauze and another alcohol pad to clean him up with. "They really did an amazing job. Modern miracle, I guess, considering there's still bits of it in the doorframe upstairs."

The blood flow had slowed, but was still too heavy to get tape to stick. I found a tube of super glue and ran a bead along the edge. "Knife wounds are usually pretty clean." I tossed the glue back in the box. Once dry, I taped a strip of gauze over the cut and stood. "I'll go see if there's anything in Charley's freezer you can put on your head."

He caught my hand and stared at the web of scars on my palm, some surgical, some not.

I stopped and stared at the wall. "She's not sane, Craig. You can't blame her."

He searched my face. "She should've been aiming for him."

I jerked my head. My jaw clenched. "It was my fault. I left the .22 out. I should've known better."

He looked like he might cry.

"Don't give me that shit. I don't need your pity." I jerked my hand free and went to the kitchen to find some frozen food that had likely expired before I'd moved out.

He followed me. I heard him, but refused to look back. Instead, I opened the old freezer and stared into it like I could see a point in the future when the conversation would be over and he wouldn't be giving me that look.

I slammed the freezer door shut and turned. "I can't find anything to put on your head."

He put his hands on my shoulders and rubbed the tops of my deltoids, trying to caress away the hurt, I supposed. "I'll be okay."

"I don't want you looking at me differently. But then, I guess you already do." I shrugged out of his arms and started pulling open drawers, looking for a plastic bag to put ice into. I found an ice cream scoop that looked like Charley had tried to cook heroin in it at some point. I tossed it on the counter. "It wasn't like I was some little waif who ran off to slay a giant. He was bigger, but he wasn't exactly Mike Tyson." I found a sandwich bag that still had bits of weed in it.

I turned, holding the bag in one hand and the scooper in the other. "I'm a better fighter now than I was then. More training, more practice. It still only takes one missed block, one wrong move, one little error and a whole fight can turn."

He hovered, but refrained from touching me while I scraped frost into the bag.

I handed him the bag and tossed the scooper on the counter. "Don't eat the ice."

He stuck it on the back of his head. He still looked like a puppy.

I went back to the living room long enough to grab my purse. He stayed on my heels, but said nothing.

"She caught him." I crossed the kitchen toward the back stairs to find some clothes.

He followed, oddly quiet.

I turned halfway up the stairs and pointed at a hole in the slanting ceiling. "She missed the first time. Second one broke the window. Third hit the wall in the hallway. Nik put a poster over it when she visited. That's the fourth." I held up my hand. "Fifth. Went through and through." I pointed at another hole, in the wall. "Sixth."

I ignored the younger version of myself I could see at the top of the stairs, screaming for Charley to stop, to listen to reason. "She probably would've done a better job if she hadn't been high as a fucking satellite."

I went to my old bedroom, found some jeans from high school.

He followed. "Do you wish she'd killed you?"

I pulled on a sweatshirt. I had no idea how to answer him.

CHAPTER THIRTY-NINE

Downstairs, I sat on a chair next to my houseguest. According to the ID in his wallet, his name was Anderson Wallace. I thought it was stupid to have two last names, but apparently his mother and mine had been having a mind meld so I couldn't fault him that.

Craig perched on the arm of the sofa. "At least I know why you weren't scared of *him*."

I jerked the kid into a semi-upright position and slapped him as hard as I could.

"Smelling salts might be easier."

"Maybe I just felt like slapping him." The kid didn't stir. I pulled up an eyelid and checked his pulse. "Fucking drug addicts."

"Do you do drugs?" His voice held innocent curiosity.

"I had beer with you at dinner."

"No, I mean have you ever done *drugs*? Like Charley? Like Lane?"

I bit my lip and thought.

"I'd understand. Believe me." He rested a hand on my shoulder.

I turned to face him. "I smoked a little pot in high school, middle school. Not a lot. Not often. Every now and then, I'd have a beer."

"While you were working?"

"It's not safe if you're fucked up, even if it makes it easier. If you're gonna make hard choices, you should know what you've done afterward." I shook my head. "I don't want to talk about that anymore. I wasn't like Charley. I got a firsthand look how that turned out."

He pulled me into him and I got the feeling he needed the hug more than I did.

"This isn't how I wanted this night to turn out." His voice was low.

"Ditto." I stood.

"I didn't really realize a night could turn out like this, frankly. I mean … is this normal to you?"

"Not anymore." I looked in his eyes. "You want to know how I was hoping this night would end?"

He nodded.

"I was hoping you wouldn't ask too many questions, that there'd be no fights, no one would cry, and that I'd forget I'm supposed to have a boyfriend in Florida and get you out of your pants."

"You have a boyfriend?"

"Only because I haven't had a chance to break up with him." I tossed the kid's wallet at his face and watched it bounce into his lap.

"Any reason why?"

"I thought that's what I wanted. I thought that's who I was." I stood and headed for the stairs.

He followed. "What does that mean?"

I stopped at the foot of the stairs. "You know, you're the first guy I ever had sex with because I wanted to. The first guy who didn't know I was a whore."

"You weren't a whore to me."

I shut my eyes. Let him hold me.

"I've never seen you that way. I never will."

"Matt never saw me like that either. He's the only other one, Matt. That never paid. Never took." I kept my eyes shut, but I was all cried out.

"So, why break up with him?"

I pulled away and walked up the stairs. At the top of the landing, I stopped. "Because of this." I pulled my shirt off.

Craig followed and ran his finger along the line running from my clavicle to my bra strap.

I turned and walked up the rest of the way. When I stopped at the top, Craig stood behind me. "He's normal. I'm not. And every time we make love he closes his eyes."

Craig's fingers danced along the webbed white lines tangled in knots on my back.

"He turns out the lights."

Craig unhooked my bra, pausing to plant kisses behind my ear, along the curve of my neck.

"He thinks I was in an accident. And he still can't bear to look." Craig's fingers caressed the exit wound above my shoulder blade. "He acts like he's afraid he'll hurt me."

"You're beautiful. Incredible." Craig pulled back and let my bra fall to the floor.

I reached for the buttons on his jeans. "I don't believe that."

He dropped his pants and followed me in his boxers. The chill in the air left goose pimples on his pale winter flesh. "Why would you be with someone who doesn't appreciate who you are?"

"I forgot who I was." I stepped out of my jeans and pulled him up the last step of the stairs. "I thought I wanted to be someone else. Someone regular."

I leaned in and nibbled his lower lip. My hands trailed the lines of his sinewy muscles, toyed with the elastic of his boxer shorts, traced the faded Invader Zim head on his taut ass.

He pulled away. "Do you still want to be someone else?"

"You want to know if you're making out with your high school girlfriend or about to fuck a hooker?"

He looked down and I felt his erection shrink against my thigh. "Is this what you really want? I don't want to be someone else who uses you."

"I've wanted to do this since Wednesday." I kissed him and tasted the remnants of calamari and beer on his breath. "You're the only person I've… You're the closest I've ever felt to… Please don't make me try to explain it."

He burrowed his face in my neck and followed the scar down to my chest. I ran my hands through his wavy brown hair and kissed him.

He was out of breath when he broke free. "Just tell me you want this."

I looked into his caramel-sauce eyes and pulled him toward Charley's room. "I want this."

"What about your room?"

"Somebody stabbed the mattress."

He raised an eyebrow.

I dropped his boxers, pushed him backward on the bed, and reached for my purse.

"You have a condom?" He pushed up on his elbows.

"Yeah." I showed him.

"You keep those on you?"

I reached for him. "Call it an old habit."

He lay back again, let me roll it on, and wrap my lips around him over it. "I remember you had the condom in high school, too."

I climbed on top of him and put a finger to his lips. "Sh. Enough old times."

As soon as he was inside me, the years melted away and I was sixteen again, a horny girl with an impossibly cute boyfriend who thought I was just another junior. But I rode him like a grown woman who needed to release a terrible week, pounded against him like a woman who needed to get just to the edge of hurt. And bit and clawed at him like someone who needed the two of us to reach the screaming together.

CHAPTER FORTY
Saturday, February 11

I'd dozed off for a while, but it hadn't kept. I watched Craig sleep and thought about our first time. Gentle. Awkward.

His hand lifted my shirt slowly and set it on his pillow. I leaned in for another kiss. His lips parted and our tongues found each other again, like desperate lovers kept apart. Or teenagers in heat. His fingers fumbled with the knots on my bikini top. Mine explored the contours of his skinny torso, the way the sheen of sweat left behind goose pimples in his parents' chilly house.

His delicate fingers cupped my breasts and he stroked my nipples with his thumbs, his eyes full of lust and amazement.

I felt desired in a wholly different way than I was used to and it felt warm, inviting. And it made me want him. It made me wet and I wanted to share that with him.

"We should use protection," I whispered into his ear before tasting the softest part of his lobe, licking the sweat and salt from our afternoon at the beach.

He swallowed, his Adam's apple bobbed against my shoulder. "Do you have a condom?"

I wasn't sure how to answer him. Did regular girls carry those? If I said yes, would he see me as practical or slutty?

Craig pulled back, his eyes searching mine. "Are you sure you want to do this? We don't have to. We could just make out. Talk."

I took his hand and put it between my legs, already half spread with one foot on the floor and the other inches from the still wet crotch of my swimsuit.

A teenage boy, he didn't need too many more hints and his fingers slipped inside as soon as his lips touched mine again.

I suppressed the sound of pleasure I'd faked for years, even though this time it was real, and ran my hands through his hair until I forced him to come up for air. "There's a box of condoms in my bag." When I pulled free and stood, I untied the side of my bikini bottom so that it slid to the floor as I crossed the room to my backpack.

When I turned, his eyes were huge and hungry.

I held up the box. "I bought these when we first started going out. I knew a girl once who got pregnant."

He nodded, and looked confused. "It's open."

I smiled, played goofy. "I may have taken a couple out to experiment with. You know, try that whole banana thing that teach you in health class."

He shook his head. "Banana?"

"Take off your pants. I'll show you. Maybe they don't do that here. I mean, it's kinda weird. Everybody laughs at it and the teacher turns a million shades of red."

He squirmed out of his swim trunks and sat on the damp spot they'd left on his comforter. His penis was clearly interested and he folded his arms awkwardly like he wasn't sure he wanted me to know.

I came over and pushed him back against the bed. "You won't think I'm a slut if we do this. Right?"

He shook his head.

I grinned because I knew he'd agree to just about anything at that point, but I crawled up next to him anyway.

Craig's hands roamed. "Are you sure you want to?"

I nodded. I couldn't explain to him how much I wanted to. It had been almost a year since the last time I'd had sex, but that felt like part of another life. This new Davis wanted the geeky kid who did well in biology and skipped school to surf when the swell was good.

I took a condom out of the box and rolled it onto him. I let him push me on my back and guide himself inside before wrapping my legs around him and pulling his face close to mine.

The phone rang while I watched Craig sleep. I pushed talk before the third ring.

"What's up, Tom?" I whispered and slipped out of bed. I wasn't dressed because I'd been curled up next to Craig, who exuded warmth, physically and emotionally. I pulled on a thin sweater and thong before slipping out into the hallway and down the back stairs. "Couldn't sleep?"

"Actually, no. I was worried about you. This Zellner character is dangerous."

I rubbed the scar behind my ear. "Yeah."

"I spent most of the afternoon working on your case. There's nothing in a database that will explain why Lane went to Sally Guthrie's house." He sounded a little drunk. It wasn't like him to do much of anything to excess, and certainly not alone.

"What's wrong?" I ran myself a glass of tap water and wandered in to check on our captive. He stirred in his sleep like a dog chasing a rabbit.

"I can't say for certain, but from what Chip could dig up—"

"Hack. He's a hacker. He hacks. You dig."

"In other words, it wouldn't stand up in court, which is why I don't do it." He paused, but if he was drinking he did it away from the phone. "Chip says those two aren't solvent on paper. That the fish business is breaking even at best. Wright's lawyer, though? He deposits and pays out a lot more money than one might expect for a small-town attorney. They're also renting dock space and storage down in Wilmington, but they're doing it through a series of shell companies."

"Drugs?" I thought about what I'd seen in Lane's room.

"There's money coming from Mexico and China. Marilyn says all but one of the bags are older-style fakes. Like, from seasons maybe six years ago. The other's a much better knockoff."

"Say hi to her for me."

He grunted. "China makes sense for the bags. Mexico could be either, but it's probably drugs. Wright does own an import business with water access."

"He's importing cheap fish and passing it off as local, but that doesn't sound like a big money maker." I shut my eyes and pinched the bridge of my nose.

"Davis, this isn't some movie. You're supposed to be helping your sister. That's all."

I leaned against the counter. "I'm trying. She seems to be at the heart of this."

"Try to stay safe."

I put my water glass on the counter and headed back up the stairs. I paused at the sixth bullet hole and ran my finger around the edges of it. Safety.

CHAPTER FORTY-ONE

I woke to pounding on the front door, followed shortly by yelling from the downstairs guest.

I slipped out of bed, still in the panties and sweater. Craig stirred and sat up. I put my finger to my lips and mouthed, *stay here.*

He looked suspicious, but nodded.

I took the back stairs, tense and ready for battle. By the time I hit the kitchen, I heard Charley screeching on the front porch and relaxed a bit.

"Let me the fuck in my own damn house!"

I flung the door open as she swung her fists to pound again and caught her wrists mid-air. "You're going to wake the neighborhood." I noticed a cab in the driveway, its driver smoking idly like he was a little stoned.

"What the hell are *you* doing in my house?" She tried to slap me and I caught her wrist again. "Where's Nik? I told her to come by. She said she was on her way."

"When was this?"

"When we stopped for smokes." She noticed the guy tied up on the couch and sauntered over. "Oh, you got me a pet." She tickled him under the chin like a cat.

I pulled her away from Wallace. "Whose clothes are you wearing?" Hospitals didn't typically discharge people after midnight and she had on a tee shirt two sizes too big, and scrubs.

She looked down. "I borrowed some from some lockers. Not really my thing."

"And where'd you get weed?" Her breath smelled like a frat house.

She smiled and pooh-poohed me. "It wasn't very good. But the liquor store was closed." She seemed shocked by this development.

"How'd you pay for it?"

She batted her eyelashes at me over her shoulder. "My charm." She made a quick sucking motion.

I planted my face to my palm and shook my head. "How much do you owe the man?"

"Little more than a suck. Little less than a fuck." She grinned and did a soft-shoe move.

I then noticed she was wearing shoes, black pumps no less. I chose not to ask about where they'd come from. "I'll go get my purse. Don't go anywhere. Do *not* untie him." I pointed at Wallace.

"I can't play with the puppy?"

"No. He bites." I went up the front stairs and came back with fifty-four dollars' worth of combined resources and Craig, wearing Charley's old bathrobe.

Charley looked at Craig and licked her lips. "Mmm…"

"Down girl." I shoved her into a sitting position on the couch next to Wallace and went outside to pay the cabbie.

He sat upright and flicked his roach on the lawn. "Well, hello sweet thang." He showed off his crooked, yellow teeth.

I realized I was still mostly naked when the cold bit into my skin. I threw the cash through the open window. "You can leave now."

"Hey, the fare's seventy. That's a long drive and I hadda wait."

"You also helped a drug addict score. So let's call it even."

He opened the door and unfolded himself in the way of tall men who wanted to seem imposing. "I want the rest of my money, bitch."

I crossed my arms against the cold. "You got all you're getting."

"The little lady said I'd be getting more."

"She's the only junkie whore here, so if you didn't get it from her, you're out of luck."

Seemed obvious to me.

He ran a finger down my cheek and eyeballed my fashion statement. "I don't think so, sweetie."

I grabbed his finger and twisted to the side. "You're so high, you probably can't even get it up."

"Bitch!" He raised his other hand to slap me and I snapped the finger I was holding out of its joint.

The screen door banged open and Craig came charging out. I knew it was him because of the footsteps, but I didn't turn. Instead, I used the cabbie's surprise against him and pulled the rest of his arm behind him and up, applying pressure on his elbow and shoulder. "Get back in the car and be on your merry way."

I shoved him as I released. He yelped and held his finger in his other hand before glaring and threatening legal action.

I stormed past Craig and back into the house.

"What the hell is wrong with you?"

Charley slapped me. "That is no way to talk to the aging matriarch of a proud Southern family. Just who do you think you are anyway?"

"You're from San Francisco."

Craig reappeared beside me and rubbed his eyes.

Wallace stirred.

"Oh, good, my pet's awake." Charley clapped and skipped down the hall.

I glanced at Craig. "This is fun, right?"

He raised an eyebrow and pointed at the stairs. "I'm gonna go find some pants."

I looked back at Wallace. "What the hell?"

"I don't gotta talk to you," Wallace said.

Charley returned with her stash box. She plopped next to him. Party time. "What'choo want, Andy?"

"You know him?" I asked.

"Andy's okay." She pulled a sandwich bag of weed out of her borrowed bra and proceeded to pack a bowl. She looked over at him. "You holdin'?"

He nodded at his pocket and she rooted around in it until she came up with a bag of whitish-brown powder. The two of them relocated to the floor.

Since he answered to it, I tried, "Andy, why are you here?"

Charley dumped some powder on a spoon and some more on a mirror.

Andy glared at me.

Charley looked over. "He ain't gotta talk to you."

He smirked.

Charley started untying him. I considered stopping her, but didn't. Andy leaned over and snorted the line of powder off Charley's mirror while she flicked her Bic under the spoon.

His eyes grew glassy and he jumped up to pace, his head twitching and his face twisted. He blinked at me and Charley until his eyes rolled back in his head.

"Hey, you okay?"

He fell backward, cracking his head on the floor. He lay there for a moment, grinding his teeth.

"Craig!"

Andy's breath grew shallow.

"Craig!"

By the time Craig got back downstairs, Andy's heart had quit. The acrid smell of heroin cooking hung in the air. My hands compressed Andy's chest again and again.

Craig took over for me. "Check his airway."

I tilted Andy's head and listened, but heard nothing, felt nothing against my ear.

Charley ignored us and dug out a used syringe.

I reached out and slapped the spoon away from her.

"What the hell?" She grabbed my arm, indignant and angry. She noticed what Craig was doing and lunged at him.

I held her, dragged her back by the waist.

She clawed at my arms. "What are you doing? Stop hurting him."

Time stretched and slowed. It felt like hours since Andy had collapsed, like I'd been battling Charley my whole life.

When I saw the tears in Craig's eyes, I knew. Andy Wallace was gone. He didn't stop, but I knew he knew.

I dragged Charley to the overstuffed chair in the corner and spun her. "Sit."

"No."

I grabbed her face with both hands and willed my voice to be calmer than I felt. "He's gone."

"He killed him!"

I shook my head slowly. "The heroin killed him. Where'd he get it?"

She let loose a horror movie scream.

I waited. "Charley, it could've killed you, too. Where'd it come from?" Again, reasoning with an addict; I just couldn't learn.

She shrugged and whimpered. "Why'd you hurt him?"

I gave up. When I turned, I realized Craig had given up, too. He was sitting next to the body, crying.

"Check his pockets for more of that junk." I walked over and grabbed what remained of the bag he'd handed Charley.

"Nothing else," he said.

"Untie his feet." I headed down the hall to flush the bag. When I got back, I squatted in front of Craig. "Get dressed. We're leaving."

"Without her?"

"Yes. I'm calling the Sheriff. He'll arrest her for possession. With her record, she should get a little time, some detox."

He shook his head, his cheeks still wet. "You can do that?"

I put out a hand to help him to his feet. "Sometimes it's the best thing for her."

"What about him?"

I lowered my voice. "You weren't here."

He nodded, but his face said I was wrong.

CHAPTER FORTY-TWO

The waterfront in downtown Morehead was deserted. The breeze coming off the water was cold, but the docks and restaurants were somewhat buffeted by the barrier island visible on the other side of the channel. The ancient brick post office stood deserted next to a converted house that sold general store type tourist crap and saltwater taffy. Many of the seafood restaurants had "closed for season" signs out front. The whole area had a post-apocalyptic feel, with blue skies and the crisp air still smelling faintly of fried shrimp, diesel, and briny water.

Craig's boss had asked him if he could go fix a central air unit Downeast. I'd encouraged, perhaps even shooed him on his way so he wouldn't think he needed to get involved in my next crazy action. I still had no idea what I was doing, but everything else had turned out dangerous. Craig seemed safer with the pipes and electrical problems.

I parked in one of the numerous empty spaces beside the Sanitary Restaurant. In the middle of the parking lot, a large map encased in scratched Plexiglas showed tourists the shoals and wrecks of the Graveyard of the Atlantic. A side note said the waters off the coast of North Carolina had proven deadly for many sailors over the centuries, much to the delight of pirates like Blackbeard.

"Great, omens." I looped my purse across me like a messenger bag and headed for the docks.

Tom might have wanted me to start with John Taylor's boat problems, but I had other ideas. Billy Guthrie's death had caused a lot of the mess I was in, so Billy's boat-fairy yacht seemed like a good place to start. The boat fairy part might have explained why a guy named Billy had a charter yacht named *Jimmy's Daydream*.

No one was around so I hopped aboard the open deck area in the back and sauntered up to the cabin like I knew what I was doing. The door was locked, but the lock was cheap and looked like it had previously been tampered with. I jimmied the broken lock and stepped down into the cabin, pulling the door shut behind me.

With the door shut, I could no longer see the deck outside. When built, a row of windows across the top of the back wall would've let in light, but someone had coated them with black spray paint and smeared on dirty grease. It made the place seem extra gloomy and smelly.

The wind outside rocked the boat gently. Urine from an unflushed head joined the diesel fumes, mildew and fish permeating the air. It smelled more like a jail than a charter boat. I opened a couple of drawers and lifted papers, shifted junk. I found the sort of flotsam I associated with Tom's friend, Rubelli, at home. The kind of odds and ends a guy who used his boat for fishing and getting away from the wife would have.

Sweatshirts, tee shirts, dirty jeans, half-eaten bags of Doritos and Funyuns, and what looked like bloated Lucky Charms covered the floor of the galley. I opened the nearest cabinet. More chips, a spilled bag of Skittles, Cap'n Crunch, the rest of the Lucky Charms. Munchies. Pothead food. Teenager food.

I stepped on a cheese curl and it crunched. Guthrie had been dead for nearly a week; it wasn't his. On the fold-down table near the stove sat a couple of pots with mystery residue that was still gooey and an oddball collection of high-end fish-finding and navigation equipment. I peered at the screen, which showed a shallow area in what looked like Raleigh Bay just off the Cape Lookout National Seashore. A dot in the upper corner blinked.

Something moved in the front hatch.

I stepped closer, hand slipping into my messenger bag for the revolver. A thin folding door at the bow of the cabin rattled slightly.

My chest tightened. My breathing slowed. I pushed open the door from the side, gun ready. Inside, a blonde, young but maybe a few years older than me, naked and goosefleshed, had been handcuffed to a low, wooden rail running the length of the compartment. She lay on a brown, upholstered bunk bed, stained and frayed at the edges.

The woman in the second email. The second "mistake."

She appeared to be sleeping. I leaned over and checked her pulse, carefully in case she woke and lashed out. It beat out a steady but slow rhythm. Her legs kicked, as though involuntary.

Boots jumped onto the deck behind me. Heavy. They crossed to the cabin door. "Fuck." The lock clicked. I turned toward it and the engine rumbled to life, mixing a fresh diesel smell to the briny aroma in the cabin. The boat rocked harder.

I looked back over at the blonde. "Let's get you some clothes at least."

She didn't answer.

I probably should have been more worried about being taken offshore by whoever was outside, but panic didn't seem useful. I went back out into the cabin and found a sweatshirt that didn't smell too bad and a pair of men's pajama pants with a reel manufacturer's logo on them. I went back to the girl and threaded her feet into the pajamas, pulled them up past the new-looking tattoo of a tiger paw on her upper thigh.

She barely stirred as I pulled them up and knotted the tie. The sweatshirt, I draped over her like a blanket.

I wasn't sure if that meant she'd been drugged, had drugged herself, or if she was just a heavy sleeper. That last one seemed more like a myth than an actual thing to me, but maybe she hadn't grown up like I had. Maybe she hadn't spent her teen years listening out for subtle changes in her environment so she could react if she had to. Maybe she was just faking, hoping whoever I was I'd go away and not touch her anymore.

I shuddered and tamped down all the other thoughts in my head.

Except, aside from the rumbling engine under us and the mystery person outside, I had nothing else to think about. And being locked in a confined space, even one with light and food, seemed like a bad beginning to the day.

I fought the urge to pace. I needed to think, to focus. Fear could be useful. Panic wasn't. Had to remember that. Had to not think about the reasons why this girl might be naked.

Survival first. Always.

The lock jiggled and the door creaked open.

I pulled out the revolver again, pushed aside the nagging voice in my head that suggested maybe it was time to stop screwing around with five- and six-shooters. Start carrying and practicing with something with more rounds. Except, I was likely only alive because Charley hadn't had any more shots that night.

I slipped out of the front berth, revolver out straight in a two-handed grip.

He saw me, stumbled back, and raised his hands. "Oh fuck. Not again."

I raised an eyebrow, but didn't lower the gun. "Who the hell are you?"

"Me? It's *my* fucking boat! Who the hell are you?"

"The boat's owner's dead."

"No, the fuckwit that asshole gave my boat to is dead. And if you're in here planting more drugs or whatever, forget it. You're gonna have to shoot me 'cause I ain't doing more—"

"You armed?"

"What? No. I mean, I had a gun on here, but I figure you bastards took that."

"Turn around. Hands on the wall." I took a step forward.

He sighed and turned. Shoulders sagged like he'd given up.

I frisked him cautiously, but thoroughly. Then stepped clear. "Turn around. Who are you?"

"I told you."

Something clicked. Damn, I needed more sleep. "You're Jimmy?"

"Yeah. Who the hell are you? Act like a cop, but you ain't a cop. Look familiar, though."

"Davis Groves."

"I thought I heard she was dead."

"She's not."

"Maybe you're lying."

"Maybe. But if I was going to make up a name, why the hell would I pick that one?"

He shrugged. "Guess you gotta point. So, how come everyone says you're dead?"

"Wishful thinking? Who told you I was dead?"

"Wasn't so much told to me as I overheard it. Something Billy told Eric."

I fought the urge to pinch the spot between my eyes. Nothing made sense.

"Look, if you aren't gonna shoot me, you mind putting that thing away?"

I studied his face. "Not until I know why you have a naked woman handcuffed to your bed."

"I what?" His voice went up two octaves.

Behind me, sleeping beauty woke screaming.

"Perfect." I jerked my shoulder and winced.

"What's up with your shoulder?"

"*That's* your big question?" I motioned for him to move around me and walk to the bow.

"What the hell'd you do, lady?" He stopped in the open doorway. "Rebecca? Ohmigod."

She jerked against the cuffs and scrambled backward against the wall of the compartment, eyes wide. "Jimmy?" The fear didn't leave her, but confusion crowded in and sat next to it.

"You okay?" I asked. Stupid question. I'd have lied had she asked me, but it was the first thing that came to mind.

Her jaw worked, but nothing came out.

"Jimmy, sit."

She moved her knees to her chest. He sat.

"You got a set of keys for those cuffs?"

He shook his head, eyes pleading with me. "They ain't mine. I didn't do this. Tell her I didn't do this."

Her face said she didn't want that to be true but wasn't sure. Which only meant she didn't know how she'd ended up in such a situation.

I knew that feeling. I didn't like it. Didn't like witnessing it even more than I didn't like feeling it. It took a lot of focus to fight through the sound of Ryan's concern in my head.

I stared at the cuffs. Pushed aside a memory of wearing them in court at eleven. Of running into the desert at thirteen.

I looked at her hands, looked at her face. Tried to figure out how to make everything right and started rummaging in my bag for something to pick the locks with. I could feel her eyes watching me. Could feel her questions charging the air between us.

Something jingled at the bottom of a side pocket I'd long forgotten.

I smiled and pulled out a handcuff key. "Think this'll work?"

She looked as afraid as relieved.

Jimmy just looked dumbfounded. "Why the hell do you have that?"

"Took it off a drunk cop at a party. Guess I forgot to give it back." I handed the key to Jimmy and watched him release her. The skin on his hands was rough, calloused, but his touch was gentle, cautious, like he knew she was scared and didn't want to add to it.

I put the gun in my bag.

She looked up at me as she pulled the sweatshirt on. "What the hell are you?"

I shrugged and ignored the short stabbing pain when I did that. "Paralegal."

Her face stayed wary.

"Bachelor party. I handcuffed him to a giant urn. Even drunk he's smart enough not to break antiques. One of his buddies unhooked him later and drove him home."

She squinted and sat up, rubbing her wrists. "Do I know you?"

"No. I'm Davis. I'm not dead."

She tilted her head at me.

"It comes up. A lot."

Jimmy nodded in agreement. She looked like she thought I was nuts, but wasn't pushing it.

Jimmy looked out one of the small cabin windows, not so much a porthole as a starboard ellipse. "I gotta go steer before we run aground."

 "You left the engine running? This doesn't have some kind of autopilot?"

He looked at me like I was stupid. "Idling. We've been drifting."

I knew why he hadn't cut the engine. He hadn't wanted to alert whoever he thought he'd trapped. I still didn't know why he thought taking his prey out to sea was preferable to dealing with them onshore, but then I wasn't exactly a boat person.

He put a hand out toward Rebecca. "Whatever they did to you, I'm sorry."

Even if he turned out to be a threat, it might be good to give him a little rope. I let him go and leaned in the doorway. "For what it's worth, I'm sorry, too."

She nodded. Swallowed. "I should be stronger than this."

"No, you shouldn't."

Her eyes met mine. "You are. Or you fake it well."

"No. I don't."

She wasn't listening. "I was supposed to find her. Alive. Bring her home. That was my job. That's what her parents paid me for."

"You're an investigator?"

She nodded and looked at her hands, studied the bruising on her wrists. "It's not like I'm some movie sleuth or anything. My uncle hired me in high school. Taught me his business. I got licensed, fully, last year.

Six months ago he had a heart attack and decided to retire."

I watched a channel marker pass the Plexiglas opposite her head.

"I'm *good* at what I do. You don't have to believe me, but I am. I'm just not… This isn't what I do. I follow the occasional cheating spouse and all, but mostly I sit at a computer. I figure out if small companies are getting ripped off and by whom. I locate old documents for little old ladies doing genealogy research. I find hidden assets for lawsuit cases, partnerships gone south." She had a genteel accent that made "south" sound elegant. Not quite the mumble of the rural Carolinas, not the drawl of Savannah. Certainly not the country-fried brogue of nearby Downeast.

"You aren't local."

She shook her head. "Virginia. Small town a hundred miles from D.C. My name's Rebecca, but I guess you figured that out."

I nodded. "The missing girl?"

"Melissa Armstrong. Junior. Her mom went to high school with mine. 'Can't Lil' Becky find her? Talk some sense into her? Woman to woman?'" She snorted and fought it turning to tears.

"The first mistake."

Her head snapped to me, her face etched with terror.

"He killed her."

"How did you know that?"

"I may have broken into a house and seen an email I wasn't supposed to."

"Eric Wright." She said.

I decided to play dumb. "The commissioner?"

"The con artist. I told you. I'm good at what I do, at financial stuff, computer stuff. I found out Melissa'd been hanging out with all these little drug addict teens. I thought, okay. I figured I'd talk to her. Try to get her to come home. Maybe she listens. Maybe she doesn't. Maybe I just call her mom and leave it to her. I'm not like whatever you are. I don't have a gun or handcuff keys or…" Her gaze caught on my hands.

I opened my mouth to correct her and stopped.

"Either way. I found her. Took me only a few days to find her. Left her phone on. Mom gave me permission to track. Ended up accidentally figuring out half her route on my way. Still…"

I watched the open ocean out the window. I wanted to know where the hell we were going, but hoped it could wait. "Route?"

"Yeah, she's been up and down the coast a few times in the past month. Anyway, I see her with a girl looked kind of like you, actually, another with an ugly tattoo on her neck, and a dorky guy in a Wright's shirt. They all pile out of a pickup truck at the Dairy Queen. Munchies, I guess. So, I decide to follow them. Like I do with the cheaters, except then I have a tracking device. Makes it easier."

I nodded. Tom occasionally caught one of those. Usually husbands, oddly, wanting to keep track of or get leverage on a trophy wife. They signed papers giving Tom permission to track their second vehicle and he did.

"They come over to the docks. Get on a boat a little smaller than this one, load up some cases of cheap beer, and take off. So, I wait. I walk around, check out the boardwalk, a few of the shops with windows facing the slip. I run into Jimmy." She smiled. "We had coffee. He seemed nice." She stopped smiling, looked unsure.

I said nothing.

"Two hours later, they come back. The two girls get off. No Melissa. The girls get in the truck. Drive off. The guy takes a while longer."

"You said 'dorky.' He have freckles? A little soft around the middle?"

She nodded. "He gets some fuel from the dockmaster, takes off again. I wait another couple hours or so, but nothing. By then it's dark, and since the restaurants are all closed up a cop comes by wondering if I'm lost or something."

"Cop?"

"Yeah, wasn't even a city guy. Sheriff's office. Asked who I was, what I was doing out on the docks by my lonesome." She made a face. "He seemed too nosy. I told him I was a tourist out for a walk. He suggested – strongly – that I might like to get some supper out at a chain restaurant on the far end of town. Seemed to think I'd want to join him."

"Well, you're a cute blonde."

"Dude was creepy. I think he followed me. At least west as far as the beach bridge. Course, there aren't that many hotels in Morehead and Newport. All he had to do, if he wanted, was wait until I'd bypassed the turn and find my rental later. It's what I'd do."

I wasn't sure whether to be impressed or worried, but she did seem good at her job. "This guy have a name?"

"Murphy."

I filed that away and turned off the alarm bells in my head.

"I got back to my hotel room that night, fired up my laptop to work on another case and find this email. Melissa. Dead and naked."

"The first mistake."

She opened her mouth a few seconds before she spoke again. "Was I naked when you found me?"

I hesitated. "I hope you don't mind. I put the pajama pants on you."

She looked down like she'd just noticed her outfit. "Thank you."

I nodded and swallowed.

"I shouldn't have let him get that close. I did so much research on Wright. I don't know why. It was just a hunch from seeing that shirt. A lot of people around here have those. But then I found out it was his boat. And the more I looked at that email of Melissa, it looked like the picture had been taken on a boat. Maybe. I figured out enough of his schedule to bump into him. Flirt with him. Get a date with him."

"He did this?" My blood boiled, then ran icy.

She shook her head. "He was charming. Knew nothing about a Melissa Armstrong. Said he didn't know much about the kids who hung out on his boats. That he leased them back to the original owners. They used them for fishing and some of them even lived on them. Dodged all my questions about how he could afford to do that, how he kept the plant in business. A natural politician, that one. But he wasn't that interested. Kept thinking I was a journalist, looking to get his name in print."

I kept my opinions on his character to myself. I angled to see what else she'd learned. "Drugs? I've heard he's running them off the coast."

"He's importing cheap fish. Bypassing all the FDA and safety regulations. Easy enough to do. And there are a lot of countries getting into aquaculture now. Some of them, Americans are turned off by. Bad reputations. He's selling that stuff as local."

I raised an eyebrow. "Isn't the FDA kind of impotent these days?" Something Nik had told me rattled around in my head.

She nodded. "The bigger problem is consumer backlash."

"That enough to kill over?" I knew it was, even as I asked it.

She nodded. "Overfishing, algae blooms, price wars. It's hard to believe that's all that's coming in on those boats from China and Mexico, though."

"You think Melissa found something out?"

"Melissa wasn't the angel her mom thought. She and her boyfriend had a case of counterfeit bags they stole off a truck in D.C. Hell, that's honestly how I tracked her after she wised up and dumped the cell phone. The two of them had been selling the things for dope money until they landed here."

I thought about the purses in Lane's room. "They recent fakes?"

"Good quality, too. Like the kind you can get busted for, not the kind you can claim is just a lookalike."

"The boyfriend's name?"

She rolled her eyes. "Rich little asshole. Had everything he could ever have wanted. He wanted to be a 'big ballin' criminal' like that stupid music he listened to."

I didn't point out that the two of us were only a few years older. "The name?"

"Anderson Wallace."

I felt bile churn in stomach. I pictured Andy's dead face and felt regret. And remorse. At the time, Andy'd pissed me off. He'd brought something dangerous to Charley and nearly killed her. It hit me that he'd just been a stupid kid.

She looked at her hands, her wrists, and the stained sweatshirt. Her eyes followed the ugly pants to her painted toes and up into my face. "Did he… Did they rape me?"

I thought about how I'd found her. I thought about how I'd found Charley more than a decade before. I thought about the morning I'd woken in my dorm room with a splitting headache and the taste of coffee still on my tongue under the bile and the morning breath. "I don't know."

She bit her lip, but didn't say anything.

CHAPTER FORTY-THREE

Jimmy cut the engine as we came out on deck. He looked around. Nervous.

"What's up?" I asked.

"I feel like I'm being watched." He shivered.

"What the hell are we doing out here?"

He looked at me like I was stupid. "I been locked up five days. Need to catch something, I wanna keep eatin'."

"Locked up?"

"Damn assholes left something on my boat. Got pinched on some petty drug shit. Cops had a warrant, which means somebody set me up."

I looked over at Rebecca. "You been here how long?"

"I had dinner – alone – on Thursday night. Had a drink at the hotel bar. Talked for a bit with a cute guy about my age. Said he went to the college down in Wilmington. Was up visiting his sister. I had planned to go back to my room. Get some sleep. I woke up here hours later. In the dark."

"It's Saturday."

Something passed over her eyes. "Someone came in. It was too dark to make out who, but he was male. He gave me a glass of water. The next time I woke up, you were here."

"How do you feel now?"

"Hungry. Itchy. Cold."

I considered Charley's various withdrawal symptoms over the years, but she was too much of an experimenter for any single thing to stand out.

I looked back at Jimmy. "The drugs weren't yours, were they?"

"I hit a joint back in the day, but I ain't touching cocaine or meth or any of that other shit."

Rebecca looked worried, pulled up her sleeve and looked at her veins.

I looked down at her bare feet. "Check between your toes."

She pulled one up and balanced like a yogi. Looked back at me, afraid.

"My mother." I didn't feel like explaining all the times we'd checked her arms, her feet, her fingers, her pupils, her temperature.

"What the hell did they give me?"

I didn't notice the pain when I shrugged. I was too busy ignoring the pain in my past.

Jimmy looked up from his own feet. "Probably heroin. Lot of the kids around here are hooked on it. Says it dulls the pain. Don't know what kind, but…"

I knew what kind. I knew what a few tokes on a joint could make go away. Problem was, it came right back when the drugs wore off. And then it was almost worse. I knew what Charley had gone through. I knew how she'd fallen from user to addict. I knew.

Engine sounds carried across the water. Jimmy spun, searching the horizon.

"What's up?"

"That's them."

"Them who?"

Jimmy didn't answer. He shoved the throttle forward.

The boat lurched forward in the water. I lost my balance and stumbled back, hitting the wall of the cabin and landing on my ass. Rebecca took two steps and went down on her knees a foot from me.

"What the hell, Jimmy?"

Rebecca scrambled to her feet and grabbed the steering column next to Jimmy. Her body tensed. "They're chasing us? That boat is chasing us?"

I pulled myself up and looked. Sure enough, out of all the available water in the Atlantic—Graveyard, my brain added—there was another fishing charter less than a football field away and it seemed to be gaining.

Jimmy jiggled the throttle and looked worried. "Something's wrong. My engine's faster than this."

The other boat closed the gap rapidly.

Jimmy's brow broke out in a sweat despite the icy wind whipping past us.

Rebecca stared at the approaching boat. When it was close enough to make out the captain, she turned to me. "It's him."

"Huh?"

"The guy from the…" The rest of her sentence disappeared. Engine noise drowned her out as Jimmy yanked the throttle back and then forward again. *Jimmy's Daydream* jerked to a near-stop before taking off again.

I landed on my ass again.

Gunshots echoed across the water. Bullets hit the wall behind me.

Jimmy yelled, hopped on one foot, and fell forward. His arm hooked the wheel as he slid to the deck and the boat spun hard to the left.

I looked up at Rebecca. "Get down!"

She stood, frozen, her face etched with a terror I could understand but couldn't process at the moment. "He seemed so…"

I reached out for her hand.

Gunfire broke through the sound of the engines and Jimmy's moaning. Everything felt like it had slowed, like I had time to solve it all, like it could be made right.

She let me take her hand.

Blood splattered my face. I shut my eyes involuntarily against the assault, and when I opened them I saw Rebecca still standing there, a hole in her neck, blood pouring from it. She reached up with her free hand, covered the hole and stared at me. Her life ran through her fingers, her mouth moved, but she said nothing. Or I heard nothing.

The bullets didn't stop. Just time.

I snapped out of my trance, willed myself back to reality, and pulled Rebecca down. The gunfire came in staggered bursts. Short pauses between shots, longer pauses when his finger tired or he was looking for targets, even longer pauses when he reloaded. Those longest pauses told me he hadn't practiced quick loading, didn't have full magazines ready.

Not that it mattered.

I pulled off my shirt and put it on her wound, used her hands to hold it tight. We were way too far from medical help for it to be anything but a pointless gesture. Her eyes said she knew it, too, but still appreciated it.

Another round of fire overhead. Suppressing.

Instinct rolled me away from Rebecca and away from the sound of the other engine. My hand slipped into my bag and pulled out the revolver without thinking about it. Instead, I thought about how I had six shots and our assailant seemed to have boxes.

He came from the stern, starboard side. Jumped. Landed on a mildewed, sun-bleached cushion. Five feet away.

He swung his gun up. Semi-automatic pistol. Sleek and black. Menacing.

Crouched in a corner between the wall and the bin holding the life jackets, I had no cover. Phil's revolver already in front of me in both hands. Waiting for a target.

His chest before my sights and I pulled the trigger. Twice.

He fired. Once. The bullet slammed into the fiberglass next to my head, kicked out minute slivers.

He fell. His face registered surprise, pain, shock.

I watched, torn between relief and horror.

His head hit a cleat and he rolled onto the deck next to Rebecca. Her eyes were wide and glassy. Next to each other I could see how she'd have been attracted to him, could see them sitting at the bar next to one another, talking.

He wasn't the dorky, doughy guy she'd seen with Melissa. He wasn't the one Lane had shot in his mom's apartment. He was the third musketeer, the good-looking blond who could probably worm his way into a lot of pants even without drugging them.

Brad.

I'd killed Amber's twenty-one-year-old brother.

CHAPTER FORTY-FOUR

I was fine until Jimmy died.

I found a towel to put pressure on his side. I elevated his leg, tied a stray pair of pants around it. He told me how to work the fish finder, how to get us back to shore. His breath grew shallow. The pool under him grew larger. I didn't have the heart to tell him the navigation equipment had a bullet hole in the middle of it.

I checked my watch, stared up at the overcast sky until I worried I'd burnt out my retinas trying to decide where in all those clouds the sun hid. Stared at the charts, trying to make sense of tides, notations, channels, and all those barrier islands.

The boat stank of blood, of urine, of feces, of fear and death. The deck was slick with fluids, sticky with the drying puddles. I busied myself, did what I thought needed doing.

I'd tied us up to Brad's boat long enough to search it—gun out, on edge, keeping the shaking under control by breathing and focusing on my pulse and potential movement. I found nothing except a self-inflating dinghy. I wiped the only surface I'd touched and kicked it loose. Only after did it occur to me his navigation equipment probably worked.

Somewhere in our drifting, I tossed Phil's old revolver into the sea. The ammunition I flung in separate directions from the top of the tuna towers. I couldn't be sure if it was because of what I'd done or what I was afraid could be found. Wasn't sure if I was afraid of myself or prison. Wasn't sure it mattered.

Jimmy died hard.

Where Rebecca had bled out or asphyxiated in minutes, Jimmy remained alive for hours. He didn't say it, but he had to have held out hope that my insufficient boating skills would find land in time, but what had taken him two hours to cover eluded me for the next four. When he finally died, it was a little after one. He should have been eating lunch or fishing. I knew I had his blood on my hands, too, and not just because I'd been applying pressure to his wounds.

I sat in my bra and stained, stiffened jeans on the fiberglass bin full of life jackets, surrounded by death. I felt I should cry, but I didn't. My skin, numbed by the cold wind, didn't seem any more real than the rain moving toward us on the horizon. I was lost in the Graveyard of the Atlantic. All around us were the invisible ghost ships, inhabited by dead sailors far more skilled than me.

And yet, I didn't try to send out an SOS. Didn't try to shoot a flare. And I couldn't be sure if it was because I didn't know how to explain the firefight or the bodies or if it was because I thought I deserved to die with them.

At twenty-four, I was the oldest one on the boat. I'd never know what Brad had or hadn't done to Rebecca. She'd never know if she had the strength to move past the uncertainty and captivity. I thought she could have. But then, I thought I had, yet I had to hold the image of his barrel in front of my mind to believe I hadn't just killed him because I'd once dated someone who seemed nice, too.

The storm rolled over us, rocked the boat that I'd left to drift, washed evidence and offal into the drain holes, cleansed my face of Rebecca's blood. I started the engine and tried to at least keep us upright as the seas grew choppier, angrier.

Eventually, I went back to the cabin to find a sweatshirt or maybe a raincoat. I was staring at the floor, at the cheese puff I'd crushed that morning and the broken things that had joined it, when my captaining failed for good.

The boat hit ground, hard because I'd left the engine running, figuring anywhere we went was better than where we were. Dumb, sure, but I hadn't cared at the time. Something under the surface breached the hull with a great grinding, splintering sound like a traffic accident with a covered wagon. The force knocked me face down onto the cheese puff and debris. The engines continued to drive us forward, pushing until they'd carved away part of the starboard side. It took mere minutes before the whole boat tilted and I fell into a wall of useless instruments.

A box of zipper-topped plastic bags fell off the counter. I picked up a few and shoved my phone and wallet into a series of them. Looped my bag around me tight, grabbed a sweatshirt and life jacket. Found the dinghy and stood knee-deep in the waves to pull the rip cord.

Before I pushed the dinghy off the stern, I saw Jimmy's body slip into the turbulent ocean.

CHAPTER FORTY-FIVE

I staggered onshore, teeth chattering, vision blurry, hands and feet numb to the point I wasn't even sure they'd bleed if I stabbed them. I dragged myself over the rocks and shells, used my elbows to pull me forward like Phil had once trained me to do. Early evening or mid-afternoon, I'd lost track of time and the sky remained black and threatening. I'd lost track of distance and everything but the blinking light that I hoped was a lighthouse or ship.

The dinghy had capsized, and after fighting to right it in the strong surf too long I'd given up and started swimming. Land had been in sight. That didn't mean it had been close.

Why I was even still alive was beyond me. Somewhere in my head I knew the stories of people who misjudged the miles on water and drowned, surfers with hypothermia, strong swimmers and fishermen swept away in currents and storms. Yet, I found myself in front of a squat, white lighthouse as it cycled through its pattern.

I pulled myself up on the fence and balanced on unfeeling, wooden feet. Staggered through the rest of the marsh, across the caretaker's lawn. Up the street, I could see the lights of houses and motels and maybe restaurants or bars. They might as well have been the moon. I'd gone as far as I could go. Possibly further.

I lay down and took out the triple-wrapped phone and, after a few tries to convince fingers and buttons to interact, called information. My mouth wasn't keen on forming words, my lips too frozen for nuance. I muttered something that resembled taxi and hotel.

"You at the ferry? Ain't gonna run no more tonight. Inlet Inn might have a shuttle if Barry ain't too drunk yet."

"Lighthouse." There was no way I could manage a sentence and I felt oddly warm and knew that wasn't good.

"Well, hell, even drunk he can get there. He's at the end of the street. Let me give him a ring."

"Please. Hu-rry." My tense, chattering jaw hurt and my brain could only think of sleep. I ended the call and curled up to wait for death, or drunk Barry.

Barry found me on the edge of consciousness. "I gotta put you in the old building, upstairs. It's already haunted." He gave me a look that said he was pretty sure I was ready to join his hotel spirits. "You look cold. What the hell made you wanna go swimming in your clothes, lady?"

I held my hands in front of his truck's heating vents and vibrated, bit the inside of my lip until I tasted copper, then mashed my mouth shut to hide what I'd done.

He looked worried, but I managed to warm myself enough to sign the credit slip. I held the wall on the way to the room, fighting the urge to pass out by trying to control the shivering with breathing exercises.

In the room, I stripped and wrapped myself in the quilt. Stripping alone took fifteen minutes since my fingers refused to follow basic directions, and as the room heated up from chilly to stuffy, they tingled and burned.

I focused on getting warm, but cold wasn't the only thing leaving me shaking. Uncle Phil had said there were people who got used to death and people who didn't. He'd always wanted me to believe he was one of the ones who didn't, but I suspected that was regret. Then, I'd had nothing to regret.

I dumped my purse, found my phone, and dialed Craig. Left a message. "I think I need you." It came out garbled and my hands shook trying to hang up.

I called Nik, but it went straight to voice mail. I wanted to tell her something, anything, but the words froze in my mouth and I listened to the static until the beep cut me off.

Craig called back, demanding to know where I was and what was wrong with me. I'd muttered something about an inn and a white lighthouse because my jaw couldn't manage Ocracoke. He hung up.

I'd curled deeper into the quilt trying to think warm thoughts. Palm trees. *Corpses.* Turquoise ocean water. *Stormy seas.* Rum runners with umbrellas. *Dead eyes.*

Craig called back ten minutes later with a name and a promise. "Boomer and I met at EMT training. He's one of the best I know. And he's been to med school. Just didn't have the cash to finish. He'll take good care of you if you let him. I swear."

I was shivering in the fetal position on the carpet. I answered by chattering my teeth.

"He should be there in a few minutes. He doesn't live that far from the inn."

"How?"

"Did I know which one? Wow, you really are messed up. It's the closest one to the lighthouse."

"Thank you."

"Call me back when you're feeling better."

"Mmm…"

"Don't fall asleep, Davis. You gotta answer the door for Boomer."

"Unlocked."

"You left the door unlocked?"

"Cold." I shivered. Things weren't going well. I should have warmed up. "Sleepy."

"Davis!"

Someone pounded on the door.

The phone clicked off in my ear and I heard ringing outside. The door opened a few seconds later.

I looked up. He was mountainous, football-player-shaped with shiny dark skin and bleached, cropped hair.

"Hi, Boomer."

"Davis?" He had a large soft-sided case looped across his bulk and held a Thermos. No sign of the phone. He dropped to one knee and poured what looked like cocoa into the little black plastic cup. "Hold this. Don't drink it yet." Like a giant Florence Nightingale.

I took the cup, staring as he popped a thermometer under my tongue, pulled a pair of shake-and-bake hand warmers and told me to put them under my armpits.

"Stay here. I'm going to run you a bath."

I waited and shivered.

Boomer returned and took the thermometer, glared at it. "Drink that now."

I gulped and burnt my tongue and throat. He eyed me but poured more. When the second cup was gone, he picked me up, quilt and all and carried me to the bathroom, where he sat me on the toilet lid.

"I'm gonna leave. Get out of the quilt and into the water."

"Aren't you supposed to be used to naked people?" I let go of the quilt and sank into the water.

He looked at me, worried.

"That bad?"

"Just try to stay awake for me." He disappeared and returned with the Thermos, handing me another cup of scalding cocoa. "Drink up."

I drained the cup and leaned back again. "You won't let me die, will you? I have something I'm supposed to do tomorrow."

He picked up a washcloth and put it over a cut I hadn't realized I had. "Craig knows I don't make promises I can't keep."

"Makes sense." I smiled at him and realized my teeth had stopped chattering.

He stared at the water. "Craig told me not to bring my partner. He likes her. But he said she'd make you go to a hospital."

"Would she?"

He gestured at the water that had turned reddish gray. "Yeah."

"It's not that bad."

"Craig's right. You don't know what's serious."

I couldn't remember a day without an ache somewhere. I only noticed when it stopped me.

He leaned me forward to check for more wounds and took a sharp breath.

"What?" Now that I had feeling again, things hurt, but not too much, so I was figured I was fine.

"Does Craig know about this?" He ran a finger along the latticework of old scars.

I tried to rub off a dirt patch that turned out to be a bruise on my shin. "Yeah. Happened a long time ago."

He opened my hands and studied the calluses I didn't remember shredding. "Can you stand to shower?"

I nodded even though I didn't feel like it.

"I'll meet you in the other room with bandages and antiseptic."

I stared at my reflection in the mirror for a long time. I didn't look any different. My eyes were still blue and my lips no longer were. I felt different, though. Not because of what had been done to me this time, but what I'd done to others. It had been the right decision.

Leaving Phil's gun at the bottom of the ocean had been the right choice, too.

It all just felt wrong.

CHAPTER FORTY-SIX
Sunday, February 12

I took the ferry from Ocracoke to Cedar Island. Watched the seagulls trail us, hoping for tourists with chips or unfinished sandwiches. They swooped in and out of the surf, white against gray. They didn't look cold or confused.

I thought I should call Tom, realized my phone was dead. Wondered what had become of my little sister, what had changed her.

In the town of Cedar Island, I "borrowed" a car from a waitress who left her keys too visible behind the counter. In Morehead City, I parked it in the lot of a church whose services were audible outside. I left twenty bucks in the ashtray, wiped my prints and walked seven blocks out of my way to get back to my rental car near the waterfront.

At a strip mall, I found a car charger for my phone.

Overall, I felt oddly refreshed. I'd slept more than I had in a week. I suspected Boomer had slipped a sedative in the cocoa, but exhaustion was also a possibility. I was supposed to see Lane in a few hours and I was hoping she would shed sudden light on everything I'd encountered since Wednesday.

I called Tom once the phone was charged enough to make outgoing calls and gave him the barest possible summaries.

"You *what*?"

I took a deep breath, sighed. "Which what? Tom, I had no choice. And every answer comes with more questions."

His voice changed to match the dismay in mine. "For what it's worth, I'm sorry."

I called Lawrence Jacobs next.

When he answered, I asked, "How'd Lane get to Billy's?"

"May I ask who's calling?"

"Davis."

He paused like he was matching my voice to some database in his head. I'd seen Tom do something similar. "Don't know. Her prints were in Guthrie's car."

"But they were friends before."

"Exactly."

I pulled into Charley's to find another rental car parked in the driveway.

The place smelled less like mold and marijuana than usual. Instead, it smelled like oranges and nag champa incense. Nik.

I followed clanging to the kitchen where I found a petite, healthy version of myself opening cans and humming something mournful and bluesy.

I leaned in the doorframe. "Hi, sis."

She spun, put down the can opener and walked over to slap me. "So, you're not dead. You look awful."

"Nice to see you, too."

She stepped back and crossed her scrawny little arms. "What the hell happened?"

I shut my eyes. She was going to get herself killed and it was going to be all my fault. "What the hell are you doing here?"

"I told you I was coming. I got here last night. I missed your call while I was driving from RDU." She walked to her purple canvas purse and pulled out her phone, pressed a couple of buttons and held it out. "I thought you were dead." Her phone beeped and played a long minute of labored breathing and teeth chattering before the bookend beep stopped it. "I tried calling you. Over and over. Nothing."

"I'm sorry."

"Right. And I guess you're 'fine,' too. What was I supposed to think? What was I supposed to do? I didn't know where you were. The cops would've just told me you butt-dialed me and to quit being hysterical. It's not like they know about your borderline suicidal tendencies."

"I didn't know what to say."

She threw up her hands. "Whatever. The sheriff came by. Said he had no interest in wasting the court's time on Charley if we'd put her in rehab. So I talked her into Brynn Marr over in Jacksonville. She's all checked in. Has a roommate who still loves *The X-Files*. They both think aliens are real." She dumped in a can of pinto beans, rinsed the can, and set it aside. "Should I ask where you were?"

I ambled closer. "No." I watched her dump in kidney beans and wash the can. The pot still had a price sticker on it.

"Then lie to me. You were always good at that." She emptied a can of black beans and stirred the mess with a new-looking wooden spoon.

"I don't feel like lying." I rubbed my temples. "This sheriff have a name?"

"Frederick something."

"He seem all right to you?"

"Better than most maybe." She described him. "What's it to you?"

Sounded like the same guy who'd come by about my car. "Things have been weird here."

"Uh huh." She sliced open a bag of frozen corn. "You know, I usually use fresh stuff from the farmers' market."

I watched her pull a cutting board out of her net shopping bag and wash it before setting to work on a variety of peppers. Red, green, yellow, Anaheim, jalapeño, finger hot. She pulled out an onion and garlic cloves to chop before throwing them into pot.

I watched her open a bag of brown rice and dump a couple of cups in after the spices.

"I keep this in bulk at home."

"Uh huh."

"Beans are cheaper than meat."

"I know."

"And healthier." She was avoiding facing me again.

I had my mantra. Nik had hers.

I walked over and took the wooden spoon. "Nik, it's okay."

When she looked at me, she had tears in her eyes. "Why?"

I clicked on the burner. I didn't have any answers. None better than I'd given Craig, anyway. "I'm a liar, a cheat, a thief and a whore. I try to do the right thing, but it isn't always possible. And sometimes it makes no difference in the end either way."

"Don't say that."

"I stole a car today." Hardly the worse thing I'd done, but maybe I thought I'd start small. "You know those people who take pens, paperclips, memo pads from the office? They never call themselves thieves. 'No one'll miss it. Everyone does it.' They're maybe right. They're still thieves." I bit my lip and took a deep breath. "Those people would never steal from a store. Never nick a pair of cheap shoes or a jar of peanut butter. They'd even tell you, self-righteously, they could do without shoes or they'd just go hungry." I let loose a guarded, airy laugh. "They *need* a box of paperclips?"

"That's not what I asked you. And I never judged that part of you."

"It's all the same at this point. I'm not the person I used to be. But I haven't forgotten what she taught me."

"Don't you ever want to know why?" A tear dripped off her nose and landed on the empty cutting board she was holding.

I shook my head slowly because I couldn't be certain of her exact why. I knew most of them I'd stopped questioning. I watched the beans bob as the liquid heated. Inside, I felt empty, drained. "Nik, it is what it is."

She snorted and tossed the cutting board in the empty sink. "Screw that."

"What do you want me to say, Nik?"

"That it's over. That it will be over. That this will end well. That you don't have to be who you were. That I don't have to be who I was. That this…" She gestured wildly at the kitchen and hurled the rest of the garlic bulb across the room. "This isn't who we are."

I pulled her into a hug. I didn't want to be who we were either, but it was starting to feel like something I wasn't going to be allowed to escape.

She left snot on my shirt and pulled away. "Where the hell have you been?"

"I did things I shouldn't have. Can we just leave it at that?" I walked away, stopped in the doorway and stared at the eggplant walls, the dent I'd left a few days before. "Things I can't undo."

"No." She grabbed my arm and spun me. Her face was set in anger and determination and a kind of motherly resolution I found it hard to argue with. "You think all your little lies held water? You want to think I don't know where the money came from? You think I haven't figured out why Charley shot you? I'm not stupid, Davis. Talk to me."

"If you knew, why didn't you stop me?" Tears sprung to my eyes and I hated myself for them. I wanted to take the words back, hoped I hadn't said it out loud.

Her eyes shone back at me. "For the same reason you did it. I didn't know any other way."

I backed away from her. "I killed someone."

She studied my face like a psychic studied tea leaves. "How?"

I stared at her. Her eyes demanded the truth and I was so tired of hiding. "I shot him. In the chest."

"You had to. I know you. You had to." She looked at her watch and back at the stove. "I don't know why I made this. We're going to be late to visit Lane. You should go shower."

I stared at her like she'd been abducted by aliens or replaced by a robot or suffered a head injury. "Nik?"

She wiped her eyes. "Go take a shower."

I nodded and went upstairs.

We took Nik's rental. She wore a lovely lavender pantsuit of repurposed polyester and cotton hand-sewn by a Phoenix artisan. I wore pants I'd owned in high school. They were black and too light for the chill in the air. Since I had no matching jacket, I'd just thrown my leather on over a tee shirt despite Nik's insistence that it smelled like a dead mermaid.

"You still handling Charley's business?"

"Some. I let the car insurance lapse. She lost her license about eight months ago. I swear she must've gotten a ticket in every county south of the Mason-Dixon line. Or, I guess Allister Connelly did."

I rubbed the scar behind my ear and tried to figure out what to say to Lane.

CHAPTER FORTY-SEVEN

We left our bags locked in the trunk of the car. Our IDs we stuffed in our otherwise empty pockets. The jail was relatively new, designed of red brick in a boxy office shape. Part of it had been built in the middle of the street separating it from the courthouse and the old ice plant so that the sally port almost shared space with an ice truck loading up to deliver to hotels and local gas stations. We parked on the courthouse side, where we could see the police station if we looked half a block down. Well, I saw it. I wasn't sure Nik saw much of anything.

She was silent as we passed through the usual metal detectors and were left to wait in a room painted an industrial-hospital beige that may have been filthy looking even in the paint can. "How's she doing?"

I glanced at her out of the corner of my eye. "How would I know?"

"You've been locked up before. I haven't. What's it like."

I thought about explaining the difference between juvenile and adult lockup. "Boring."

"That's the best you can come up with? You think she's bored?" She glared at me, back in mom-mode.

"I don't know. I don't know her. Not anymore." I stared at the tile. "Maybe not ever."

We were eventually herded into a room resembling a high school cafeteria, except the cheerleaders and jocks had been replaced by uniformed corrections officers and the furniture was all bolted to the floor.

A burly man of maybe thirty-five gestured at a table near the corner. "Sit here. You pass anything to the prisoner, I will arrest you."

Other family members were already waiting at other tables, but were spaced far enough apart that I couldn't make out what anyone was saying. Most waited quietly, but a few of the older women cried.

Two girls and four boys, ranging in age from late teens to mid-twenties, came in with the boys spaced further back. All wore ankle and wrist chains and gender-coded jumpsuits. Lane, like the other girl, wore dark blue.

Nik's breath caught when she saw Lane, but she otherwise maintained her composure.

One of the women at another table burst into hard sobs. A young male officer with a bald brown dome of a head led the tallest boy to her. She reached out for a hug, but the officer motioned for her to sit, untouched.

Lane was the last to be led over. The jumpsuit hung on her like they'd tried to dress a skeleton. Her eyes were shifty and hard, set in dark cavities seen on overly made-up models and old insomniacs. Eyes like an addict. She sat where she was told, metal clanging, and stared at us, mouth twisted in disgust.

"I like the hair color," Nik offered. "Is that a tiger paw?" She pointed at the tattoo on Lane's wrist.

Lane didn't acknowledge her. She slouched as best she could on the attached stool, hands on the metal table. She stared at me and the disgust grew. She tapped a foot and the chains jangled. "What?"

I put a hand on Nik's to discourage her input. "You do this?" I asked Lane.

She leaned forward. "Wha'd'you care?"

Nik gave her the mom glare. "She's trying to help." Hateful ingrate, the tone implied.

"I don't need that bitch's help." She swiveled her gaze to Nik long enough to deliver her point before refocusing her venom toward me. "You through running scared?"

"You're in too much trouble for this foolishness. You want to think you're grown, act it. Maybe this seems fun right now, but you're looking at twenty-five to life, if you're lucky."

"What the fuck do you know?" She leaned back again and drummed her fingers. "I'm a juvenile."

"Crime like this? They'll direct file, transfer it to the adult system. By the time a verdict and sentencing comes through, you'll be at least eighteen. Adult crime. Adult time."

"They can't do that." Defiant teenage face.

"They will, Lane. And if you did this, you probably deserve what they give you. But if you didn't? If you've got a different explanation, spit it out before visitation's over."

Her features morphed. The teenager slipped away, replaced by a harder woman I knew too well. "They all got what they asked for. We all do, don't we?" She held my gaze for several seconds, her jaw set to the standard Groves response to fear.

Nik put her hand on mine and let her fingers trace the surgical scars along the back of it.

I pulled away and crossed my arms. "Tell me how Billy Guthrie asked to be shot."

She doubled down on the hard stare.

"Wha'd'you know? You left." She leaned forward. "You ran. Charley's right. You're dead."

I ignored her. "Why'd Billy load the gun?"

Lane squinted at me. "Who told you that?"

I cocked my head at her. She suddenly seemed worried, almost afraid, but not of prison this time. "So, it's true."

She tried to glance over her shoulder without turning her head. "Coincidence. We were shooting it in the woods last month."

I nodded like that made sense. "So, last month you were friends and this month you blew his brains all over his mother's wall."

Brief sadness crossed her eyes before they hardened again. "What's it to you?"

Nik backhanded me in the chest, probably because she couldn't smack Lane. The guard eyed us, but said nothing. She pointed at Lane. "If you don't let us help you, you're going to prison."

I watched her jaw stiffen. "You don't get to know about me. Not anymore."

I thought back. "The purses. The old ones. You get those from Vince?"

Her eyes betrayed her, but her face didn't. I'd asked the wrong question.

"The car. You pimping out those girls alone or someone pulling your strings?"

Lane looked at Nik. "Fuck that bitch."

CHAPTER FORTY-EIGHT

Outside, I looked at Nik and held out my hands for the keys.
She sighed and stared at the car while I retrieved the purses. "She shot that guy, didn't she?"

"She meant to shoot someone. I haven't decided if she meant to shoot Billy." I got in and started the car, adjusted the seat to make room for my legs.

She got in, folded her hands on her lap. "What happened to her?" Her eyes watched things pass out the windshield. She didn't seem to have noticed we weren't heading back to Charley's.

"I don't know."

I felt her eyes on me. "I think you do. I think you know damn well what's wrong with her and you're hiding it like you always do."

"You seem to know everything, Nik." I stopped at the Live Oak Street light.

She shifted in her seat and looked over at the instrument panel behind the steering wheel. "I had a friend in college. We lived across the hall from each other." She unfolded and refolded her hands. "A guy raped her at a frat party. Her friends scattered. Some said she'd asked for it. Some seemed to lack the words."

"She wasn't expecting it. She thought she was safe." I knew that feeling, more from theory than reality.

"Some days I feel like a floating island in a sea of the damaged."

I thought about the difference between the stories that made me feel less alone, and the ones that made me feel worse, like it was never-ending. "Your friend. I'm sorry. She should have been safe."

"You should have been safe, too."

I shook my head. "Coulda-shoulda-woulda is bullshit, Nik." The light changed and I turned, drove us toward the waterfront.

"You were raised to be my fucking bodyguard. Do you not realize that?"

"It was my choice. To protect both of you. And I failed."

"You were a kid, too!"

I didn't say anything. There wasn't anything to say. Nothing we'd agree on, anyway.

"You think someone molested Lane."

I looked over, watched her face fight the words. I swallowed the fat spit that showed up before tears. I blinked slowly, changing my breathing to a deep, meditative style. I waited.

"You know something."

"I don't. Not for certain." I parked in one of the spots between the inn and the old post office on the empty end of Front Street.

"Then what do you think." Her tone was angry but her eyes were still sad.

"I think Lane is more of a survivor than we know, maybe too much so. I think she got into something, in over her head."

"That's not what I asked."

"It's all I've got for now." I got out and stood on the cracked sidewalk. Nearby, the few sailboats rocked gently.

Nik got out. "You need to talk to me."

I tried to look at her but couldn't.

She reached for my hand, but stopped just shy of touching, as though she were afraid I'd burn her. "What happened to you?"

"Nothing." It came out automatically.

She worked her jaw around the words. "What happened when you were eleven?" She put her hand to her face, closed her eyes and rubbed the spot between them. She took a deep breath and looked at me. "At the foster home. What happened?"

I looked out at the water. Studied myself from within. I felt solid in my stance, my arms crossed, my feet, planted on the ground beneath them. Thought back to that day, without the filters of adulthood. "I saw the way he looked at you. I knew it was wrong, but wasn't sure why. And I was jealous."

"What?" I heard her heart break under that word, a sharp crack of air escaping her throat with the letters.

"He wanted to play. That's what he called it. He wanted to experiment. He wanted to act out… things." I thought about things he said and did and how they weren't all things he'd heard from peers. "Some of the things hurt. Sometimes they felt good. And I was confused."

"Davis, why?"

"I guess I was curious, too. You always had me reading adult books. And sometimes I snuck some of my own in."

Her breath caught. "You blame *me?*"

"No. I've never blamed anyone but me. Him." I wanted to comfort her, but I couldn't. "He told me not to tell, so I knew it was wrong. I knew it was something he shouldn't do with you or Lane. But still, sometimes it was…almost fun."

Her face twisted to disgust.

I understood. But I didn't say it.

"I fell asleep in class and the teacher asked me why. I made a mistake; I told her I'd stayed up playing with our brother." I watched a pair of pelicans skim the surface of the water. "Her tone told me it was wrong. Her face told me to lie. So, when she asked what we played, I named toys. Games. And I learned I needed to lie better, or say nothing.

"I don't know what she told him, the dad, but when he punished me, it hurt. A lot. And I learned my lesson. I learned not to tell."

"Davis—"

"And I learned that the things he'd taught me to do, the things I'd done for free? I learned other boys would pay me for those things. And even if it hurt, it didn't hurt for long. Later, I learned it wasn't just teenage boys who'd pay. That the more a guy thought he had to lose, the more he was willing to pay. Or the more he was willing to kill. So I learned to read people. Just not well enough."

Nik's body held its shape, but only barely as her sobbing bent and swayed her in the stiff onshore wind. I wanted to hold her. I wanted to tell her it was fine. But I'd just told her it wasn't.

When I saw her knees buckle, I caught her and hugged her to me. She pushed me away feebly. "Your jacket stinks."

I let go.

"I knew. I knew something happened. You changed. I knew you…I knew."

I looked at my feet, which no longer felt solid.

"Why didn't you talk to me? You had to know I knew. Why lie? Over and over and over?" She started to hit me with her fists, at first lightly on the arms, but it grew to a pounding on my chest.

I let her. Let her fists pound the stab wound Charley had made and gritted my teeth, because I knew I deserved it.

When her fury exhausted, she pushed me. I didn't budge. "Why?" she asked.

"If I'd told you the truth, you'd have wanted to report it or fix it or stop it. You'd have had a burden you couldn't carry."

"Except I carried the back end of that thing across half the states. I carried all the stuff you dropped." She studied me. "You're bleeding again."

"It happens."

"Why didn't we stop this from happening to Lane?"

"I don't know."

CHAPTER FORTY-NINE

I drove the rest of the way to Rex Whittman's in silence.

In the driveway, I pulled a Beretta and a .22 caliber trail revolver out of my purse. I handed her the Taurus. "Anyone tries to take you out of this car, point this in their ribs or stomach and shoot until it clicks. If I get killed, drive away. Don't mess with the cops. Call Tom. And go back to Arizona." I handed her my phone.

She gave me the look she used to give me when we were kids. The one that said "don't do it and be careful and fuck you" all at once.

I got out and took Phil's pistol to the front door with me. I wasn't sure what I was doing besides coming unglued, but it felt right.

I beat the door three times with the side of my fist. "Rex, I want answers!"

I immediately ducked to a squat to the left side of the door.

Footsteps pounded from the back, followed by a boom that ripped a melon-sized hole out of the door. The second blast tore out a chunk of wall over my head.

I pushed open the door, staying low, and rushed him, jerking the gun barrel to the side as he fumbled to reload. I stuck the sleek 9mm against his cheek and yanked the shotgun out of his hands as I kneed him in the crotch. "Sit down."

He sat. Right on the stack of yellowed TV Guides and a pile of remotes cluttering up the end table. "What the hell, lady?" He rubbed his nuts and scowled.

I realized I was breathing too hard, slowed it down to an even, calm pace. "That sums it up. What the hell indeed?"

He held up his hands, realized he still had a shotgun shell in one and threw it away. "Shit."

"Tell me what the hell happened. No bullshit this time."

He spread his hands wider. "I don't know."

"That sounds like bullshit. Strike one. Who shot Billy?"

"If it wasn't Lane, I don't know." He must've seen the shift in my face because he added, "But I heard someone else was there."

"Who?"

He looked sad. "Amber."

"Why'd you try to shoot me?"

He looked down at his lap. He mumbled. "There's a reward."

"Someone put a hit on me? In the sticks?"

"Reward."

"Uh huh. How much?"

"Six grand." He glanced at me to see how I'd take it.

"Really? That's it?"

He nodded again. Maybe he wasn't sure what to add.

"Who's paying?"

"Vince said Eric."

"Has anyone even *seen* Eric?"

He shrugged.

"Then you don't even know if it's good or if he's even still alive. You willing to risk jail time over that?"

He hung his head.

"What the hell'd you do to Melissa Armstrong?"

"Who?"

I considered shooting him just for the blank look on his face. "The girl passed out on a boat a week ago. You and Lane and Sylvia went out to party it up? Ring any bells?"

"That skank?"

"Strike two."

"What? Look, lady, Davis, whatever. I was supposed to get the girl on the boat. The girls helped because, you know, I'm such a looker. The bitch wanted nothing to do with me."

"She had a boyfriend."

He snorted. "Some boyfriend. Didn't stop her from screwing everyone else."

"So, what'd you do to her?"

"Nothing."

"Strike—"

"Wait! Fuck. I didn't. I swear. I was told to get her on the boat and get her out to sea."

I studied his face but all I saw was the loser no one wanted to let into the group, the guy who did all the work, got none of the glory, and for once wanted a piece for himself.

"How'd she get dead?" I asked.

"Brad, I guess."

"You guess?"

"Yeah. Brad. It's his fucking boat. He lived on it."

"Billy's boat? Jimmy's boat?"

His look said that was bullshit.

"His own boat. Used to belong to John Taylor." He looked at me like I was stupid. "Brad lived on the boat to keep Taylor's kid off it. Damn brat kept coming around, snooping."

"Brad killed her? Melissa?"

"I guess. She passed out. I had a few more beers. Helped him throw her over when he was done."

"Done?" If my finger had been inside the trigger guard, I'd have shot him. I took a long, deep breath. "And Billy?"

"I heard he was leaving Amber."

"Who said that?"

"I don't know." He up-turned his hands. "People. Around. Gossip. You know."

"Why?"

"Someone said he was planning to nark on Vince for what he did to Amber." He looked bitter about it.

"What'd he do?"

"You don't know?" His eyes got big. Finally the fat kid had something over someone else. "He fed her habit. Got her to work for him."

"He pimped her." I cocked my head. "You sure this wasn't about that crappy Chinese seafood?"

He shook his head like that explained it. "It wasn't like that. She wanted it. They all did."

Uh huh. "They're *teenage* girls."

"Most of them will do anything for a fix." He sneered. "Like your mom."

"You say that like I don't know."

He looked at his lap. "Look, Billy and Lane? They were best friends. They told each other everything. *Everything.* But she liked Vince. Thought she was using him." His doughy face looked almost sad. "Vince was using her."

"How'd they even meet?" I wanted his take. As a litmus test.

He shrugged. "Some party over on the beach. Billy brought her places back before he got tight with Amber. Course, Lane seemed to know Vince already, so…" He shrugged again.

"Why didn't you just tell me this before?"

"They'd have killed me."

"And not now?"

He glanced at me. Sheepish. "Someone's gonna kill you. They maybe won't know I talked. Besides, you been to see Lane, right? Maybe she talked."

"That's what you plan to tell people? To save your ass?" I thought about how he could've known where we'd been.

"Wouldn't you?

"You think she told me anything?"

"If she had, you wouldn't be here." He seemed pretty sure of that and it made sense, provided he didn't know where else I'd been since I last saw him.

"How'd you know I saw Lane?"

"Hell, everyone with a drunk in the family knows when jail visits are." He looked at the floor, the wall behind me, and at his shoes. They were drugstore boat shoes worn to holes. Something about his demeanor had changed. Deflated.

I picked up the shotgun and walked toward the door. "You move, I shoot."

Rex looked at me like a puppy who'd left a puddle on the floor. "For what it's worth, I'm sorry."

I wasn't sure how much of him I hated and how much I pitied.

"My cousin used to run with them. Kelly. She wouldn't talk about it. Got pregnant."

"Suicide?"

"Supposed to look that way." He sighed. "I'm done with this mess."

I held up the shotgun. "This'll be in the yard. Don't point it at me again."

I was almost across the hardscrabble yard when I heard the screen door open. I turned, ready to kill him, but he was standing with his arms up and harmless. He looked as forlorn as his sagging porch. Gray clouds, accumulating in the distance, only enhanced the portrait of rural poverty.

I wondered what he'd do with the shotgun.

In the car, Nik looked at me with her mom face. "My friend tried to kill herself once. She's better now. I think you're still trying."

CHAPTER FIFTY

Back out on Lennoxville Road, I pulled out my phone and made two calls. The first was to Tom and went to voice mail. I hung up and called Lawson.

As we passed the abandoned fish factory on the corner, I noticed a faded wooden sign with Wright's name on it. The old menhaden place. I couldn't imagine it running. It looked about the same age as Rex's house, but was in even worse shape.

Lawson answered on the sixth ring.

"Lawson. It's Davis. I think I just figured out your defense. Lane wasn't there alone. Physical evidence bears that out. The other person, rumor has it, was Billy's girlfriend, Amber Martin."

"The girl with the missing brother? That isn't your doing, is it?" His voice sounded strained, annoyed.

I wondered if he actually thought that. "You really don't think much of me, do you?"

"You *have* worked for Dick for nearly two years."

"Point taken. Look, you know as well as I do a good defense is a good story. The burden is on the state. You just have to confuse the jury enough to have reasonable doubt."

"Somehow I remember that from law school, yes."

"What's going on around here is confusing as hell, so doubt should be easy." My tone strained civility. "Here's your story. Two girls showed up that night in another girl's car: Billy's best friend and his girlfriend—who was being pimped out by someone, maybe Lane."

"That doesn't help."

I kept going. "One stabbed him. One shot him. Or one had a gun and it accidentally went off when he reached for it. A sheriff's office guy showed up before the locals. Murphy. He's related to the Martin kids. Another deputy was with him. Probably Lamar." I spelled out the rest of the connections and oddities I'd discovered.

"How do you know all this?"

"If you believe me, so will a jury."

"So, you're making it up?" He sounded exasperated.

"I'm telling you the things I've been told. Someone has a vested interest in making sure Lane takes the fall for Billy's death. And she's angry and guilty enough to think she should."

"You talk to Dick like this, too, don't you? It's why you're still around? You don't take 'no' for an answer and you call him on his BS?"

"I also type real fast."

Nik looked over at me after I hung up. "I thought you were dead back there."

"Only inside."

"This isn't funny."

"I didn't say it was."

"Now what?"

I bit my lip. "We go see Wright's lawyer."

"What does he have to do with anything?"

"Money. He has control over it and I've heard it's the root of all evil."

CHAPTER FIFTY-ONE

The weather was changing again as we drove across town. Clouds rolled in from the ocean and the wind chill dropped. The aging streets were mostly deserted. I followed Live Oak to an intersection just past the courthouse, turned, turned again, ending up on the same street as the police department. At the bridge end sat a pale yellow house with a blue and white historical plaque out front. The address Tom had previously given me for Wright's lawyer gleamed above the door.

Rayford Jackson answered my knock, holding the squeaky screen open as we stepped inside. "Come on back. I made coffee and tea. Suppose you'd rather just have a Pepsi."

I smiled and followed him, Nik close at my heels, down a dark hallway to the kitchen. "Coffee's fine."

I'd been expecting a movie villain, someone who instilled much fear in the hearts of men and teenage boys. Instead, I had an elderly man dressed like Mr. Rogers leading me to a kitchen, which was surprisingly bright even on a dim winter evening.

He poured coffee from an antique coffee pot. I must have been staring because he commented. "You like? It was my wife's favorite."

"It's very pretty." Nik smiled, playing the good girl.

He offered sugar in a tiny pot with a matching pattern. "I have milk in the fridge."

I declined both.

He dumped in sugar and went to the fridge. "Mr. MacQuayde mentioned you had some questions. I'm not sure how much help I can be."

I sipped my coffee. It was good. Nik continued smiling.

"Would you like to move to the office or are you two comfortable here?" He put the coffee pot back on the counter. "Since my wife died, I'm afraid I haven't been much of a housekeeper."

I smiled. "I'm fine here, if that's okay."

"So, where should we start?"

I started to open my mouth but Nik beat me to it. "Your client is trying to kill my sister and I think you should tell him to stop."

"My client?" He looked properly confused, appropriately stunned even.

"Yeah, Eric Wright." Mama Bear protecting her cubs.

"I'm afraid there must be some misunderstanding." He picked up his coffee cup and sipped.

I looked around at furnishings from the early 1900s mixed with appliances from the seventies and eighties. The wood paneling along the bottom wall of the kitchen weighted down the cheery yellow wallpaper on top and the green linoleum was faded and stained. "You make good money protecting Wright?"

He shifted his focus to me. "I beg your pardon, young lady. That doesn't seem like polite conversation."

I leaned back. "I'm not that polite."

Nik added, "She's really not."

"Maybe you should leave."

I didn't budge. "So, about my question? You live in a pretty good house, but you're not putting a lot into the upkeep. The car out front is high-end, but not late-model. Wright's is faltering. Or it's not. Depending on who you ask. Which is it?"

"I cannot discuss that."

I glanced at the fridge again, and the photo under the Seafood Festival magnet. "He have the money to have me whacked?"

He set his cup down. "Hear me out, Miss Groves."

"Davis. Please."

"Davis, then. My client, Mr. Wright, is not who you suspect he is. He couldn't do these things you're accusing him of doing." His accent was softly Southern, the kind where you can hear the British roots in it, but his phrasing kept borrowing from old gangster movies. It made me wonder whom he was trying to fool.

"Your son works for Wright, too. He just bought a nice house in Surf City. Ocean views, I'm told." Chip the hacker was handy.

"My son is none of your business. Or Mr. MacQuayde's, for that matter." His tone made it clear he knew where I'd gotten that information.

"Who started the rumor about the hit?"

"Mr. Wright would never do that."

"He's missing. So, was it you? Tanner?"

"You know my client records are confidential."

I raised an eyebrow.

"Mr. Wright is a smart, shrewd businessman. He offered jobs at a time when everyone was hearing about this great economy but not seeing the evidence. Between the flooding, the storms, and the pollution, the locals couldn't afford to live here."

"How noble."

He looked at his caramel-colored coffee. "His father left when he was three. I understand you lost your father at a young age also. That must have been hard."

"Didn't make me a drug dealer or a murderer." I thumbed over at Nik. "And she's not even a prostitute." The fact that he knew about our father wasn't lost on me.

"Eric isn't a strong person, never has been. Good at business, but, well, he's most certainly not a drug dealer or a murderer."

"Maybe, but he *has* been passing off cheap seafood as local."

"Even if he were, that's a matter for the FDA. And if his customers have no complaints, why would you?"

Nik made a face, but kept her soap boxes stored.

"His father was a good man. But he died. And Eric's mother remarried. All of this you could probably find out from any waitress or hairdresser Downeast, so I'm breaking no confidence. His mother was not a strong person. Probably not so unlike yours."

"Some of us don't get that luxury. Being weak."

Nik caught my eye, but I pretended not to see her.

"Her father owned the seafood business. When she remarried, she changed Eric's last name to her father's because her new husband wanted no children."

"That's awful," Nik said.

"Again, all part of local lore. As is her father leaving her the business on the condition she let the general manager remain and that her new husband never touch it. When the manager retired, Eric took over. The gist of that is in the public records."

I blinked at him. "And the part that isn't?"

He sighed. "That would be the part protected by client privilege. But something tells me you can guess how well young Eric was treated by his stepfather."

I watched his eyes grow sad with the weight of things he'd carried too many years.

"I did the best I could." He got up without a word and walked down the hall.

I glanced at Nik. She mouthed for me to behave.

He shuffled back in, carrying a snapshot of a boy standing in a kitchen and clutching a small, stuffed rabbit. His face was purple and swollen, his chest bare.

Nik looked over my shoulder. "You never called social services? You never told the police?"

"I was not at liberty to interfere. There's no guarantee he'd have been better off. At least I kept an eye on him."

"What happened to the stepfather?"

"Eric killed him. Or had someone do it."

I looked up. "You said he wasn't a murderer."

"I have no proof of it and I'd never testify in court. Three years ago, when he came back from school permanently, the man disappeared. A body was never found. I just know."

Nik's breathing changed next to me.

"Uh huh."

He ignored me. "Most of the town thinks he's nearly a saint." Jackson rubbed at a liver spot on his wrist. "Eric bought a salon for an old girlfriend. When they broke up, he fired her. I never got the feeling they were…compatible."

"Sweet guy. She still around?"

"Sort of. Her parents buried her in the family plot in Newport."

I raised an eyebrow. "Car accident?"

"Boat. She drowned while on Shackelford Banks with her brother and his wife."

"When?"

"Two weeks after the break-up."

I thought of Jackie. Dead in the snow.

Nik looked incredulous.

I jerked my chin at the photo on the fridge. "They don't look much alike, do they?"

He looked over his shoulder and back at his lap. "I may have been unfaithful once. It was a long time ago. The baby was little. We were stressed. I had to go to Raleigh on business. Things happened."

I raised an eyebrow. "Vince Zellner?"

He looked at his thumb, stroking the handle of the mug. "He was a troubled kid from what I understand. Needed a father figure, perhaps. His mother got caught up in an accounting scheme, did some time. Tabby and I took him in when he was seven. He went back to his mother when she got out. Vince was," he furrowed his brow, "thirteen."

"He ever meet Eric?"

He gave me a weird look. "No."

"Tanner threatened a family man near Newport."

His jaw was stone. "I didn't endorse that. I don't condone it."

I looked at the picture of a boy with a bunny and a black eye. "He really missing?"

His face sagged. "I just hope he's not dead."

In the car, Nik shuddered and flicked on the heater. "How much of that do you think is bullshit?"

I put the car in gear and turned on the windshield wipers to clear the icy mist. "Doesn't matter. Matters who believes it." I turned onto Turner Street.

"He has the money. If he wants you dead, Davis…"

"He won't be the first."

CHAPTER FIFTY-TWO

We pulled up in front of Charley's without speaking. Nik hadn't said a word since we'd left Beaufort, and while I could guess what she was thinking I wasn't sure I wanted to hear it out loud.

The front door wasn't locked, was barely pulled shut. I looked at her and pulled the Beretta out of my purse. She moved behind me like we'd done this dance before and both knew she wasn't waiting in the car any more than I was.

We found Eric Wright sitting on the couch, wrapped in a clear plastic parka, holding a small-caliber pistol on his lap. He looked like a tired version of the college athlete Jackie had fallen for; a dejected form of the small-town politician who'd convinced voters he could be trusted. Sun-bleached hair flopped over his forehead, damp and greasy, and his lavender polo shirt showed signs of having been worn too many days.

I pointed the 9mm at him. "What the fuck are you doing here, Eric?"

"I need your help." He didn't bother embellishing. He barely looked up from his lap.

"Excuse me?"

He searched my face. "He hasn't broken you yet, has he?" He looked at Nik. "You?"

"Where the hell have you been?"

"Hiding."

"Clearly." I picked up the gun off his lap. He didn't even seem to notice. "Eric, I really don't have the patience for this kind of crazy. And frankly, since you were armed I'm pretty sure the only reason I haven't shot you is the mess."

"My lawyer's trying to kill me. My employees are ruining my reputation. My friends are… I don't have any friends." He sagged into the stained couch and looked at home under the dingy, spray-painted wall.

I stared at him. "What about Vince?"

A wave of fear and sadness and longing crossed his face and a dozen things clicked into place in my brain. "Vince is your lover."

Nik's head whiplashed in my peripheral vision.

Eric's face twisted. "I'm not gay."

I thought about the video and the man with the tiger tattoo. I thought about Jackie and Rebecca. I thought about denial and abuse. I thought about his stepfather. "It started with your stepdad, didn't it?" My voice sounded calm, understanding, even to my jaded ears.

"I'm not gay."

"I didn't say you were."

His lower lip, split from too much sun or cold wind, quivered. "I'm not."

"Eric, let's be clear when I say I'm quite certain there are things you've done that I don't agree with—"

"I'm not."

"Yes, but if someone did something to you as a child, that's on them. Not you. It doesn't make you one thing or another."

He just shook his head. "I just wanted to be normal."

I glanced at Nik. "Some of us don't get to be."

"I went out with the guys one night. After a game. We tried some bar downtown. Partied until late. A guy chatted me up. We talked baseball. The last of the team left and this guy asked if I wanted to get another beer or two at his place.

"I told him I wasn't gay. I told him I wasn't like that. He laughed. Said it was just a couple beers. The night was young."

"But you liked him. You *were* attracted to him."

"I'm not gay. I'm not like that." He wouldn't meet my eyes, "But he was so nice, so gentle."

"Look, let me be real clear with you. I'm sorry for anything that happened to you that you didn't want, but I'm about two minutes past my patience for the homophobia. Some of the most important people in my life have been gay and that didn't make me love them less and it didn't break my heart less when they were gone. You wanna hide your shit publicly? Fine. But drop the act with me. If you knew—"

"I was confused. And it's the South. I had a reputation to protect. I have a business. People who depend on me."

"You didn't think a gay politician would get very far."

"I do *good*, Davis. I've done good."

"And Vince? He do any good?" I asked.

"Being with Vince was great, but scary. I tried to help him. I thought I could change him. He just had too much hate. Pain I couldn't heal."

"When did he make the video?"

He turned pink. "He loved me."

"Blackmail isn't love."

"You don't understand. I've tried so hard. I loved Jackie. I did. Just never like that. And she was okay with it. She wanted just enough sex to have kids. I figured I could do that. I could."

"You hit her. You used her."

He shook his head. "I never."

"Vince?"

He nodded. "He took his anger with me out on her. Sometimes on me. Mostly on her."

I pictured the "mistakes" and the dead women in the Wilmington newspapers. "He hate all women or just the ones with you?"

He shut his eyes. "He wasn't always like this."

"Like what?"

"Dangerous. Evil."

"Melodrama much?" I asked.

He gave me his best earnest face, but the greasy hair messed up the look. "He's got a streak. He likes to find people's pain points. And push them. Their fears. Their nightmares." He wiped a tear. "I don't know what happened."

I flexed my right hand, worked the ache out of it. "I don't care what happened. His mommy went to prison. He didn't get enough cupcakes. Whatever."

Eric looked up, eyes full of fear. "He knows about that guy in college, in Boone. The one who drugged you. I don't know how, but he does."

Only one way. I'd only talked about it once before my conversation with Tom on Thursday. Ryan was dead, but when our apartment had gone up in flames my paperwork from the clinic had still been sitting on my desk.

"That's gonna be his plan, you know..." He looked at me, earnest again, but also cagey. "He wants to break you."

Nik's breath caught next to me.

He lowered his eyes. "You're the only one who can stop him."

"I don't have a fucking cape, Eric."

Nik squeezed my arm "What is he talking about, Davis?"

"He's saying Vince thinks roofies will push me over the edge, turn me into a quivering mess like Charley."

Nik relaxed. "Well, that's just stupid."

He looked up at me. "I never meant to hurt her. Jackie. Our relationship, it made Vince so angry sometimes. He wanted us to be together, didn't understand what I was doing with her."

"You used her and you let him hit her." I stared at him for a long time.

He picked lint or dust or stray pot off the couch cushion. "I'm sorry. I'm sorry for what he did to you. I know you were just trying to protect her. I know she didn't understand."

"Davis, what're you thinking?" Nik asked.

I shook myself out of old memories. "You have a tattoo?

"Vince does. A tiger on his shoulder. It was his old high school mascot." His eyes grew sad. "You saw what he did to Jackie."

"Why?"

"I wanted to marry her. He seduced her. Said he'd ruin her for both of us. That she'd know how awful I was, how good he was. That she'd never be able to show her face in a white dress. He blackmailed her. Told her if she didn't leave, he'd show the video to her mom."

"Why? Marriage would solve your image problem, right?"

"He didn't like sharing. He didn't like that I loved her. Even as a friend. He wanted me to himself."

I thought about the video, about Jackie's attitude toward sex, about how she'd talked about Vince. "Seduced? Or raped?"

Eric wouldn't look at me. He either didn't know or couldn't bring himself to say. Maybe it no longer mattered.

I waited for Eric to catch my eyes again. "Who killed that woman? In Wilmington."

His jaw worked a little longer, then stopped. "How?"

"No, who?" My disgust was bubbling over.

"What woman?" Nik asked.

"I thought it was you. I thought it was you lashing out when you fought with Jackie. It was him."

He looked at the ceiling, worked his mouth like he was hoping an answer would find its way in there on its own. "He started those fights. Then, when she ran off, I was upset. I didn't want to even look at him. He was ruining it."

"Your perfect image." I said.

His face crumbled. "He said he had to blow off steam. I didn't know, then. I mean, I knew he had his own issues with—"

"You're as complicit as he is."

"You don't understand. I love him. Loved him. You don't know what it's like."

I wanted to shoot him so badly I had to rub the side of the slide with my trigger finger to keep it outside the guard. "I know all about abusive relationships. I know all about power and control and excuses. That shit don't change if you're gay or straight or bi or trans or a fucking teen hooker. You don't have to hurt yourself and you don't have to hurt other people to be happy. You don't."

Nik put a hand on my shoulder. She didn't pat or rub or speak. Just let me know she was still there. That my anger wasn't the only thing in the room.

"What about Melissa Armstrong?"

"Who?" he asked.

"The first mistake."

His eyes widened. "It wasn't like that."

"Did you fuck her? Try to marry her, too?"

Nik punched me in the back of the shoulder.

I flinched.

"I don't know. I never met her. Rebecca, that investigator, said she was hanging out with Lane and Billy. I liked her. Rebecca. She was nice. Smart. Smart enough to know we weren't going any further than dinner and drinks, but she was fun."

"Why'd Vince kill Melissa? She was a kid."

"Because I found out what he was doing and tried to help Rebecca get that girl home."

"Allister Connolly?"

"Lane's idea, which was really Vince's. He used those girls. Getting them drugs, pimping them out. He'd get Lane and Amber to find him runaways, addicts, people he could exploit. He just likes pain. He wants to see other people hurt." He tried to suppress a sob. "I see it now."

Nik hit me again. I wasn't sure why but it sounded like she was trying not to cry.

"He hurt them, hooked them, turned them out." I left just enough room for him to take it as a question, but it wasn't. I knew too much about guys like that.

Nik hit me again and I felt the cut underneath start to bleed.

"I didn't mean to do anything wrong." Eric looked defeated.

"How'd all this start?"

Nik leaned her head on my shoulder and I heard her swallow. I wondered what was going on in her head, but was afraid to ask.

Eric looked at her and then his hands. "Purses. Vince got a line on some purses working at the port. Sold some, made a little money. Guy who had the purses asked if he wanted to make even more. Told him about a dealer. Vince thought it made him seem tough. Liked the idea. Liked the pain drugs caused even as they promised to make it all go away."

"But you stayed with him."

"I thought he'd stopped. After Jackie died, things settled for a while. I inherited the seafood company and I tried to—"

"You used his contacts to import cheap fish."

"You make it sound petty."

"It's illegal. That doesn't make it glamorous."

"It was supposed to be a win-win. I could afford to pay my guys—well. I could afford to help out local fishermen. I could stay in business. It wasn't just a campaign promise. I meant it."

"You ran for office so you could pretend to be a big baller."

He glared at me. "I meant well. I did. Brought it in on cargo ships under a shell company Jackson set up. Used the smaller charter and fishing boats I bought off the guys who needed help. Loaded the imported stuff in their hulls and brought it into Wright's like they'd caught it."

"And the money to buy the boats?"

"Jackson said we had it. I didn't know he was padding my accounts laundering Vince's dirty money. I never asked where it came from."

Jackson. I had a feeling Zellner had targeted Wright all along, had known about him for years. And maybe been jealous.

"Why?" Nik asked. "Why not just use trucks?"

"Keep up appearances," I said.

He nodded. "Small town. Illusion is fact even if every gossip knows the truth. Consumers get picky at the store, but they'll eat it in restaurants and not think twice about where it came from."

"Anyone quit?"

"Just one."

"And?" I waited.

"He died. House fire later that month."

"Arson?" I asked.

He looked aghast as best he could. "Fire department didn't think so."

"The local *volunteer* fire department?"

"Fine. So I may have paid off a few guys over the investigation. It's not like I killed the guy."

"But you figured Vince did."

"We weren't supposed to be bringing in drugs anymore. That was the deal. I didn't know he was still doing it until then. It could have jeopardized everything I'd worked for. It could have sent us to prison. And for what? The seafood fraud was bad enough, but it was profitable."

"You know why," I said.

He hung his head.

I remembered something Sally had said—her son had been a proponent of local seafood. "Did Billy find out?"

"I don't know. I didn't kill him, if that's what you're suggesting. I thought Lane did."

Nik lifted her head. "If Lane worked for Vince, would she kill someone because he asked her to?"

Eric shrugged. "Vince is the best kind of drug. And the worst."

I thought about drugs and why people did them. "What happened to Lane?"

Eric mashed his lips together.

"You don't get to plead the fifth on Charley's couch." I put the gun barrel on his forehead. "Talk."

Nik sucked in oxygen, but didn't tell me to stop.

"I don't know. Not for sure."

I pushed against his head with the gun. "Lane."

He held up his hands. "Okay. Vince fucked her. I only know because he told me about it. Proud of himself. Told me all the kinky shit she was willing to do for him, like I wasn't good enough for him. Hell, that's—"

"Did he rape her?"

His eyes widened and his mouth worked silently.

I grabbed his throat and bounced the back of his head against the drywall, shoved the gun barrel into his eye socket.

Nik screamed.

"Did he?"

He gagged, sputtered, croaked out a no.

I loosened my grip slightly.

"I don't think so." He coughed, swallowed with a wince. "He acted like she wanted it, wanted him. Around that time is when he killed Charley's boyfriend."

"When?"

He shook his head.

I pushed against the gun, could feel his eye's resistance.

"Davis!" Nik yelled, her voice on the verge of anguish.

"Two years ago! Maybe less. Look, she was already messed up when she got to him. Girls like her, they don't find a guy like Vince by accident. They find him because they're running from something. Because they want something to dull the pain."

I grabbed his greasy hair and yanked his head backward, shoved the gun barrel up under his chin. "What happened to her?"

He shook his head as best he could. Tears leaked out of his shut eyes.

Nik sobbed beside me. "Davis! Please! Stop."

I took a deep breath and stepped back, lowered the Beretta.

He shook his head, eyes still closed. "I don't know."

I handed Nik the .22 from my purse and headed for the door.

"Where the hell are you going?"

"You can't leave me here." Eric jumped up.

Nik swung the .22 and caught him on the chin with it.

He lost his balance and sat heavily.

In the car, Nik looked at me. "You're an asshole."

"Yeah," I agreed.

"That's no way to get information."

"I know."

"I'm not leaving." She stated it simply. Like it was fact.

"Nik, these people are dangerous."

"Which is why I'm staying. Someone's going to have to identify

you at the morgue. Someone's going to have to keep Charley clean.
Someone's going to have to talk to Lane's attorney."

"It all fell apart."

"We've been unraveling a long time. What are you going to do?

"Nik, if shit goes down, promise me. You do you. Let me do me."

"What the fuck does that even mean?"

"Let me take the hits. Let me take the bullets. Just pick up the
pieces and run."

"And if there's nothing left?"

"Lane's going to prison. Charley's going to end up with a hot shot
or the sharp end of a blade. I'm tired of trying to stop her. I'm tired."

"And if he kills you?"

"You really want to count up all the times I should've died before
now? Because I lost count, Nik." I handed her the Beretta. "I'm done
with this."

My phone vibrated in my pocket as I got to the end of the street.
I pulled it out and looked at the screen. Lawson. I looked at her and
answered.

"You've lost it," Nik whispered.

"I don't know how to say this." But he did. "Lane attempted
suicide. She's being treated at Carteret General."

"What?"

His voice said he thought this was as routine as a continuance and
just as benign. "Tried to choke herself with a sweatshirt. She's being
treated. They'll probably get her some anti-depressants. This sort of
thing is fairly common in the jails. It'll be okay."

"No, it won't." I hung up.

Nik watched me. Her expression was already etched with worry
and fear. I turned onto the highway and made it worse by telling her
what Lawson had said.

When I looked at her again, her eyes held a steady resolve I hadn't
seen in years. We were all just moments from the people we'd learned to
be as children. And Nik and I had learned to be survivors in more ways
than one.

Outside, the wind was picking up, the sky ominous above the tree
line. Storm smells hung in the air. This would be no summer shower.
No cleansing rain to relieve plants and people of the heat. What was
coming would be cold and punishing.

CHAPTER FIFTY-THREE

We were halfway to the hospital and the sky hung heavy with big, fat, angry puffs of gray that matched my mood and threatened to put another layer of water between my eyes and the road.

At the light, when I could see the brick structure off to my left, my phone rang again. I answered without looking.

"Davis? You okay?" Craig.

"Yes. No." I stared at the light, willing it to change.

"I haven't heard from you since… Look, I know I'm not supposed to be worried, but are you okay?"

The light finally changed and I made the turn. "No. Just no."

"Davis, what's going on?"

I told him. I told him everything. A lump formed in my throat. The light changed and I willed myself around the corner. "I gotta go. I'll call you later."

"I have an emergency call over in Beaufort. Heater's busted and it looks like a storm. Call me, though. Anytime."

I parked and dialed Lawson. "I need to get in to talk to her."

"She's still technically in custody. She's still—"

"Yeah, I didn't ask for your legal opinion. I need to talk to her. You need me to talk to her. Figure out how to make it happen. Otherwise you're going to be defending me too after I steal scrubs and an ID."

He sighed into the phone. "Dick said you were a bitchy pain in the ass."

"I know. Those are my good qualities."

"I'll meet you at the hospital."

Nik didn't question me when I left her in the lobby. She always knew when not to.

I hung out near the entrance long enough to inhale a lot of secondhand smoke and collect a few names of patients. The one that seemed most likely, an elderly woman with Alzheimer's and few kids, I used to get in as a visitor. Once in, I roamed corridors until I stumbled upon a wing and a floor that seemed promising and started looking for a room with officers posted outside.

Lawson called from downstairs while I was slathering makeup over my recent bruises and unbuttoning my shirt so my bra showed. "You're my assistant. You need to act like an assistant. Can you do that?"

"Yes sir, Mr. Lawson," I said in my best fifties cartoon secretary voice.

He gave me the room number and told me he'd wait for me by the elevator on that floor. He sounded like he was fighting the urge to drink.

I met him at the elevator, hair fluffed, chest puffed. "How do you do, Mr. Lawson?" I smiled a smile I didn't feel and held out my hand.

He was dressed in jeans and a surf tee shirt under a navy blazer. He didn't look happy. "You drive Dick nuts, don't you?"

I pulled out the gift shop legal pad and reading glasses out of my purse and winked.

He led the way down the hall. "I know you tried, but you still look like crap."

Lane was handcuffed to the bed. She a black eye, and dark bruises around her neck that looked hand-shaped.

Lawson made nice with the deputy, explained the whole attorney-client confidentiality stuff with his generous smile and handshake and a healthy dose of lawyer slime. I overheard something about drafting and competency and hearings. I wasn't really paying attention because I was watching Lane's face as she sorted through the new development.

Lawson shut the door and walked over, mouth open ready to speak.

I cut him off and turned on Lane. "What happened?"

She looked from Lawson to me and glared.

"He's your attorney, Lane. You need to start talking. Soon would be good. Those bruises don't look self-inflicted."

"I hate you." She curled her lips. Perfect imitation of a teenager. Wouldn't help her in adult court. Assuming she made it that far.

I crossed the room and got in her face. "Yeah, you hate me, Charley hates me. I should be dead. I got it. It's not going to stop me from trying to help you. Talk."

She swallowed, winced like it hurt. "I'm pregnant."

I sat on the edge of the bed. "Whose?"

She picked at the blanket. The handcuffs rattled against the plastic bed. "It wasn't my fault. You don't have to believe me, but it wasn't."

I looked over into her eyes. "Let me make a guess here. Hear me out. One of Charley's boyfriends or johns or stray drug dealers molested you. Maybe not the one I scared off with a knife. Maybe not even the next one to come around. Maybe he touched you. Maybe he raped you. Either way, it was wrong. Either way, how you felt was how you felt. But you couldn't tell anyone. Couldn't tell Charley. She'd throw you out and tell people you were dead like she did me. Couldn't tell Nik because she lived too far away. Couldn't tell the school because you'd end up in foster care and we'd instilled a lifelong fear of foster care."

Her eyes looked to Lawson, narrowed at me. "What the fuck do you know?"

"A lot. Especially about this. More than I should. More than either of us should. Some other time, I'll give you the whole speech about how it's not your fault and how blah blah blah. The bottom line is, I've been there."

She shook her head. "You don't know shit. You weren't there. You left."

I pulled aside the top of my shirt, showed her the long white scar running away from my collarbone. "The guy who did this didn't touch me. Some other guys did. The scars on the outside don't always match the hurt on the inside."

She sniffed at the window, still not buying it.

"So, you did something to try to make the hurt go away. Based on your friends' hobbies, I'm going to guess drugs. Very traditional. You guys probably didn't talk about all your whys. Talking makes it too real."

"Fuck you."

"Along came promiscuity. Had to prove to yourself you were over it, didn't care."

She swallowed again and winced.

I took a deep breath. "Except, it didn't go away. Except, you didn't really feel any more in control. Except someone misunderstood your intentions, took things too far. You lost control again. And then you felt worse than ever."

Her eyes glared, but her jaw was trying not to cry. "Fuck you."

"You felt worse because you thought this time you were to blame. You played with proverbial fire, right? No one would sympathize when you burnt yourself. So you put a cork on the pain. But your anger? It didn't die and it didn't like being bottled up and you weren't just angry at him, but yourself. So you got more self-destructive. Did things you knew you shouldn't, terrible things to hurt others because you didn't want to feel alone with all that pain."

"Shut up!" She squeezed her eyes shut and I could see the colors of the shiner spread out, layered atop one another. "Just shut up." Her chest shuddered with sobs.

I looked at Lawson and let my own tears go, felt them tumble down my face, bounce off my cheeks, leaving streaks in the makeup.

He started to speak. I shook my head.

I put a hand on hers, waited for her to jerk away, but she didn't.

"I didn't do it. I didn't mean to do it." She sucked up snot and let a breathy sob. "He was my best friend." Her face crumbled and she sagged against the bed.

"What happened, Lane?"

She shook her head. "I'm gonna go to jail. For like ever. And Billy's dead and Amber's probably already dead. And it's all your fault."

"I know," I said.

"I made those girls. I was in charge." She pointed at her chest with her free hand and I noticed the tattoo again. Orange and black with claws. "I thought I could handle it all."

"You belonged to Vince." I'd known girls who'd been converted to property. They were often tattooed with a name or symbol, branded like cattle.

"He took care of us. Which is more than I can say for you or Charley."

"Only as long as you did what he said."

Her face fought with the tears. "How do you know? How did you know?"

"Because I've gotten into fights I knew I couldn't win just so there'd be a reason my guts ached. Because I've been locked up with girls who thought they knew what they were doing. Because I always thought I did."

She mashed her lips together. They were cracked and tear-stained. "Charley went nuts."

"I'm sorry."

"It was all because of you. But then she really lost it."

"You needed a new home. You needed to feel wanted."

Lawson grabbed the legal pad from my lap and started scribbling. I wasn't sure what he was thinking, but I had a feeling the shitstorm was growing.

"He wanted us to kill Billy. I didn't want to, but you don't go against Vince. He said Billy was going to betray us. Amber had miscarried, blamed Billy. She stabbed him. He grabbed the gun. It went off." She squeezed her eyes shut and shook her head.

"What happened to Melissa Armstrong?"

Lane opened her eyes and snarled. "That girl with the purses? She didn't want to work. Thought she was too good. Said she was going home. Vince said that wasn't an option. Told us to get her out to sea and let Brad take care of her."

"That didn't ever seem like a bad idea?"

"She got in over her head. You don't tell Vince no. Shit happens." She shrugged and the handcuffs rattled.

Lawson looked up from his paper, trying to keep the look of horror off his face and doing a bad job.

I wanted to be horrified. I wanted to stare, mouth gaping, but I couldn't. My own moral ground was shaky at best. "Why didn't you call me? Before all this?"

"Charley said you hated us, that you left because you couldn't stand to look at us. You never called or visited." She shrugged again. "I lived at Amber's for a while. Sylvia's. Ricky used to hook Charley up with dope. Vince had better stuff. It just came with a price tag."

"Always does."

"Don't look so sanctimonious. I know all about the shit you've done."

"From Charley? Or from Vince?"

Her look said both.

"I've done stuff much worse than anything they've said, but they don't know anything about it." I thought about the things she'd done. "Why'd Billy load the gun?"

She sniffed. "He and I used to go shoot it in the woods sometimes. For kicks, you know."

"How'd Amber get out of there?" Lawson asked.

"I don't know. Her cousin showed up. Knocked me out."

"Murphy?"

She made a face like she'd eaten a turd. "Yeah."

Lawson let out a low whistle and looked at me. "Think we should angle for a plea?"

I had no idea. I handed him Tom's contact info. "If anything happens to me, get what you need from him."

He looked at the business card. "I'm gonna kill Dick."

CHAPTER FIFTY-FOUR

In the lobby, I checked my phone to find a message waiting. Craig.

"It's weird. There's no one answering at this house I was supposed to be at. Guess I'll head over to the hospital and meet up with you. Maybe talk you into some food at the cafeteria. They make a mean mac and cheese."

I looked at Nik. "She's alive. Go meet Lawson. See if you can talk to her." I gritted my teeth, not sure how much to tell her yet. "Look, Lane's done some shit she really shouldn't have. You gotta forgive her."

"You're not gonna tell me, are you?"

"Not yet. Call Tom if you need to." I rattled off his number. "Don't go anywhere else. Seriously. I'll see you later."

"Where are you going?"

"I gotta make a phone call."

She gave me a face that said the phone worked fine there.

"And I gotta think."

She tilted her head like she knew what that meant. "Stay safe."

I called Craig from the parking lot. He didn't answer. I put the rental in gear and headed east.

Craig called back as I waited at an intersection. "I just got pulled over leaving Beaufort. Still want to meet up?"

"Since when do you speed, Craig?" I got in the eastbound lane.

He was quiet a minute. "I think Charley's house is on fire."

"Excuse me?"

"It was on the fire-rescue channel."

"Who pulled you over? What were you doing?" My bad-things-are-coming senses were working overtime.

"I don't know. Guy's checking my license. Why?"

"You weren't speeding? Swerving?"

"No, Davis. What's going on?"

"Get out of there. Just get the hell out of there. Don't stop to get the license. Just go." I picked up speed heading toward him. Rain started, fat drops hitting faster and heavier.

"Davis, don't be ridiculous." His tone changed. He had seen something. I heard him put down the window and the guy tell him to put down the phone. Craig didn't hang up, just set the phone down. Then I heard the guy ask him to step out of the car.

I floored the rental. I wasn't sure what I thought I was going to do. I wasn't sure what was happening, but as I listened to the guy arrest Craig without mentioning a specific charge, I knew I was about to get my prom date killed.

The wind buffeted the car going over the high-rise bridge. The rain blew horizontal. The rental car said the outside temperature was in the low thirties. And night had fallen as I raced through Morehead.

When I saw the lights in my rearview mirror, I wasn't surprised. We were on the causeway, between towns, but close to both. And I was indeed speeding.

The rental car's tires sank in the icy mud as I turned off the asphalt and the windshield wipers tried to clear the sleet-rain mixture from the darkness ahead of me.

I called Tom, put the phone on speaker and set the phone upside down in the notch under the radio.

The cop got out, a bright yellow slicker flapping behind him like something out of horror flick.

I sat and watched him in the rearview and the side mirror. When Tom answered, I said, "Don't talk. Just listen carefully. Record if you can. Won't hold up in court but it may not need to." I rattled off a location.

I put the window down and glanced up, offering innocence and a willingness to cooperate. He was already pointing his gun at me. "Get out."

"Officer, what is this about? Was I speeding?" Sweetness.

"Get out. Now."

I hadn't been arrested since I was thirteen. Not really. I stepped out cautiously. By the time I was half-standing, I was drenched and shivering.

He grabbed my arm and twisted me, slipped on the first handcuff quickly like he'd been practicing. I could've stopped him, but I'd have ended up full of bullets and bleeding out in the rain. I was tired of bleeding in winter.

He banged me into the side of the car.

I shouted, not because it was hard to hear, but because the window was still open. "You can't arrest me for speeding. I wasn't even going that fast. That bridge is huge. It's not my car. I can't be responsible for rentals. It's raining."

He leaned in close. "Nothing personal."

"What's not personal? What the hell? Where are you taking me?" I twisted enough to catch his nametag through the gap in his slicker. "Fuck you, Murphy."

He marched me toward his car, my opportunity to feed Tom more information lost. He tossed me into the back seat and climbed behind the wheel. "It's not what you think." He turned in the seat so he could get a better view of me, sprawled and wiggling into an upright position. "I don't want to be doing this."

I planted my feet on the floor and righted myself. Ordinarily, sitting on handcuffed hands was uncomfortable, but my hands were so cold and numb I barely noticed.

"I'm sorry. You have to understand. I just don't do things like this." He wiped his face and looked weary. "You should know I didn't mean your sister any harm when I arrested her. I had to. She was there. She was covered in blood. What did you expect me to do?"

"And the other girl there?"

"I'm sorry." He started the engine.

I kicked the partition. Hard. Hard enough to hurt my teeth. "If you're carting me off to get executed, you owe me answers."

"I'm sorry."

I looked around at the doors, the windows. All standard police fare. No handles to grab. No cracks in the seats big enough to find hidden weapons. I kicked the partition again. "Talk to me!" I angled myself so I could kick the Plexiglas. Having my hands under my ass gave me enough leverage to kick it where it had been bolted to the metal partition.

"I have to."

"Who called you that night? Amber or Vince?" I kicked again, both feet.

His answer was quiet, so quiet I almost didn't hear him with the storm raging outside. "I was told to wait nearby."

I kicked and kicked. "Where the hell is Craig Silvano?"

"Who?"

I leaned sideways and twisted around for a different angle. "The guy you kidnapped earlier this evening. The one your little puppet masters told you to grab like you did me." I kicked the window. The glass spider-webbed but didn't shatter completely. "The innocent father you plan to murder if you haven't already." I kicked again and the pane turned to confetti. Cold, wet wind whipped into the back seat.

He slowed. "It wasn't like I wanted to."

"Fuck you and your fucking conscience."

"We were gonna lose the house." He had to say it louder than he wanted to because of the wind and rain now swirling into the car. Outside, thunder and lightning fought the sky for airtime.

I sat up, so I could scream near his ear. "Live in an apartment. You don't murder people over the fucking mortgage."

He gripped the steering wheel. Ten and two, like a good boy. He had great posture for someone who claimed he was doing things under duress. "I can't let my kids be homeless."

"It builds character." I rolled and kicked out the other window. When I sat up again, I positioned myself in front of the rearview mirror. I noticed I'd managed to crack the Plexiglas where it was bolted to the metal partition. Another weakness to exploit.

"How can you say that?"

"Because living in a car didn't kill me." I kicked. "Apparently you thought that was your right." I kicked.

He stopped at a light.

I could've gotten out. I didn't. I needed to know where Craig was.

"Where the fuck is Craig?"

He turned and looked at me, his face etched with worry by the dull glow of the street and dashboard lights.

"Why take *him*? He's not part of this." I kicked the partition.

Murphy was silent.

"Where?" I kicked and watched the tiny spider web crack grow.

He hit the dashboard with his fist. "Dammit!"

I rolled into my back, straightened my legs in front of my face and slipped the cuffs over my butt. Sat up and pounded the Plexiglas with the sides of my fists.

He was young. He didn't deserve what had happened to his family.

He didn't deserve what I was doing to him. I didn't deserve any of it either. It just was.

The Plexiglas began to give. My hands were bleeding. My wrists were bruised and circled with grooves and cuts. I kept pounding.

He opened his door. Opened mine. Grabbed my shoulder and dragged me out into the rain. We were both already soaked. Both shivering, but maybe neither of us from the weather.

"Why?" His face was next to mine. I could've pulled his gun and shot him. I could have kneed him in the balls. I could've broken his nose with my forehead.

I stared at the tears in his eyes.

He went for his gun.

I bent, hit him in the gut with my shoulder.

We landed on the median, skidded in the icy rain into the oncoming lanes, but we were the only ones on the road. The area too rural. The weather too rough.

He pulled the gun free, managed to shoot his own window out of the car.

I bit his hand, sank my teeth deep into his tendons using my hands to hold his arm somewhat steady.

He grabbed my neck with his free hand, squeezed until I saw spots.

I couldn't breathe, couldn't swallow. I couldn't keep my grip on his hand. I pulled the cuffs up, wrapped them around his arm and tried to tighten them as the world went black.

CHAPTER FIFTY-FIVE

I woke up in the trunk. It was warmer than the backseat, but that was my own fault for kicking out the windows during a nor'easter. The trunk was sturdier than the backseat, but my hands were still in front of me.

I found the taillights. Took what seemed like forever, but I found one and kicked it out. It was black, wet and freezing outside.

Under the spare tire I found the tire iron, but couldn't pull it free without getting the handcuffs caught on something. Every time I yanked on the tire iron, the cuffs dug deeper into my wrists. I should have been in pain, but I was too cold and too angry to feel more than the dullest ache.

The car stopped and I fell forward, hitting my head on a random metal piece of car. I struggled to prop myself up again, to roll over, and to finally pull the tire iron free. I settled for one of three as the trunk popped open.

Vince stared down with a flashlight in one hand and a dark, long-barreled handgun in the other. "Hi, Davis. So nice to see you again."

He backed up and motioned for someone else to grab the handcuffs and yank me out. I kicked him in the crotch and took off running into the darkness.

The bullet hit me in the back of the left thigh, high, almost my ass. It was a fluke, a lucky shot out of the half-dozen he made. I tumbled, skidding in the mud until a rock stopped my face. It sliced open my forehead and tore out a chunk of eyebrow.

I lay still. Mud in my eye, left pinky twisted backward from the fall. Waited as male voices echoed in the air.

"Get him out of there."

"What the fuck is this shit?"

"Hold him."

I could barely make out words in the pounding rain.

The next gunshot was singular.

My heart stopped, but not because the bullet had hit me.

I wanted to stay there, pretending to be dead, hoping they'd think I was. I knew I'd roll over to find out who'd they'd shot. I knew it wasn't over.

I took a deep breath, willed myself to ignore the pain, the fear, the baggage. I closed my eyes and took in a long, slow, slightly muddy breath and sent it to my fingers and toes and aches. I let it out slowly, bubbling the puddle under me, releasing everything but my will to survive long enough to take some of them down with me.

Then I rolled over.

CHAPTER FIFTY-SIX

Craig stood next to a younger version of Rayford Jackson, staring at the ground. On the ground would be Murphy. I couldn't see him, but I knew. Craig, even from a distance, looked terrified.

I pulled myself into a sitting and then standing position. My left leg refused to work properly, but I convinced it to at least support the rest of me long enough to hop my right leg forward.

They couldn't see me yet. Couldn't hear me.

Vince pointed his gun at Craig's chest.

"No!" In my head, the noise was a roar, but what came out couldn't make it past the rain and wind.

Vince pulled the trigger. Craig stared at the hole, high on the right, and sank to his knees. Vince aimed, pressing the long barrel to Craig's forehead. My immediate thought was selfish: everyone who cared about me died.

I swallowed my pain, the raw emotion clawing at my throat, and stopped in my tracks. "You think you've broken me?" My voice came from some rage-filled part of me that rarely saw anything but the inside of a gym or a dojo. "Leave him alone! You wanna dance, motherfucker? Come dance! You promised to fuck me up, right? I'm still standing, you sonofabitch!"

Barely standing, maybe, but he couldn't make out the wobble in my stance from where he stood. My heart thudded in my ears and my breath kept catching on the way in.

Craig turned his head to look at me, but I couldn't make out his expression. He sank to his knees and fell forward. My heart sank into the mud with him.

I had nothing left to lose.

I took another hop-step toward Vince and Tanner, my leg a strange mix of fire and ice. "What are you waiting for? You killed him, right? Big boys. Killing unarmed men. You should be so proud." The only thing keeping me upright was adrenaline and anger. I was sure of it.

Maybe too sure. Training maybe helped.

Phil's voice in my head telling me I wasn't done yet. My sparring buddy, Franco, taunting me to push harder.

The two men I'd let push me, punish me on purpose, when we sparred, trained.

Vince motioned for Tanner Jackson to stay by the car, walked toward me. At first I thought he'd just shoot me like he had the other two, but as he got closer, his face betrayed him. He stepped in with a single blow. I blocked it as best I could, but my arms were inefficient as a team. The gun collided with my cheek and pain exploded in my head.

CHAPTER FIFTY-SEVEN

I came to as we boarded a boat. My head ached like a bad hangover. My face felt swollen, disconnected. My legs didn't work right so they dragged me over the side, banging my shins on the cleats. I kept my eyes shut and fought the urge to vomit.

They dropped me on the deck. Footsteps walked away.

"I got this, boss."

Hands unbuttoned my jeans.

Panic rose from my toes and blossomed in my head. Memories banged on the bars I'd hidden them behind.

Rough hands yanked my jeans over the wound in my thigh, let them catch on my boots, and left them there.

You were a whore for years. You want to get upset about this now? Phil.

Get up. Fight them. Franco.

Hands grabbed the front of my shirt near my throat. A knife slipped under my collar and down the length of my shirt. When the knife reached the bottom, I jerked my hands up, wrapped the handcuff chain around his wrists and rolled to plant my knees in his ribcage. I turned my wrists, my arms, until the knife pointed away from me and bucked upward, using my body to force the blade in to the hilt.

My feet kicked frantically at the boots and pants but couldn't seem to break free of the laces.

The face over me belonged to a younger version of Rayford. It held fear and pain, but also surprise. Mine must have bordered on animalistic, a lumpy mask of purple and red.

I jerked one foot free, rolled, and wrapped my right leg around his neck, followed him over until I was looking down at him. I tightened my grip on his neck and pulled out the knife. His arms grabbed my elbow, tried to push me off. I brought the knife down into his chest, where he'd have pledged allegiance. Yanked it out and brought it down again between his collarbone and neck.

I watched the light go out of his eyes and felt the weight of what I'd done hit me. Felt the cuts on my arms and hands, felt the thick wound to the muscles across my stomach.

A hand yanked me backward by my hair.

"Dammit, bitch." He hurled me around into the wall of the cabin. It wasn't hard. I was cold, bloody and broken. I tripped over the pants hanging from my left leg, which still leaked blood.

"Always in everyone else's business. Always where no one wants you."

I tugged my hands against the cuffs. The metal dug into my skin, ripped at the flesh. I pulled harder.

"Just give up. Give in."

"Never."

He smiled. "Good. Don't make it easy. Let me tear you down slowly."

He held a pistol, what looked too much like a SIG Sauer P226, at his side. Uncle Phil's missing gun. My missing gun. He held it out slightly and fired three times at the deck. Two kicked up splinters near my bare feet; one took off my smallest toe before hitting the wood below.

"Ah, saw you flinch." He grinned.

My ears rang. "Did you kill Eric?"

"Eh. It's tragic to lose a lover like that. But he was weak. Couldn't handle changes in the business model."

"Why hurt Charley? Why bother?"

"Men always want to protect their women, daughters, wives. They'll do anything you ask if you threaten the people they want to protect." He leered at me. "Women? They won't even fight to save their own kids."

"You had Charley confused with a mother?"

He held up a small, white pill. "I suppose you recognize this? Well, maybe not. GHB and ketamine are easier to spike coffee with."

"Why? Look at me. You need drugs to kill me?"

"I still hear your spirit. I want to hear it break."

Don't panic.

Kill him.

He rested the barrel of the pistol on my nose, on a bruise I didn't remember, and left a burn. "Open wide."

I shook my head slightly, my own actions earlier that day not lost on me.

"Oh, you'll take it. And then we'll have some fun, you and I. Or, maybe just me."

Run.

Fight.

"Ah, maybe you're thinking you've been here before. That I can't teach you anything new. But that's the point, isn't it? You need everything to be on your terms. You need to be in control."

I stared at him, evaluated which parts of my body could still respond to commands. Which parts of him were vulnerable and within reach.

"Even now, you're thinking you're strong enough."

He leaned into the gun, pushing my crooked cartilage until it gave. Pain erupted in my face and I cried out involuntarily.

His hand slipped past my lips, my teeth, like I was a dog in need of heartworm medication. His fingers shoved the pill into my throat.

I bit, clamped down on his fingers.

He jerked free, hard enough to dislodge a tooth. His stance shifted.

I stepped to the side, brought my arms up and hit his forearm with mine. The gun discharged. The bullet tore through the top of my ear. I kneed him in the crotch, nearly blacked out, kept the gun off to the side as best I could.

Standing wasn't where I was strongest. I wrapped my injured leg around his, tangled him and toppled him backward. His head bounced off the deck, my elbow came down into his sternum.

He tried to lift the gun. I grabbed his hand and torqued his wrist. His finger, jammed inside the trigger guard, squeezed off a wild shot. His finger broke. I pulled, off-balance, and fell back, the gun still in my grip.

The muscle in my thigh stretched as I fell. Agony-induced nausea roiled my system and I fought the urge to black out.

Vince pulled himself out from under me, placed a hand on my naked thigh, his thumb over the exit wound.

I spun the pistol in my hands and got the deadly end of it pointing at him.

He jammed his thumb into the hole.

I screamed and pulled the trigger.

CHAPTER FIFTY-EIGHT

The urge to vomit hit again, but when I tried, I failed.

I managed to drag myself out from under Vince before the pill started taking effect. It had been maybe five minutes, no more, but the adrenaline rush could have accelerated it. Or, maybe it wasn't the pill making me feel woozy and drunk, but rather the blood loss and overwhelming agony.

The boat had a flare gun mounted to the wall with the instruments. I changed channels on the radio until I heard voices. What sounded like the local rescue squad responding to a traffic accident near Otway.

Otway. Downeast. I was so far from a hospital. Maybe as far as Jimmy had been.

I hit the talk button. "Help? Please. Help."

No answer.

"If you can hear me and you know Craig Silvano, please go find him. Please save him if you can. He's been shot."

"Ma'am, who is this? Come back."

"I'm on a boat. I think Craig was in the yard. With a deputy." My eyes felt heavy. "I don't know where I am. Eric Wright might own the place. Or Vince Zellner."

I hobbled outside the cabin and fired the flare. I needed to get to a road, flag someone down. I needed to find help before I passed out.

I drank the coffee and made small talk while the bill arrived. He smiled too much, encouraged me to finish the coffee before we left. Made small talk about sports with the waiter.

I stumbled off the boat and onto the dock, narrowly avoiding landing in the water instead. My legs gave out. I pulled off a tattered piece of shirt and tied it around my leg. Used the wooden slats to pull myself forward. Found a broken piece of pottery and gripped it as I pulled myself along the grass.

My coordination failed. My vision blurred. My eyelids drooped for longer and longer. Every time I snapped back, I dragged the filthy ceramic along the inside of my forearm. The pain brought me back, but briefly. I decided not to think about the effect the blood loss was having.

I reached the cop car in the driveway on the verge of consciousness. I knew I wouldn't remember more than flashes later.

The dash color in the car.

The street sign near the restaurant.

The texture of the couch.

The look on Ryan's face.

My ruined fingers pawed at Craig's neck, begging the universe for a pulse. "You have to be okay," I whispered to him. "If I'm still moving, you have to be okay."

Murphy lay next to him, cloudy eyes staring sightlessly at the cloudy sky. His gun still at his side with his phone. I pulled the phone loose and pressed the emergency button. Put my head on Craig's pelvis while I waiting for an answer.

"Officer down." I set the phone next to me and let my eyes slide closed.

CHAPTER FIFTY-NINE
Tuesday, February 14

I don't believe in miracles. Miracles are for people who overcome near-fatal diseases. Miracles are for kids who think some deity's helping Santa deliver gifts. Miracles are unicorn poop.

They're also waking up after being shot and left for dead—again. It's probable I should start believing in miracles, or at least unicorn poop. Maybe after more surgery and rehab to relearn using parts that worked fine before. Maybe after the nightmares passed.

I woke with tubes sticking out of my nose, my throat, my hand.

Nik sat on an orange plastic chair staring at me. She looked like she'd been there awhile. I wanted to ask her if Lane was okay, if she was really there.

She stood. "You still can't talk. Tomorrow maybe. Tomorrow's Wednesday."

I nodded.

"I won't yell at you until you can yell back." She pointed at the contraptions.

I nodded.

"Does it hurt?"

Everything everywhere hurt, but I didn't want to tell Nik that. I shook my head slightly.

"Liar." She wrung her hands and scrunched her face. "They were sure you wouldn't make it. You didn't for a minute." She looked mad about it. "Stubborn."

I nodded.

"How? Davis, how did…?" She mashed her lips together.

I had the same question. How, indeed.

"Tom's nice."

I nodded again. My eyelids felt heavy.

Nik stood. "I can't do this right now. I just can't." She left.

I fell asleep.

Friday, February 17

My hands didn't work so great because of the bandages and splints, one on my left pinky finger and one on my right thumb. I pulled off as many bandages and I could using my teeth. My face hurt. My hands hurt. My hands I could stare at, see the hurt. Stitches crisscrossed old scars and I could guess where they'd later tingle or register only numbness or pressure.

My left arm was fitted with casts and hinges such that it looked like I'd stolen it from a fifties robot. I didn't remember breaking it.

Cindy, the physical therapist I'd insulted the day before, popped in while I was staring at the mess of surgical tape and stitches around the GSW. I was thinking it was pretty in a grotesque sort of way, all the different colors and patterns.

She must've thought I was thinking something else. She ambled closer, giving me a tentative smile. "It's going to heal up just fine." She didn't even chastise me for ripping the hospital gown.

I nodded because that seemed like better than my usual responses. "When are we going to walk?"

"Well, you have a broken leg, quite a bit of muscle damage." She smiled, changing gears. "I actually came by to see if we could reschedule for later. There's an FBI agent wants to talk to you. Doc wants you to talk to the hospital psychiatrist first, make sure you're up to it and all. Formality, I'm sure."

"I don't need a shrink." My voice sounded gravely.

She kept the grin. "I don't believe it was an option. The hospital feels it's in the best interest of the patient in situations like this that we make sure your total well-being is considered."

She sounded like a fucking brochure.

"Just what kind of 'situation' am I in?"

"We find that patients who almost die in surgery, patients who… Well, just that they need someone to talk to." She pulled the blanket up to my chin, covering the wounds I'd been looking at.

I wanted to tell her it was fine. It was okay. I wanted to reassure her. I knew from experience with Nik that wasn't likely.

"They did a kit."

I nodded. "They won't find anything." That certainly wouldn't help my defense.

"They found flunitrazepam—Rohypnol—in the tox screen."
"I know."

The hospital shrink was busy and young, likely fresh out of school and doing some sort of rotation before moving on to a private office in the suburbs. She wore khaki slacks and a tight pink sweater, from which she pulled loose brown hairs as she walked in.

I watched her open a manila folder, study the contents quickly and smile broadly. "I'm Sandy."

Sandy. Cindy. Seriously? "Davis."

"How are you feeling today?"

"Can we just cut to the chase? I feel fine. I mean, mentally, fine. Physically, I feel like I got shot and beat up, but that'll heal and then I'll be fine."

"You know if there's anything you want to talk about, anything you tell me is completely confidential."

"Just tell me what to sign."

Tom opened the door with a blonde in tow. The blonde introduced herself as Special Agent Martha Stewart and dared me to laugh at that.

Laughing hurt, so I stuck to nodding.

"The boat offshore? You do that?"

"I need a lawyer?"

She shook her coif and looked like she needed a cigarette. "Don't give me that. I have DNA, witnesses who saw you drag your ass onshore."

I thought about telling her I could find witnesses who'd seen her bake a cake, but decided against it.

"Up to the prosecutor. You took away part of her payday killing Zellner and Wright."

"I didn't kill Wright."

"So you admit to killing Zellner. Your gun killed both of them, you know."

Tom buried his face in his hands. "I'm going to get Lawson."

"I left a whole lot of DNA there, too, you want to go all *CSI* on me." I glared at her even though my face was probably still too puffy to pull it off.

"There's also a destroyed police car, a dead officer—"

"What about Craig Silvano?"

She mashed her already-lipless gums together.

"I'll wait for that lawyer."

"You know that just makes you look guilty."

I stared at her, watched her fingers. "You planning to quit smoking?"

"Tanner Jackson. He worked the night shift at a packing plant."

Rayford's kid.

"You buried a knife in his carotid. Takes a lot of strength and a lot of hate to do that."

"Or fear," I said.

"Silvano's alive. Awake. We'll see if he backs your story." She flicked an imaginary cigarette and left.

CHAPTER SIXTY
Friday, March 17

Lawson got himself a team. The team set to work drafting things, getting evidence independently analyzed, asking me a lot of questions about what I did and didn't do, why Charley's house was a pile of ashes, why Wright's body was in the ashes.

A plastic surgeon explained how he planned to repair my face—broken bones, lacerations, burns from the shot that tore a hole in my ear—and my leg and my hand. Again. He told me there was nothing he could do about the toe or the ear. I didn't care.

Cindy kept my mind off all that by trying to keep me from pushing myself back into intensive care and convinced me to get my arm working again slowly instead of punching the wall until I broke something else.

The nurses ensured I weaned myself off the morphine slowly rather than my cold turkey plan of yanking all the tubes out as soon as the swelling went down enough to grasp stuff. They still couldn't talk me into the pills. I spit them out, threw them away.

I needed to be in agony. I deserved it. And the physical torture almost kept the torment in my head and heart in check. Almost.

Nik wandered in and out, looking alternately forlorn and pissed. She sat on the bed. Most of what she said involved updates on Charley's progress with rehab.

I said little, too. Lawson might keep me out of prison, but the best deal he'd been able to get for Lane had been twenty years. Part of that was my fault. I'd killed three of the people she might have testified against. Still, she'd killed Billy, whether she'd meant to or not. She'd helped kidnap Melissa Armstrong, which made her legally responsible for the girl's death. She'd hurt too many others. She'd earned the time.

I missed her sentencing, but Nik said her eyes had looked dead.

"She won't come out the way she went in."

Nik wrung her hands. "Maybe that's good." She left before I could see her cry.

At some point I called Matt. He asked how I was. I decided to give him a taste of the truth. "I don't think we should see each other anymore."

"Is it someone else? You met someone up there?" He was quiet for a moment. "I know I haven't been the most attentive. I can do better."

I swallowed. "I just remembered who I am is all."

Eventually, the hospital discharged me. The various agencies told me not to go anywhere. I checked into a hotel across the intersection from the hospital, so I could get back easily for Cindy's therapy, and tried not to go stir crazy. Nik got a room on one side, and spent most of her time on the phone with professors, doing online research, writing her thesis and an article on a nesting swallow.

I was lost in my own head. I replayed the things I'd done. I replayed the things done to me. I wallowed, without the booze and pills Charley used. I was trapped without my usual coping mechanisms and I was coming apart. For all his efforts when alive, I feared Zellner had finally broken me now that he was dead.

Nik knocked on the door, stood in the chill, arms wrapped around her, looking unsure and almost skittish.

I leaned against the open door.

She took my arm, looked at my hand. The stitches were gone, but the scars still looked like angry reddish purple lines. "Put on shoes."

I looked around the room, not sure I owned shoes anymore. My duffel bag had been found in the rental car, but my boots were evidence. All I had were some fuzzy slippers from the hospital gift shop despite Cindy's insistence I wear sneakers to PT.

Nik looked at them, looked my leg, the crutches leaning against the doorframe. "Come on. We'll take the elevator."

At the elevator, she looked up at me. "Run."

"Excuse me?"

"Run, Davis. You've done it before. We've all done it. Just, this time, fake who you are. You've barely got any fingerprints left. Get a new identity. Go back to school. You're young. Study astrophysics or something. Just go."

She was crying, and seeing her tears, I couldn't stop my own.

"Just go. I got you some clothes. In the car. I rented it under my name, but you can dump it like we used to. Steal another. Keep going until you're clear."

I shook my head.

"I know what you did. All of it. I'm sorry. Let me do this to make it up to you."

"No. I ran alone once. I won't do it again. They want me to do time, I'll do time. You need me, I'll figure out how to be there."

She looked up at me, her eyes pleading. She was trying to tell me she'd been a big girl when I thought she wasn't. That she wasn't a vulnerable teenager or a drug addict. That she'd be okay if I split.

I shook my head, shuffled back to my room.

Lawson knocked the following afternoon. Agent Stewart was with him, looking pissed.

I left the door open and went back to sitting on the bed.

Lawson went directly to the windows and opened the blinds. Stewart stood in the doorway, hands on her hips, ready to pull her gun.

I gave her a look that I hope dared her, but wasn't sure I pulled it off.

Finally, Lawson sat on a chair. "We have a deal. We're waiting for the prosecutor. Normally, we'd do this at the office, but this is more convenient given the circumstances." He gestured at my leg and off in the direction of the hospital.

Stewart glanced at me like she wanted to pinch my head off and chewed her gum harder.

The prosecutor was a middle-aged woman stuffed into a power suit like a sausage. She introduced herself in a rush and I promptly forgot her name, her exact title, and to say hi back. Instead, I stared out the newly opened blinds.

"The same gun shot a commissioner, a deputy, a volunteer EMT, and a suspected trafficker. You fired it, but so did the trafficker," Sausage Woman said.

Lawson said, "They can't tie you to Wright because Murphy already had you and Silvano. Silvano stated Zellner had the Sig."

I didn't respond.

Lawson added, "They found some girls, younger than Lane, hanging out at Jackson's house, shooting up. Watching TV. They heard it all. Ignored it. Turned up the TV."

I kept staring out the window. The part of me that had lived my whole childhood outside the boundaries of normal and safe hoped they'd be okay. The part that had seen the look on Lane's face, had really listened to Nik for the first time in a long time, wasn't so sure.

"Ms. Groves, are you listening to me?"

"No."

"Do you think maybe you should?"

I looked as far as her strained jacket buttons and shrugged. Shrugging still hurt, but for new reasons.

"Are you okay, Ms. Groves? Have you taken anything?"

"Just tell me what you came to tell me."

Sausage Woman looked at Lawson. "You need to get your client some help."

He looked at her like she was an idiot.

Stewart had taken to lounging on the wall, still ready to shoot me if necessary.

I was sick of all of them. Their self-righteous stares. The false concern. The tiptoeing like I was a dying toddler. "You know what? Fuck you. You want to arrest me? Do it. If not, spit it out and get out."

Sausage Woman huffed and clasped her hands together just so. "I came to tell you we're clearing you of any charges."

I looked at the carpet. It seemed clean enough on the surface.

After the women left, Lawson pulled a chair across from me and sat. "She makes it sound generous, but they had no case. The evidence isn't clear-cut. Our side brings up roofies and the fact that you were nearly naked when they found you, there's no way a jury will convict you. Besides, your blood's all over the trunk of the deputy's car. No way that got there innocently."

I looked up.

"Craig's, too. Not as much, but it puts him there."

I nodded and looked at the carpet again. The whole time I'd been asking, Craig had been inches away. He'd live, but he'd made it clear he'd never talk to me again. It was just as well. I'd hurt him long before I'd gotten him shot.

"There's still a question of whether you should keep your concealed weapons permit. Other than that, you're free to go home."

Home.
I went back to staring out the window.

ACKNOWLEDGEMENTS

Books don't happen in a vacuum, though it feels that way when you're writing at 2am alone. This would not be remotely readable without the help of editor Elizabeth A. White and friends like Holly West, Thomas Pluck, Elizabeth Amber Love, and Josh Stallings. Early readers Joelle Charbonneau, Laura K. Curtis, and Andrew Thompson deserve thanks and an apology for having been subjected to such awful drafts.

So many other fabulous people have offered support, advice, a laugh, someone to walk with or hang out with, a shoulder, friendship, or necessary social media shenanigans. First off, I'm not sure anyone believes in me more than Keary Cunningham, despite all evidence he shouldn't. As for the numerous others, I am sure the following list is not complete, so please forgive me if you feel you've been forgotten:
Lisa and Wes Rider, Meredith Texeira, Skye Cleek, Gloria Smith, Vic and Barb Smith, Erin Mitchell, Hilary Davidson, Owen Laukkanen, Kent Gowran, Steve Weddle, Sabrina Ogden, Clare Toohey, Stephen Blackmoore, Ben Leroy, Todd Robinson, Bryon Quertermous, Jerry Bloomfield, Jen Conley, Ron Earl Phillips, David Cranmer, Alex Segura, Chris La Tray, Lauren Winters, Joshua Atkins, Elaine Ash, Joe Myers, Chris Holm and Kat Niidas Holm, Dan and Kate Malmon, Daniel O'Shea, Rhonda Hicks, EC Lamb, Michelle Isler, Charles and Dianne Cunningham, and so many others.

I'd also like to give a shout out and thanks to Judy Bobalik and the Crimespree Clan, Jon and Ruth, as well as all the other organizers and volunteers of Bouchercon where I've had the pleasure of meeting so many great people in person. (I'm not talking about the giant, drunken Ginger Ape.)

ABOUT THE AUTHOR

Neliza Drew used to write ad copy before turning to crime (fiction). She spent more than seven years in juvenile detention (as an English and math teacher). When not writing, she regularly teaches kids how to punch each other (at a dojo). She eats a lot of tofu but makes up for it with the booze and swearing.

Her short stories have appeared in the charilty anthologies *Protectors 2: Heroes* and *Feeding Kate*.

Neliza lives in South Florida with her husband and too many cats. She can be found online at nelizadrew.com and on Instagram and Twitter as @nelizadrew.